# RECYCLED

The first General Jack Hospital
mystery by Jo Bailey

**BAGGED**

# JO BAILEY

# RECYCLED

## A General Jack Hospital Mystery

St. Martin's Press . New York

*Design by Basha Zapatka*

Library of Congress Cataloging-in-Publication Data

Bailey, Jo.
    Recycled / Jo Bailey.
        p.   cm.
    "A Thomas Dunne book."
    ISBN 0-312-09901-0
    I. Title.
    PS3552.A3722R4    1993b
    813'.54—dc20                                              93-29096
                                                             CIP

First edition: December 1993

10 9 8 7 6 5 4 3 2 1

For Pip, Toots, W.B., and the Block

## Acknowledgements

My thanks to Clark Piepho for the many hats he wears, and for the use of his vehicle.

# PART ONE

# ONE

AT FIVE PAST THREE THAT MORNING an alert came over the radio in the hospital's communications center. The private patient had arrived at the city's international airport and was being transferred to a helicopter for the hop to General Jack, more formally known as Jackson General or Jackson County Medical Center. With news of the arrival, Jan Gallagher fought off fatigue by focusing on the bank of twelve closed-circuit TV monitors before her. A small woman with a girlish figure, she had a full head of black hair and dusky eyes that were burnt out from watching the monitors for the past several hours. As a rule, her mouth was generous with a smile if the opportunity arose, but at the moment, the line of her lips was perfectly straight and her expression one of intense concentration.

Activity on the upper-right monitor, which showed the hospital's parking ramp and the helipad atop it, picked up immediately. All total, the ramp had a half dozen low-light cameras, whose transmissions the monitor rotated through at ten-second intervals. The first picture Jan saw showed two hospital guards barricading the ramp entrance with a sawhorse. Next came a pair of guards jogging beside the DEA agent who handled the black Labrador retriever brought in to sniff for explosives. Camera three caught Security's Ford Escort playing its spotlight over empty Elder Care vans. Scene four: the guards at the Twentieth Street pedestrian entrance had intercepted a nurse who had most likely just finished pulling a half-shift of overtime and was trying to go home. They weren't taking any chances though, and detained her. The fifth camera showed a hospital guard pacing in front of the ramp's exit, a radio pressed to his ear.

But it was the view from the last camera, the one focused on the helipad, that drew Jan's strongest attention. Up there, the activated landing lights now made everything appear garish, as though caught in the glare of a magnesium flare. Five DEA agents had armed themselves with rifles, and the overweight agent in charge was spinning around like a dervish. He distributed orders to everyone, including four hospital guards, who positioned and repositioned themselves outside the metal railing that marked the edge of the landing pad. An ambulance had been backed up an incline leading to the pad, and it waited to drive the patient two blocks to the emergency room where she would be stabilized before being rushed to her intensive-care bed. At least that was the usual routine. How everyone knew the patient was a woman was an unknown, but it seemed to be common knowledge throughout the land.

The only person resisting all the excitement atop the ramp was Jan's boss, Eldon Hodges, who was also known, among other things, as the Little Admiral, this thanks to a merchant marine background and a salty air that accompanied him everywhere. He stood off to the side, scanning the skies. From the rear his outline looked decidedly Churchillian, except for the way the swirling wind tweaked his hair on end like that of a circus performer named Bozo.

It was mid-April with a low ceiling of clouds. Everyone but the Little Admiral and the head DEA agent in the trench coat wore windbreakers that said either DEA or JCMC SECURITY on the back. The Little Admiral was snug in a heavy winter coat, fur collar turned up, pudgy hands buried in deep pockets. Never once did Jan see him move, not even when the main DEA agent bugled in his ear.

On the next rotation through the views of the ramp, the special agent in charge showed up at the parapet, looking down at the street, or at least Jan assumed that's what he was studying. Before she could decide for sure, the monitor switched its view to the blockaded entrance where the driver of a light-colored Beamer stood beside his open door, reaming out the two guards who wouldn't let him pass.

"Doctor," Ginger commented from behind Jan. There were three guards posted to the communications center for the patient's arrival. Two of them were women; the third was Leo Kennedy, the oldest man in security. The basement communications center was no plum assignment. Out of boredom they'd quit speaking to each other hours before.

The monitor switched to a view of empty parking spaces. The Labrador and handler had disappeared for a final sweep of the stairwells, or at least that's what Jan heard over the two-way console, which had come alive with transmissions. Leo was handling the radio. Since the cameras in the ramp stairwells were all dummies, installed as psychological deterrents, Jan couldn't track the agent and his best friend there.

The monitor before her switched to another empty view, then cut to the Twentieth Street door where the nurse, if that's what she was, continued arguing with the guards without getting past them.

Switch to the ramp's exit where two guards now listened to their radios while watching the night sky.

When the monitor's view returned to the helipad, the head agent was still leaning over the parapet, peering down at the street.

"What's he see?" Jan asked, pointing at the agent's flapping coat-tails.

No one in the windowless communications center had an answer.

Of the other eleven monitors before Jan, ten showed dim, empty halls stretching off toward heaven, or maybe not quite that far. The nurses who occasionally passed before the cameras were more likely to be carrying cups of coffee than harps. One of the ten screens caught an orderly sneaking into a bathroom with an as-yet unlit cigarette dangling between his lips. The eleventh screen, situated in the middle row, showed the emergency room's entrance, where, in preparation for the incoming patient, security guards were locking doors and herding visitors to a lobby away from the entrance. At least the bar rush was over for the night, and all the drunks had been stitched up, put in cabs, tied to gurneys, or collected by the tank truck and sloshed over to detox.

Watching the twelve screens silently, relentlessly, advance through their stations, an apprehension began to build inside Jan with each shift of view. She felt as though they were steadily approaching a calamity she was helpless to prevent; worse, she would have to observe it in its entirety. The doomed, trapped feeling reminded her of watching the evening news during the Vietnam years, and she found herself wishing she could save the day by spotting a man in a ski mask skulking along a little-traveled hospital corridor. None showed up.

In the next shot of the helipad, the overweight DEA agent was nowhere to be seen. With that discovery, Jan joined Ginger in watching that monitor alone. A minute later, on the next cycle through the cameras, the agent showed up at the Little Admiral's side, wildly shouting and gesturing his bulky arms in several directions. Jan reached for the switch that controlled that monitor and locked in on the transmission from the helipad camera.

On the screen above her the Little Admiral turned and barked orders at the hospital guards, two of whom raced toward the panning camera mounted above the helipad's receiving room. Just as the guards passed out of sight at the bottom of the screen, the surgical caps of the medical staff passed them from the opposite direction, rushing toward the landing pad. Within seconds the doctor heading the medical team was bellowing at the head agent and gesturing at the ambulance, where one of the security guards appeared to be helping the paramedics cut out paper squares to tape over the ambulance's rear doors.

"What the hell's that asshole doing?" Ginger wanted to know.

The asshole in question was the security guard cloaking the ambulance's rear windows with squares of paper. He also happened to be Ginger's ex-fiancé. His nickname was Studly, and he had recently given her the heave-ho for a younger woman. On the monitor the Little Admiral lifted his two-way to his mouth and Jan heard his voice theatrically rumble over the radio console.

"Dispatch two men to A Building, sub-basement."

"What's down there?" Ginger demanded.

"Nothing," said Leo.

"No cameras," said Jan.

"There's gotta be something."

"Water pipes."

On the screen, Ginger's ex-fiancé was climbing in the back of the ambulance. He stopped long enough to gaze upward as if hearing something.

"Where the hell's he going?" Ginger demanded.

And then the monitor showed the helicopter swooping down out of the sky.

The powerlessness that Jan felt at that moment mirrored the same feeling of weightlessness she'd once experienced before a car crash. Whatever she reached for drifted away, whatever she saw seemed to be hurtling toward her, whatever was going to happen didn't care if she was seat-belted in or not.

# TWO

IN THE EARLY MORNING DARKNESS HE paced back and forth, talking trash to his portable rocket launcher. Not that the assemblage of stainless steel and polished wood was a brilliant conversationalist, but the man had gotten into the habit of moving his mouth before the action started. A rut of sorts. It pumped him up, prepared him, and he unconsciously fell back on the ritual now that the game clock inside his head was nearing the two-minute warning.

"Hotstuff, time for a little red-dogging."

Hotstuff was his pet name for the rocket launcher, which actually looked like little more than a three-foot length of pipe outfitted with a sight and trigger. He'd positioned himself on the second floor of a warehouse, in a vacant space directly above a free clinic that tested for social diseases. All quiet down there now. Nothing but confidential files and fermenting petri dishes. His location overlooked the spot where Twentieth branched off Charles Street. He also had a prime view of the back side of Jackson General's oldest building, a seven-story hodgepodge of senile brick and barred windows, and of its newest addition, a ten-story parking ramp crowned by a helipad. It was the space reserved for helicopters that drew the man's interest;

he viewed everything else as a possible decoy. Jackson County Medical Center had an ER rated as a level-one trauma unit, which meant that patients were airlifted from hundreds of miles away to be hooked up to its advanced machines or sewn together by its highly skilled tailors. The man talking to the rocket launcher awaited one of these arrivals.

"Straight to the quarterback, Hotstuff. No messing around."

He'd been bivouacked on the vacant second floor of the warehouse for three days. The source his employers had bought and paid for was nowhere near well-enough connected to pinpoint the target's arrival any closer than a week. Buying better information ran the risk of revealing intentions, and in his profession surprise was half the battle, strategy the rest. So he sat with his airport scanner turned on low, seven days worth of dried backpack food, and a mummy sleeping bag for the twenty minutes of nod time that he stole every fourth hour.

Outside, the April night sky had a low ceiling of clouds that threatened drizzle. Weather fit for roots and earthworms. Inside, he could see his breath most of the time. As he'd heard over his scanner, there had so far been two medivac deliveries during his vigil, a rock climber who'd lost her footing and a drunk traveling at seventy miles per hour who'd mistaken a cement abutment for an exit ramp. Each time a chopper alighted, the man had gone through a dress rehearsal, using the stopwatch function of his wristwatch to record the seconds, on average three hundred and ten of them, that it took the medical team to move the patient from the top of the parking ramp to the street level in an ambulance. A cumbersome arrangement, but apparently the best the hospital could deliver in the congested center of the city. On Twentieth Street the ambulance turned right, away from the warehouse and toward the emergency room entrance two blocks distant. With its flashers and siren on, the rig made a colorful bull's-eye as the man zeroed in on its back doors, and at a distance of roughly forty yards, the target was well within the range of the rocket launcher. Smiling at the un-armored doors of the ambulance, the man had told his metal sidekick, "They ain't blocking you out, Hotstuff. Not the way you blitz."

He always conferred with his weapons, no matter how dumb they might be. From sap to laser-guided scope, he refused to discriminate, believing that a close personal relationship with his tools imbued them with character and the will to succeed. Naturally he conversed with himself too, for he certainly qualified as a weapon. At six-two, he weighed in at what he liked to think of as two hundred and five "treacherous" pounds. His knuckles were the broad, fractured humps of a brawler's; his neck had the stoutness of a battering ram, an impression that the bluntness of his facial features did nothing to alleviate. His nose had frequently been introduced to unforgiving surfaces, and his blue eyes had a guarded flatness to them. He wore leather gloves, a weathered aviator's coat, a hooded, navy-blue sweatsuit, and high-tech running shoes that were two sizes too large in case a forensics team later managed to get a footprint. After three days, the tissue stuffed in the toes of his shoes was rock hard. The sharpness of his words betrayed a keen intelligence even though the content of his messages wasn't always brilliant.

"Motherfuck, Hotstuff. We oughta renegotiate the contract, all this dicking around."

He knew the game clock was winding down when the helicopter dispatcher cleared the way for a Dr. Purcell to communicate with the nurse on board an incoming chopper. Purcell headed the liver transplant team at General Jack and was expecting a patient named Carmen Romero-Muehlen, who was otherwise known as the target. The dry runs were over.

Increasing his radio's volume, he stepped nearer to the warehouse's grimy, green windows, to gaze upward toward the helipad. Incandescent floodlights now capped the parking ramp with a hard, white glow. Above the elevator bank beside the landing pad, an orange wind sock was filled by a northeasterly breeze off the lake. A sweatiness in his crotch, a hitch in his heartbeat, let him know he was ready. Alerted, he could now detect the distant pulsing of two choppers lumbering over the miles of dense city. One craft for the patient, one as escort. Everything was first class when the DEA put on a spread. As the pounding blades neared, the man ceremoniously removed two square windowpanes whose caulking he'd already chipped away. Hefting the rocket launcher to his shoulder, he rested the muzzle on the open grid and said, "Batter up." Mixing his sports metaphors didn't bother him a bit.

Over the man's airport scanner the head surgeon and the transport nurse were conferring.

"Come on lady," the surgeon was complaining, "you're not up there for the sights. Now give me the rate. Over."

"About one-ten," answered the nurse. "Over."

"Save the *abouts* for baking a cake. What rate? Over."

"One-fourteen."

"Better. Now the pressure?"

"One hundred over eighty."

"Neurological status?"

"We just went through that, doctor."

"Is there something else you'd rather be doing?"

"Checking," said the nurse. Speaking to the patient, she said, "Open your eyes."

No response came over the radio.

"What's your name?" asked the nurse.

Apparently the patient wore a headset to communicate with the nurse, for suddenly came a stream of Spanish invective that made the man in the warehouse smile. He'd heard the words before. For that matter, he'd heard the voice before, in person. Carmen Romero-Muehlen had five times hired him to take care of headaches for her, and now her bosses were paying him a bonus for more of the same type of pain relief.

"Your name?" repeated the nurse.

"The pain," the patient moaned in English.

"What year is it?" asked the nurse.

"The goddamn pain."

"Where's the pain?"

"Everywhere, you fucking whore."

And then came the doctor's voice, as if he couldn't hear everything the man in the warehouse could. "What are you finding, nurse?"

By the time they hovered over the helipad, the nurse was probably wondering which turkey below them was the surgeon and what heavy object she could drop on him. The patient, for starters. The man in the warehouse hoped she didn't.

The top of the parking ramp was lit up like a stadium as the helicopter settled down onto the landing pad. For three hundred and fifteen seconds the man peered down his spotting scope at the street. Then came the ambulance, flashers on and moving slowly—for the patient's comfort, he supposed with a chuckle. As soon as he squeezed the trigger, he knew. It just felt right. And a split second later, when the explosion gutted the ambulance, he let out a single victorious whoop. The flames erupting from those back doors were far too intense for survivors.

In rapid succession, he stuffed his sleeping bag, toothbrush, eating utensils, and chamber pot into a double-strength plastic bag and was running down an empty hall with a flashlight in one hand and the plastic bag in the other. All he abandoned was his friend the rocket launcher.

On the far side of the nearly vacant warehouse, he pulled a shopping cart out of a recess beneath a stairs. The cart held grocery bags bulging with aluminum cans, had discarded shoes tied together at the laces and dangling over the handlebar, and on the lower shelf had stacks of bundled newspapers. He deposited his plastic bag on top, pulled a ratty winter parka on over his aviator jacket, and tugged a tired red stocking cap with a yellowish fluff ball and a reindeer pattern down over his ears. Ready, he checked his wristwatch, nodded to himself, and opened the nearest fire door to push his cart into a night resplendent with sirens and flashers.

Two squad cars passed him without slowing. And when the DEA's escort chopper drifted overhead, fixing its spotlight on him, he stopped pushing his shopping cart to give them the finger. They moved on, interested only in someone fleeing the scene. He hustled that cart another mile and a half over curbs and around derelicts conked out on the sidewalk before reaching the white Thunderbird he'd rented. Making sure he was unobserved, he loaded his plastic bag in the trunk, ditched his street-person coat and cap, which were beginning to make him itch, and calmly drove out of the city, headed to the next urban center large enough to have a commercial airport.

Halfway to his destination, he stopped to replace the Thunderbird's stolen license plates with rental-agency plates. He sailed the stolen plates out over the small lake he'd parked near. Lifting the plastic bag out of the trunk, he tossed it on the front seat, and then, turning toward the lake, inhaled deeply. Pasture ran down to the edge of the water, and he whiffed growing grass and cow flop and spawning fish. It all added to his sense of well-being.

"Hoo!" he shouted into the night.

When no one answered, he laughed. Not that he'd expected an answer, and if he'd gotten one, he would have grabbed his gun and gone out there, as he'd once done when a holstein had bellowed back at him. He'd dropped the heifer with a single shot between her huge brown eyes. That was his prerogative at the top of the food chain, which by the way was the only place he ever planned on being. Life had taught him that much. Second place might as well be printed on a menu. When his turn for second place came—as he knew it eventually would—he wanted one between the eyes. That's all he asked.

After savoring one last breath, he checked his wristwatch, climbed behind the wheel, and drove on, spewing the contents of the garbage bag across the countryside one piece at a time. Here and there in the graying dawn he saw lights go on in barns, a sight that filled him with great contentment. His workday was done while everyone else's was just beginning.

Three hours later, at the next airport, he booked the first flight to Las Vegas, where he checked into his favorite casino, laid twenty grand and twenty dollars down on the next Super Bowl champ, and called a catering service he knew of for a little something special named Suzie. While waiting, he asked room service to send up a half-dozen toothbrushes and an equal number of small tubes of toothpaste.

When the Suzie arrived, he made her stand still at the center of the suite for inspection. Circling around her white, scalloped-hemmed wedding dress, he was pleased to see that the satiny material had been dry-cleaned since his last trip west. He'd had trouble with that before. These days everybody wanted to cut corners. Lifting the veil, he saw that this Suzie had full, red lips, a diamond nose stud, and a wild gallop to her silvery eyes. When he checked her teeth, he was pleased to see they'd recently been cleaned and polished.

"They told you what to expect?" he asked.

"Sounds like a good time to me."

She had a fake Southern accent that had probably been picked up from TV, but that was all right with him. Imagining that she was addicted to TV only added to the reality.

"You ever worn a wedding dress before?"

"I've been waiting for the right man."

"You ready to tie the knot?"

"Let's get on with the show."

Good answers. Crossing to the hallway door, he let in the retired liquor salesman who always performed the ceremony. The Seagram's Seven preacher wore a floral tux and sometimes forgot the rice, but he always bore down real hard on the part that went *by the power vested in me by the State of Nevada.* . . . You could tell he got a charge out of saying that. After the vows, the groom slipped a hundred in the preacher's liver-spotted paw and shoved him back out the door. Sweeping his bride off her white, needle-heeled shoes, he carried her to the king-sized bed and started unlacing her gown. Right away he ran into a problem.

"What's this?"

"A garter?" she said, ceasing the little encouraging coos in her throat.

"And what color is it?"

"Whatever color you want?"

"You got that right."

Rolling off the bed, he called the catering service and told them he didn't want any goddamn hussy-red garter belts on his bride and they damn well better get it straightened out or he'd burn down the third-rate hotel where they did business. The Suzie lay still on the bed until he ordered her out, at which point she fled.

He spent most of the next hour and a half brushing his teeth. When a small knock came on the hall door, he let in the next Suzie and this time they got it right.

A day later he felt sufficiently unwound to call his phone contact and arrange to pick up the hundred and fifty thousand still owed him.

"You missed," the voice at the other end said.

"Don't joke me around."

"We wouldn't do that," the voice assured him. "We know this has never happened before."

"It hasn't happened now."

"What do you plan on doing?"

"Give you a money-back guarantee: If Carmen gets out of that hospital alive, you not only get a refund, I'll put myself out of my misery."

He set the phone down in its cradle as gently as someone returning an egg to its nest. The tension headache didn't hit until he raised his arm to check his wristwatch. Then it felt as though his skull was shrinking and his brain swelling. Out of eighty-four contracts, this was the first one he'd dropped.

# THREE

Within an hour of the explosion, the Little Admiral relieved Jan of her duties and instructed her to take Ginger with her. Glassy-eyed, Ginger stood staring at the upper-right monitor, looking as though run through by a spear and waiting for the pain to catch up. Survivors of the accident, as Jan was still thinking of it, hadn't included Ginger's ex-fiancé, Studly, which left Jan feeling shell-shocked herself. No security guard at Jackson General had ever been killed in the line of duty.

Only the patient had gotten through the attack unscathed, and that was because she hadn't been on board the ambulance. At the last moment the head DEA agent had insisted they bring her over through a maintenance tunnel rather than risk the open street. The rest of the night's sordid business had been decoys, fireballs, and screams, all uncaptured by camera, since none were trained on Twentieth Street. For that much Jan was grateful. All they'd heard in the communications center had been a rumble, muted like distant thunder, and then came a garbled radio report that there were flames on Twentieth.

"Do you mind if I ask you a question before I go?" Jan said to the

Little Admiral. Formality provided her the strength to talk to him at all. Two years before she'd sued the county for sexual discrimination in its promotional practices. She'd won, forcing the Little Admiral to promote her into her current non-position as Security's head of special projects. There were no special projects. The Little Admiral made sure of that.

"Better you than your lawyer."

"Why did you assign me down here?" It marked the first time since promoting her that he'd actually given her something legitimate to do.

By that time of the morning, nearly 4:15, Eldon Hodges had the spun-dry look of someone who had spent the night circling a drain without being sucked down. A pink puffiness ringed his small, watery eyes, and a cockeyed jolt of stiffness had him listing slightly starboard. Despite the closeness of the communications center, he kept his winter coat on, collar up.

"Orders," he said, stepping around Ginger as if she was a potted plant.

No doubt he'd been waiting all night to deliver that line. Jan knew if she held out long enough, a witty response would occur to her, but she didn't have the heart to leave Ginger stranded in the middle of the room a minute longer.

As Hodges filled the seat she had vacated, Jan led her coworker away, guiding her by the arm. She felt as though helping a sleep-walker back to bed.

"Is there anyone I should call for you?" Jan asked.

Ginger stared straight ahead without answering. A slender but busty blonde, she kept her frizzy hair tied back like a cheerleader and imagined her black-cloth uniforms were intended to be worn tightly as spandex. She'd just turned twenty-nine, a year Jan remembered as clearly as if it was yesterday, which it wasn't. Creeping up on thirty-nine herself, Jan knew that any number ending in nine bore watching.

"Would a cup of soup help?"

Ginger managed to shake her head *no* a fraction.

"Something stronger?"

Another shake.

"How will you get home?"

Ginger suddenly cupped a free hand against her side as if in pain, but before Jan could reach for her, Ginger lowered her hand and shuffled on. Jan walked her to the woman's locker room and watched her change into street clothes. There was a small silver flask on the top shelf in Ginger's locker, and Jan made her take a sip, then had to stop her from taking a third sip. The liquor helped, though, allowing Jan to lead her to the hospital's taxi stand where Ginger stood motionless on the curb as Jan opened the cab door. Glancing over her shoulder and seeing how lost her charge appeared, Jan silently closed the door and led her onward, saying, "I'll give you a lift."

Seeing Ginger's distress enabled Jan to put most of their differences out of mind. Still, there was a niggling irony in having to help the woman at all. The two of them had never gotten along, especially after Jan's successful lawsuit. Ginger had been far less than supportive of what she slighted as "Jan's crusade," and afterwards she had let Jan know that every woman in the department—there were three—could now look forward to everyone thinking they all got special treatment.

Jan expected a rough passage across Twentieth, where squad cars and crime-marker ribbon sectioned off the charred rubble in the middle lanes, but Ginger floated by, oblivious. They reached Jan's Pontiac without incident, and for once it started without her having to threaten to kick anything.

It took three tries before Ginger dredged up her address on Hargrove Street. She lived in a high-rise apartment complex near the downtown and within two miles of the General. Her building had the tiny balconies and underground parking and tennis courts fancied by single, young professionals who didn't have time to play tennis or step on the balconies, nor, most likely, to do any hand holding with a neighbor they probably didn't know anyway. Punching in the front door's four-digit security code took Ginger over a minute, but figuring out which floor to stop the elevator on required less than a minute, and finding the door key went even faster. Once inside, Jan almost had to exhale to have enough air for her next breath. The efficiency's cozy size helped explain how Ginger afforded the address on a security guard's salary. The single room's messiness also made it clear she didn't have any money left over for a maid.

The first thing Ginger did was turn on the TV set and stare at it as if expecting Studly to reappear. She didn't object when Jan led her away from the early-morning test pattern and put her to bed without removing anything more than her shoes. She didn't object but neither did she take her eyes off the TV screen.

"Is there someone I can call?" Jan asked.

"Absolutely not."

Jan finally convinced her to take a sleeping pill, and leaving the tube on, eased herself out of the apartment. The last thing she heard while closing the door was Ginger saying quite clearly, "I'm glad he took back his ring."

She arrived at her suburban ranch house before six, which meant she was home in time to catch her sixty-nine-year-old mother snoring in the bed next to her own and clutching the golf putter she always slept with when Jan happened to be away.

The house's two other bedrooms were brimming with daughters—three of them teenagers—who were no doubt dreaming about rock stars, breast implants, video games, or wherever a young girl's subconscious carried her these days. Jan claimed no insights there. Surprisingly enough, despite the cramped quarters, or maybe because of them, she managed to feel overwhelmingly and devastatingly alone, so alone that she didn't bother crawling into bed but turned off the nightstand alarm clock and drifted out to the kitchen to make everyone breakfast. As she put water on to boil, it felt as though a part of her was missing. Not a physical appendage, but a hidden slice of her mind or heart or spirit. Since winning her court case this missing quotient had at times cast a malaise over her that could linger for days. The events of the night increased her pulse, but also widened the slice that was missing within her. She knew that her chances of finding anything meaningful to do about what had happened were next to nil.

Sighing silently, or nearly so, she filled a plastic bowl with scalding tap water and dropped a can of frozen orange juice in it to thaw. At the back of the refrigerator she found some strawberries that were salvageable, and began slicing away the bad parts. Cutting out the mushy, dark spots improved her mood, a fact that she refused to analyze any farther. At 6:00, she wound up the two yellow toy ducks she used for reveille and sent them quacking into her daughters' rooms. One duck had a chipped beak, the other a broken tail. Better them than her.

By 6:15 the wrangling over bathroom privileges had commenced, and by 7:00 her daughters were grumping about having oatmeal and fruit again. Come 7:30, everyone but Claire, the grandmother, was out the door. Claire remained behind, wrapped in her house robe and shaking her gray head at the last one to depart; she didn't appear to believe that any of them would survive long enough to return. Three of the girls caught school buses, but the youngest, Tess, age eight, hadn't yet budded to the stage where having a mother was a total scandal, and Jan gave her a ride to school, gaining a few more minutes with at least one of them. At the school-side curb, Tess leaned back into the car to press an inch-long rubber toad into Jan's hand, a good-luck charm to help her mother through the day.

"Chin up, Mom. Mr. Right's out there."

Before Jan could deny that she was waiting for Mr. Anybody, her daughter dashed off, leaving Jan to close the passenger door.

From Lincoln Elementary, Jan returned home to crawl into bed at about the same time her mother turned on "Donahue". The last thing she thought of before nodding off was a comeback to the Little Admiral's one-word answer as to why she'd been involved in the patient's transfer.

"Short orders," she mumbled into her pillow with satisfaction, too weary to care if it made sense or not. She hadn't worked a graveyard shift for months and was totally spent.

\* \* \*

When Claire shook her awake at 1:00 that afternoon, Jan pulled a pillow over her face and wouldn't let go of it.

"I said, it's the hospital."

"Tell them I'm dead," Jan said through the pillow.

"I already did. They say it's urgent."

"The Little A?"

"No. It's some woman who sleeps with a pea under her mattress."

Poking a hand out from under the pillow, she let Claire slap the bedroom extension in her palm. After a moment she got the right end of it pressed against her cottony mouth and said something related to, "ThisisJanGallagher."

"This is the secretary for Roger Averilli."

Jan bolted upright. Roger Averilli was the hospital's executive administrator, the man providing Jackson County Medical Center its sense of purpose and direction. In other words, the man ultimately responsible for the circles they went around and around in, although Jan realized that was a bit like blaming the meteorologist for the revolutions inside a tornado. The county had a momentum that was far greater than the sum of its parts.

"Are you there?" the secretary asked.

"Yes."

"Mr. Averilli would appreciate it if he could schedule a meeting with you this afternoon. Is that a possibility?"

"When?"

"The matter is an urgent one, or I wouldn't have been instructed to bother you at home, Ms. Gallagher."

"It'll take me at least an hour to get there," Jan said, waving off her mother, who was already objecting.

"That will be acceptable. I'm instructed to ask you to bring a notebook."

"Well," Jan said, hanging up and running both hands through her thick hair. She'd felt Roger Averilli's shadow before and recognized the chill. "This should prove interesting."

"Not half as interesting as what's going on around here," her mother commented from the doorway. Claire's eyes wanly drifted toward the window and her lips flattened against one another in her air-of-mystery expression.

"Are they stealing each other's clothes again?" Jan asked, in no mood to find out whose Barbie doll had a hatchet buried in its back.

"Don't stay home for me," Claire bravely said.

Propping herself against the headboards, Jan cradled her arms across the front of the red football jersey, number 00, she wore as sleepwear. Claire remained half shadowed in the doorway, wearing yellow plastic cleaning gloves and a green plaid apron she'd owned since the fifties—the century's, not hers. Jan hadn't seen the cleaning togs for a decade, not since the time of her mother's divorce. Checking further, she discovered that Claire had traded in her housedress, the one with a small flower print and deep waist pockets, for a simple A-line skirt and a white blouse with a Peter Pan collar. The blouse looked like one borrowed from a GD, as Claire referred to her granddaughters. Near the apron's strap was a delicate maple-leaf pin that Jan had never seen before.

"What happened, Mother?"

"Something happened?"

"And why are you dressed up like you're going to meet somebody's teacher?"

"I am?" Claire said, sounding innocent as her granddaughters when passing contraband down the line behind their backs.

"I'm supposed to be the one talking to the teachers," Jan said.

"At least you remember that much."

"Listen," Jan said, swinging her legs off the bed and standing, "I've got to get back to work, but I'll be home for supper. We can talk about it then. That's a promise."

"Don't get me started on your promises."

"So what *do* you want?"

"Don't get me started on that either."

"It didn't go well last night?" Jan guessed. It was the first time in months that she hadn't been home to help with the girls.

Claire ignored the question, tucked her plastic gloves in her apron's pocket, and circled behind Jan to start making the bed. A creature of habit, she always began with the pillows, fluffing them out, and today she really socked it to them. Claire was sixty-nine, another number ending in nine. Lately she had started wearing bright ribbons in her thinning hair and sneaking calcium tablets because of a friend's osteoporosis. At times she left a room in a snit because a granddaughter didn't show enough respect; minutes later she would stare distractedly out a window as the same granddaughter tried to apologize.

Taking the pillow out of her mother's hands, Jan sat her down on the edge of one bed and lowered herself to the other bed so that they sat facing each other, knees almost touching.

"What is it, Mother?"

"Maybe I want something for myself," Claire said, her voice embarrassed but stubborn, her eyes lowered.

"Any ideas on what?"

Claire turned her gaze toward the vanity where she kept her family pictures, even the ones that included Jan's dad, who'd years before left Claire for a younger woman; sixteen months younger, as it turned out.

"Are the girls getting to be too much?"

"That goes without saying," Claire said, trying to laugh but actually sniffling, which meant it was possible that whatever she was dressed up for might not involve the girls at all. She generally hung tough with them.

"You want to move back to your house?" Jan softly asked.

"That neighborhood's not safe for an older woman and you know it."

"You could sell the place and buy a nice townhouse somewhere out here. One with a fountain."

"A fountain?" Claire crossly said. "What kind of nonsense is that?"

"Did the doctor tell you something last week?"

"That he wished he had my constitution."

"So what, Mother? I'm done guessing."

"I don't know," Claire said, clenching her puffy hands together in her lap. "Do you have to be in such a hurry about everything?"

"Look," Jan said, standing, "I'm not sure we're fighting, but if we are, I'd like to know why. Maybe we should put this on hold until we can pin down a few details."

Crossing the hall to the bathroom, Jan closed the door before Claire decided to follow. She figured it would be easier to find out what was toast, as her kids said, from her second daughter Amy than by badgering her mother. Claire and Amy had been thick as thieves since discovering that Leah, the oldest daughter, didn't want them to be. Everybody but Tess, the youngest, had trouble with Leah. When Jan left for work, Claire had moved to the kitchen and was dicing onions to hide that she was crying. She'd been resorting to that ruse since Jan was a kid.

# FOUR

THE MAN IN LAS VEGAS RETURNED to his sports book to double his bet on next year's Super Bowl. Keeping a positive attitude was essential. Anyone who'd ever heard of California knew that much.

"A long shot," said the cashier.

"I used to play for them," the man said. "In their glory years."

"Those bums never had any of them years," remarked the cashier, counting hundreds in his drawer.

It took two security guards to pry the man off the cashier's throat, but at least it felt as though he'd asserted himself, which had to be a step in the right direction even if he was escorted all the way to the street. In fact, the man had enjoyed a brief stint in the NFL, three preseason games to be exact. He'd been cut from the team and blackballed from the league for ending a rookie sensation's career by chopping him off at the knees well after the scrimmage whistle had been blown. He took perverse pride in being the only man he knew of who was banished from the NFL for being too mean. The next day he'd enlisted in the army, an event that he now looked at as the real start of his life. It was there that he finally found his niche. Not that he'd lasted all that long in the military, but it'd given him a taste of something real, something that football, with all its rules and referees, had only hinted at.

From the casino he traveled to the bus depot to collect a suitcase he'd shipped to himself before he'd started his vigil in the warehouse overlooking General Jack's parking ramp. That'd been almost a week ago now, but the shipping clerk had no trouble finding his luggage, not the way it had stickers from every NFL team plastered all over it.

The clerk, needing both hands to lug it to the counter, made a joke about what must be inside it.

"The only thing funny about dead bodies," the man who'd blown up the ambulance said, "is how little space they take up."

Hefting the suitcase with one hand, he easily carried it across the terminal to the baggage check-in counter. Behind him, the baggage clerk unconsciously made a sign of the cross. Once he'd shipped the suitcase right back to the city he'd just left, he hailed a taxi for a ride to McCarran International.

# FIVE

FOR THE FIRST TIME IN MONTHS, Jan drove in the passing lane on her way to Jackson General. Once at the hospital, she tried to gauge wind direction by asking the Little Admiral's secretary if she had any messages.

"Hardly," Miss Pepperidge answered, no more forthcoming than usual.

From her cubicle, Jan dialed the executive's office and was promptly informed that Mr. Averilli would be notified she was available. While waiting, Jan carried on the brave front of doing something worthwhile by occasionally turning the pages of her dictionary, which she normally spent her days reading, line by line.

For the first three months in her current non-job, which she'd been promoted into so that management could keep an unblinking eye on her, she'd been assigned the rewriting of Security's procedural manuals. Her second three months were spent reworking the three-volume magnum opus that she'd updated during her first three months. Now, in the third three months, she no longer bothered to rewrite the manuals, but simply opened them up on her desk before spending the day reading *Webster's Ninth New Collegiate Dictionary.* To date, she'd reached the top of page 754, the entry *milium*, which was a *small whitish lump in the skin due to retention of secretion in an oil gland duct.* All in all, not a bad creation myth for how the Little Admiral had come into existence.

When her phone rang only minutes later, she half expected it to be her mother, calling to complain that a household appliance had gone belly up, or that one of the girls was missing, or that some illness was impending. Some days the smallest bump in her routine could set Claire off. But the caller was the executive administrator's private secretary, who informed her that Mr. Averilli was ready. Putting a pencil check beside her current word, and marking her place in *Webster's* with a sacred-heart picture of Jesus, another early-morning gift from her youngest, she visited the rest room to splash water on her face and make sure nothing was sticking to her teeth.

Fear of taxpayer revolts insured that county officials maintained a poor-as-a-church-mouse air of humbleness. The big shots got around such anonymity by replacing overhead lighting with floor lamps; by hanging original oil paintings, preferably of workers cast in a heroic glow; by making absolutely sure they obtained an office with an outside window; and at the highest levels by making sure their secretaries had fresh-cut flowers every day and not just once a year for secretary week.

Roger Averilli's secretary had fresh irises on the corner of her desk and spoke with so much confidence and elegant good cheer that she must have thought she worked at a suburban hospital. That may have been a snap judgement about a woman Jan didn't know, but something told her that the string of pearls around her neck had been made the old-fashioned way. When the secretary recorded Jan's name and arrival time in a scheduling book, she did so with a flourish that far outstripped the county's normal here's-your-number-take-a-seat reputation.

Anticipating a further wait, Jan settled into an armchair with a magazine, *Healthcare Financial Management*, but had barely skipped the table of contents before the exec's polished door was opened by the man himself.

"Come in, Officer Gallagher," Roger Averilli said, waving her forward with an encouraging gesture, one that Christians at the Colosseum would have recognized. Everything else about him was twentieth century, though, from his natty dark suit to the alloys in his perfectly capped teeth. His pinkish face had the soft cheeks, high forehead, and brimstone eyes of a TV evangelist. Jan felt some drag in her heels.

He guided her by the elbow to an uncomfortable-looking seat in front of his Quaker-simple desk, which was completely cleared off, uncluttered by even the simplest skull-shaped paperweight. The office had a high ceiling, the only one she'd ever seen in the hospital outside of Mulrowsky Auditorium, where the cadavers were wheeled out for lectures. Along the walls were enough wooden shelves to build a rowboat, if anyone wanted one of walnut. Barely a quarter of the shelves were filled, and the tomes present were dressed in black leather that looked as though it had been handed down from the time of the plague.

To see that much empty space in a county office was disorienting. Normal county operating procedure called for saving every scrap of paper against the day a person had to cover his or her bottom and point a finger at someone else, preferably someone in another department. No film of dust covered the bare wooden surfaces; a clean, piney scent curled about the room. All the ordinary sounds of the hospital, the rolling carts, overhead pages, wheezing patients, were shut out. The padded silence added to Jan's discomfort.

There were two squarish chairs before the desk, the second one overflowing with a large man dressed like a cereal-box leprechaun who'd gotten into the supergrow. He sported a wide, chem-lawn green tie, a beige suit coat with yoked shoulders and gold buttons, and black pants whose cuffs were straining to catch up to his ankles. His beady eyes had a feverish skip to them, his smile a calculated angle. Beneath the outdated clothing was a glint of machinery, and his right ear had an earphone plugged in it, one of the unobtrusive kind favored by news anchors. With a muffled grunt, he hoisted his considerable bulk upward to greet her. For the last several weeks Jan had observed him barrelling in and out of the Little Admiral's office, and although she'd once or twice caught him gazing directly at her as he came and went, there had yet to be any formal introductions. It was the head DEA agent.

"Jan," Roger Averilli said, "am I right that you were on duty last night?" He rested a small hand on the back of the chair reserved for her. The rhetorical way he asked led Jan to realize who had given Hodges the order to involve her.

"I was."

"Good," he said, gesturing for her to be seated and returning to his own chair behind the desk. "Good. That means you're up to date on everything." He hurried on before she could object. "We were hoping you might be willing to help us out of a tight spot."

"If I can," Jan said, guessing that the "we" included the man squeezing himself back into the chair next to hers. At least he was nodding vigorously, in agreement with the exec.

"Excellent," Averilli said, lightly rapping the top of his desk with a knuckle. "Jan, I'd like you to meet Special Agent George Windish."

The man beside her struggled upward again, offering his hand, a cold, clammy thing that Jan let go of as soon as possible.

"George is with the Drug Enforcement Agency," the exec explained, applying absolutely no special spin to the agency's name. He might have been introducing someone from the local PTA. "He's here with a special unit to provide us assistance in protecting a patient, and he's specifically requested that you be the hospital's liaison person assigned him."

Jan processed that a moment before asking the agent directly, "Why me?"

"Because you look perfect for the job," the agent said, trying to sound winsome. The effort wasn't entirely unsuccessful.

"Are looks important for what you have in mind?" Jan asked.

"All that he's trying to get at," Roger Averilli smoothly explained, "is that he's lost faith in our head of security and is searching for talent elsewhere."

Jan silently pointed a finger at herself, to which the exec nodded, acting a quarter-step—if that much—behind the agent in his reassessment of Eldon Hodges's capabilities. All around, it sounded like a major crisis of confidence. With such upheavals happening two or three times a month at the county, Jan wasn't as unsettled as she might have been.

"What I'm trying to get at," Jan said, now gazing directly at the exec, "is how you came up with my name."

"Easy," Agent Windish said. "You were recommended by a homicide detective I've worked with before."

So the exec hadn't selected her, which was essential information to know.

"Why have you lost faith in Hodges?" she asked, preferring not to discuss the only homicide detective she knew.

"He wasn't up to the cosmic nature of our struggle," the agent answered with a straight face and the crazed glint of the totally committed.

"Two paramedics and a security officer died last night," Averilli added. "Some foresight might have prevented it."

Looking from one man to the other, Jan said, "What kind of cosmic explosion was that last night?"

"You realize this is confidential?" the agent asked in a half-whisper.

"I do now."

"I'll take your word on that," the agent said. Looking down at his green tie, he thought a moment before revealing, "A portable rocket launcher was used, a Russian model popular with terrorists."

Jan nodded as if she'd expected as much. "What makes you think I can do any better than Hodges?"

"We don't expect you to," Averilli said. "After last night, Agent Windish has convinced me that we're not equipped to manage this situation. Effective as of this morning, he is in complete control. All that we're looking for is someone to act as a liaison between the hospital and his men. You'll be reporting directly to Agent Windish and will have the full cooperation of the entire hospital staff."

"And if I pass?" Jan asked, smiling over the idea of the hospital's entire staff cooperating over anything.

"Entirely your decision," Averilli said, reflecting her smile back. "Should you decide not to get involved, you can return to your duties without giving our dilemma another thought."

"But I hope you won't," Agent Windish spliced in. "Believe me, a piece of information like this one doesn't come along but once in a career."

"Whose career?"

"Anyone's. We're protecting a woman who's been running U.S. distribution for one of the Medellín cartels for years."

"She's cutting some kind of deal with you?"

The agent nodded vigorously, saying, "With her help, we're going to take down a whole network."

"And where's Jackson General come in?"

"Your hospital's the reason she's cooperating." The agent leaned forward, lowering his voice still further. "A little over a year ago Carmen discovered her liver was shot. Hepatitis. About the only place she could get one of those put in was in the States. When we found out what she was shopping around for, we naturally wanted to lend a hand." He flexed open his palms and grinned boyishly. "For some reason, she's been having trouble getting a transplant center to take her."

"Because of you?" Jan asked, wanting to be certain.

Windish shrugged modestly without answering.

"Who's after her?" Jan asked.

"The best. She skipped with a suitcase of green, and the money probably means less to her family than the loyalty, that and what she might spill."

"I've four daughters to think of," Jan pointed out.

"My men will be handling all the risks," the agent assured her. "Yours will be strictly a support position."

"How long's this going to last?" Jan asked while gazing out one of the executive's windows. The office had a view of a small courtyard landscaped with evergreens that were popular for passing out under. Early every morning Security had to make a sweep of the area to roust any drunkards. At the moment it was empty except for a pair of gray pigeons.

"Not long. Her condition has turned critical, which moves her to the top of the transplant list. Even we couldn't bump her up there." He said this last with some malice, and Jan caught the two men eyeing each other coolly. "So now we're waiting to see if she gets a donor. Either she lands one soon, or she dies."

"And if she dies?" Jan asked.

"She's signed an affidavit," the agent said with a philosophical shrug. "But I probably don't have to tell you we'd prefer a live one on the witness stand. Juries buy it better. If you want my two cents, the little lady will be in the witness box. She's got a thing about living."

Jan nodded to show she appreciated such sentiments.

"May we have your answer?" Averilli said, sounding detached, as though he'd already moved on to considering his next meeting.

"Why's the hospital getting involved?" Jan asked, shifting her eyes to the exec.

"It's our responsibility to care for those in need," the exec automatically pointed out.

"Is that the only reason?" Jan asked, thinking the answer flowed too smoothly.

"The patient has agreed to donate a million dollars to your transplant unit," Agent Windish filled in.

Averilli covered up a wince by glancing out the window, a reaction that made up Jan's mind.

"I'll do it."

"Perfect," Windish said, rubbing his hands together.

"I'm sure it will work out," the exec added, standing and angling toward the door.

"The first thing," Agent Windish said without rising, "is for you to pick two other seasoned people, one from each shift. They have to be trustworthy and team players. You'll be in charge of them, but one of you will be on duty at all times to assist my men with anything they need here at the hospital. We need to move quickly on this, but not so fast that we make mistakes. My men have everything covered right now, so we'll interview your candidates in the morning and go from there. This is big, Officer. The statistics generated from this one operation will be high side. You'll feel good about participating in this for years, believe me. Years and years."

As she watched the agent spread his hands wider and wider to show how many years he was talking about, she found herself wondering how big a rube he thought he'd found. Big enough, she guessed, because for some reason that part of her life that had been missing for the last few months suddenly seemed within hailing distance.

In the lobby outside of administration Jan plugged the pay phone and dialed the fifth precinct police station. She avoided her desk phone, not wanting the Little Admiral's secretary to sprain an eardrum eavesdropping.

"Detective White," she told the desk sergeant who answered.

The clicking of lines told her the call was being transferred. Behind her, two pensioners were reminiscing about the days when cod-liver oil took care of most everything.

"Detective White," a man answered in a voice that was bored, tough, and needy, although Jan may have been applying that last adjective unfairly. Her second ex-husband had been a city cop.

"All right, White, who told you it was OK to pass my name around?"

"You didn't appreciate that?"

"Tell me about this guy," Jan said. "How much of what he says is straight?"

"Is that the only reason you called?"

Sighing heavily, she said, "Over the last six months how many times have you asked me out? And how many times have I said no?"

"Eleven."

"You're keeping track?" Jan said, miffed.

"But after your last refusal," the detective said, "I promised that I wouldn't bother you again."

"I'm glad you remember. So why'd you sic this Agent Windish on me?"

"I thought you might appreciate the boost."

"The last thing I need down here is people thinking somebody's pulling strings for me."

"Listen, Gallagher," and now the detective sounded more normal, more put out, "the guy called me a couple days ago and wanted to know if I knew of anybody he could trust at your place of employment. Hey, he's got a job to do too."

"More," Jan prompted.

"What if that's all I know?"

"How about if we were to meet somewhere for dinner? Would you know any more then?"

"This supposed to be my big chance?"

"That's a little optimistic, Detective."

"Enrico's tonight at seven," he said in a hurry.

"I'll be there."

"You make it sound like armored combat."

The wounded way he said it made her lighten up enough to back off. "OK, White. Truce. Enrico's at seven."

"Ciao."

*"Oh please,"* she said, annoyed with how the detective was forever trying to be something he wasn't. Next he'd be wearing gold necklaces.

For the rest of the afternoon she worked at selecting one candidate each from the evening and night shifts to help her accommodate Agent Windish. Considering that the number of guards in Security who would even talk to her after she had sued the department was minimal, finding two of them whom she could trust ought to be amusing. Pulling out an employee call-in listing for the entire department, she started crossing names off to see who would be left. Luckily, she worked in pencil. By the bottom of the list, she'd drawn a line through every entry. Armed with the eraser end of the pencil, she started backtracking and eventually came up with three names, two on the evening shift, one on the graveyard. None of them were home. Once she'd tried dialing their home numbers a second time, she had put off the inevitable for as long as possible and called her own house to tell her mother she was dining out and would be a little later than expected. Strangely enough, Claire didn't even object.

# SIX

THE MAN WHO'D MISSED CARMEN ROMERO-MUEHLEN bought his way onto a return flight to Jackson General within two hours of learning of his failure. Finding a gambler willing to believe his luck had about-faced was never a problem, not when he offered twice the going rate for a ticket. His only complaint was that the hotshot he'd bought the passage off had tried to save money by going economy class, and no one in first class would let him upgrade even though half the people up there had to be airline employees taking advantage of perks before their carrier went belly-up thanks to leverage buyouts, salad makers' wages, and deregulation. He had a shrill argument with the ticket taker about the whole sorry business. By the time he boarded the flight, it felt as though he had a busy signal pulsing between his ears.

He still refused to believe he hadn't subtracted Carmen; a part of him thought it possible that the bastards who'd hired him were trying to cut corners like everyone else and save a hundred and fifty thousand. But that didn't make sense either. That amount was nothing compared to the havoc he'd cause if they were jerking him around. He knew it, they knew it. So he glared out his second-class window at the highways and ranches etching the mountains and valleys below him as they flew eastward. Thinking about blowing up whatever he saw helped ease his headache.

The airline stewardess serving lunch in his section had to touch his shoulder to get his attention, and when she did, he whirled on her so fast that the businessman dining beside him swallowed wrong and gagged. Before the stewardess could apply a Heimlich maneuver, the man returning to Jackson General delivered a karate chop between the businessman's meaty shoulders. A square chunk of chicken breast flew out. Nodding his thanks, the businessman reached for his Chivas on ice and sipped to still his cough reflex. That triggered another coughing fit that the man headed back to Jackson General ignored in disgust. When the businessman regained his composure, he tried making conversation.

"I owe you one, mister. What will you have?"

Waving off the offer, the man returned his attention to the window, bothered that he'd so thoughtlessly saved this fool's life. It seemed a bad omen, particularly when his headache suddenly abated.

"Business deal gone sour?" the businessman guessed.

"Not in business."

"Now isn't that interesting," the businessman said, on automatic chummy now, the way a salesman reflexively would be. "If I'd had to say, I would have guessed you were some kind of entrepreneur. If you don't mind my asking, what is your line?"

"Sportsman."

"That so," the businessman said, intrigued. He leaned back for a secret appraisal of the man. "Fishing, hunting, that kind of thing?"

"Big game," the man said, sighting up on his neighbor in a way that made the businessman laugh nervously and flag the stewardess down for another double.

"Trophies and stuff?"

The man only nodded, staring at the businessman's gray suit coat as if it was an unfamiliar pelt.

"I'll drink to that," the businessman said, draining his plastic glass.

"These days a little something to hang on the wall is the only way to get any satisfaction."

"What'd you say your line was?" the man asked.

"I didn't," the businessman answered, breaking into a grin broad enough to leave stretch marks. Reaching inside his suit coat, he produced a business card that announced he sold maritime insurance. Everything after that became predictable, including the fact that they were flying over some of the most arid real estate on the North American continent.

As the miles slipped by beneath him, the land began to flatten out and take on the geometric shapes of agribusiness. At intervals he saw tractors combing and tending the earth; they looked no bigger than red fire ants and made such straight lines that they appeared to be on remote control.

# SEVEN

Jan's date with Detective Frank White was unsatisfactory in every way she'd expected and in a few that she hadn't. He was a large man with ugly good looks, if such a thing was possible, and for some reason, with men it was. Some months before, the homicide detective had gotten it into his head or heart, or wherever such things occur, to be smitten by Jan and had since been persistent enough about it to be flattering, she supposed. To date Jan had steadfastly refused his invitations, telling herself that she disliked droopy mustaches, nicked faces, and aspiring eyes, particularly in men nearing age fifty. But as their meal progressed from Chianti toward espresso, she found herself being charmed despite herself.

To start with, he'd picked Enrico's, where so many cops brought their families that he wouldn't have dared show up with a one-night stand. The owner knew the detective's first name and showed them to a private booth, lighting the candle bowl himself. The restaurant's sky-blue walls were decorated with poorly-drawn Tuscany village scenes, and over the booth branched twigs that had fall-colored leaves glued to them and tiny red-and-green lights woven throughout them. If the decorator had been aiming for a summery garden feel, at least the occasional moth flickering by was buying it. Maybe the patrons were too. Laughter and agreeable conversation covered up the faint cricket and bird music filtering through the brittle leaves above them.

When the mustached owner bowed at his prosperous waist and told Jan that she was a vision of loveliness, she couldn't prevent a rose petal or two from rushing to her cheeks, even if he had just gotten through repeating the same line to the women in the two booths before hers. Jan had changed into the simple black skirt and white blouse she kept in her locker for those times her uniform wasn't appropriate. The outfit reminded her of First Communion, but at least she'd had time to touch up her eyes and lips so she didn't feel entirely twelve years old.

For his part, the detective worked hard at telling self-deprecating stories and actually listened to her when she spoke. Whenever a lull overtook them, he folded and refolded his red napkin. It was the nervous gestures that weakened her the fastest. Jan knew that the last time she had sworn off men forever, she hadn't really meant it. What she didn't know was if she didn't really mean it yet. There were problems, historic ones. Obviously enough, Detective Frank White was a cop, and that was a species of maleness she had a strong allergic reaction to, as her second marriage had proven.

"So let me get this straight," she said, trying to stick to the point, "you worked with this Agent Windish for three weeks."

"Assisted him," the detective corrected, rubbing a blunt thumb against the stem of his wineglass. "It was three weeks, give or take a day, with my other investigations thrown in too. So I wasn't actually with him every minute."

Whenever Jan brought the conversation back to the DEA agent, the detective's eyes turned spaniel and slid to the side as if searching for the waitress or spotting someone he knew. His answers came back carefully phrased though, so she knew he was paying close attention.

"You were working with him on a homicide?"

"That's what I do, yes." His mustache tilted, which meant he was grinning. When he sneaked a look to see if she would allow him to lighten up, she gave him a blank expression. Failing there, he put on his undertaker's face and said, "One of his informants bought it."

"That's all you can tell me about it?"

"There's not much more, really," he said, apologetic. "The victim's name was Richie Denmark, and he had some kind of South American franchise that the DEA didn't care to discuss with me."

"How'd he buy it?"

"Lots of bullets. Looked like a grudge match."

"And when was all this?"

"This past winter, over the holidays. Matter of fact," the detective said with a hangdog smile, "I spent Christmas Eve tracking down leads that led nowhere."

"If you put in three weeks," Jan said, refusing to comment on the detective's lonely holiday, "there must be a little more. Don't you think?"

It was Jan's turn to smile, but the detective pretended to be watching a passing dessert tray and failed to notice.

"You'd think so," Frank White said, back to folding his napkin, "wouldn't you? But we didn't turn a thing. It works that way more than anyone likes to admit."

"You're sure?"

"Of that much," he said, and this time she let him get away with a smile, which emboldened him enough to ask how her girls were. She answered briefly as possible, avoided inquiring about the detective's private affairs, and got back to matters at hand.

"Are you working the three that got blown away last night?"

"We're keeping an eye on it," he said with a disgusted shrug. "The feds are pretty much boxing us out, and word's come down to let it ride. Let's leave it at that."

"Fair enough. So what's this Windish like to work with?"

"Not nearly as much fun as an eighty-hour workweek."

"Well, thanks for sending him my way," she quipped.

"I figured you were a big girl and could make up your own mind."

Score one for the detective. That was exactly the kind of grown-up answer that would get Jan in trouble with the guy yet.

"One more question," Jan said. "Is the homicide you worked with Windish connected to this business I'm involved in?"

For a moment the detective's thick fingers pinched the stem of his wineglass as though he might snap it. As he gazed down at the sip of red wine left in the glass, a troubled crease settled across his wide brow. He sat there so long that Jan considered repeating herself but didn't, unexpectedly wanting to give him a chance.

"I hadn't thought of that angle," he admitted.

"Care to think about it now?"

"I really don't know what's going on at your place," he said, hopeful that he'd found a way out of answering.

"We can take care of that," Jan answered, and without an invitation she filled him in on the basics.

The detective periodically shook his large head as she spoke, and at the end said, "Sorry, I don't see any tie-ins."

Too bad he didn't sound as convincing as he should have, although Jan realized that her doubts may have been nothing more than her personal history catching up with her. She'd once or twice dined with her second ex at Enrico's. He'd taken her there whenever hoping to convince her that she hadn't caught him red-handed.

She managed to eat half her veal scaloppine and spent the rest of the meal assuring the detective that the food was delicious but the servings too large.

On the way to the parking lot neither of them spoke. He stood a foot taller than her and outweighed her by a hundred pounds, so he really couldn't help it if he loomed. Nonetheless, she didn't like the feeling and kept her distance. Once they reached her car, she formally thanked him and climbed into her Pontiac so fast that she felt a little foolish. He remained awkwardly outside her door until she rolled down the window.

"What do you say we do this again?" he asked.

"All right," she said, surprising herself as much as him. Before he could pin down any details, she rolled up the window and drove away, catching a glimpse of him standing where she'd left him. It looked as though he was still staring at where her car had been parked.

On the way home she tried selling herself on the notion that the only reason she'd agreed to see him again was to find out if he was holding back anything about Agent Windish. She also found herself thinking that was exactly the kind of crock that a divorcée afraid to take another chance would try to peddle herself. Those thoughts kept her busy enough to forget that something strange was going on with her mother. The reprieve was short-lived though. It ended when she opened the front door at home.

She was greeted by a jangly blast of Guns 'N' Roses, a wave of burnt popcorn, and a living room that looked tidy as a landfill after the seagulls had been in. Whenever the house got this out of control, she expected to find Claire holed up in the kitchen washing dishes no matter what the hour, but tonight her mother wasn't there. In her place stood Amy, Jan's second daughter, the one who'd been masquerading as a grown-up since her tenth birthday. Her arms were buried up to the elbows in soapsuds and a martyred downturn had crimped her lips. The house had an automatic dishwasher, but no one used that when they had a point to make.

"Where's Claire?"

"On a date," Amy said, pausing in her labors long enough to rub her nose with the back of her wrist and leave a dab of foam behind.

"A *date?*" Jan said, covering up her astonishment by crossing to the refrigerator to look for something, perhaps something edible. She wasn't sure. Seeing an apple in the crisper, she reached for it, realizing only then that she was still hungry and that vanity had been behind her unfinished meal at Enrico's.

"With Mr. Kinsey," Amy said, addressing the soapy sink. "She left Leah in charge." Her voice cracked a little over that injustice.

"Mr. Kinsey?" Jan said, still holding the apple.

"The retired navy man on the next block."

"Oh." Jan took a bite of the apple, chewed, and casually asked, "Where'd she meet him?"

"Community center."

Another bite. "How long's this been an item?"

"An item?" Amy said. "I wouldn't call it that. Grandma's a woman who likes to keep her options open."

"Right. I forgot." Doubting that the household could handle simultaneous romances—hers and her mother's—she tried to change the subject. "So what went on around here tonight?"

That was a classic mistake. Amy delivered several rehearsed paragraphs on how childish her sisters could be, particularly Leah. It was all finger pointing from then on. Jan ordered lights-out at 10:30, well before Claire made it home, and long after having decreed that she was disappointed in all of them.

By then she'd also given up on reaching any of the candidates for her special assignment at home. She could have checked to see if they were currently on duty, but knew her luck would be much better if she caught them away from the boys at work, where macho hormones were easily triggered. To get to sleep, she had to count various fluffy objects. In the morning Jan let her mother sleep, even though there was an orchid corsage in the refrigerator that hadn't been there when she had gone to bed. After a sniff of the orchid, she headed out the door to work, determined to find a supporting cast for her new assignment.

# EIGHT

FROM THE AIRPORT HE TAXIED TO a downtown hotel.

"A new one near the convention center," he told the driver before settling in to watch the tourist billboards and jockeying cabbies. A departing aircraft drowned out the driver's answer. As they merged with traffic on the freeway leading away from the airport, they passed a state trooper who'd pulled a speeder over.

"That bastard's always hiding right there," the cabbie complained, his words suddenly audible in between the roar of jets. "You in town with all the other shrinks?"

The man smiled as he looked down at his Ivy League suit coat, dark turtleneck, and briefcase, but then a more practical thought occurred to him as they shot past the highway patrol car.

"How many hours a day are you behind that wheel?"

"Counting pee breaks or no?" the cabbie asked.

"You have to know the city pretty good?"

"What? You thinking of changing careers, Doc?"

"Dreams aren't they used to be," the man said.

"Being a hack ain't either. There's only a half dozen places it's safe to take a fare. If they want somewhere else, I start speaking Arabic. It moves 'em along."

"How long to get hired?"

"If you had a chauffeur's license you could start this afternoon."

"How long to get the license?"

"You're dealing with the state there, Doc, so you're on your own. Six weeks, maybe, or two months if you're lucky." The cabbie lifted a palm to show it could be longer. "How about giving a dream of mine a whirl?"

"I'm a child psychiatrist."

"You want the truth, Doc, my dreams are pretty goddamn childish."

The cabbie frowned a half minute, shifted lanes, and started in on his story. In the distance the city's downtown looked no bigger than a skyline in a glass ball. It was a chill, gray day. If anyone had given the scene a shake, snowflakes might have swirled down. The driver had to speak up to be heard above the heater's fan. By the time they reached the newest hotel in the city, the cabbie had laid his nightmares all out—vampires, underwater castles, and people who spoke backwards but somehow made sense. The man tipped him modestly and told him his dream was pretty standard fare but not to worry, the entire human race was going through a bad time.

Before entering the Yorkshire Hotel, he crossed the street to a camera shop and bought a pair of high-powered binoculars, then stopped at a drugstore for a supply of toothbrushes and toothpaste.

The black doorman at the Yorkshire was dressed up like frilly old England, and the desk clerks wore blue blazers with a coat of arms stitched on the pockets. Fortunately the psychiatrists' convention hadn't absorbed all the available hotel space, and the man didn't even have to start flashing green to secure a room. He turned down a suite with a view of the lake, which was the city's chief tourist attraction, and chose a room on the fifteenth floor that overlooked the far side of the downtown. As in every other U.S. city where he'd ever gone on safari, the scene before him included a clock tower, an Empire State Building knockoff, and a sprinkling of modern glass structures that managed to look windowless even though constructed of nothing but windows. Hanging on in the city's shadows was the sooty courthouse, the vine-covered walls of an old boys club, and an abandoned train depot. Jackson County Medical Center fit right in with all the other has-beens.

For most of the afternoon he sat motionless at his room's window, meditating on what had gone wrong as he watched the hospital through his binoculars. At intervals he tried to think of some bit of wisdom his father had once told him, but the truth was, he couldn't remember a single worthwhile thing his old man had ever said. They'd been a small, terribly formal family, and his father would have turned a murderous red to think of his son calling him his old man. Both his mother and father had been professionals, the old man an electrical engineer, the old lady a commercial real estate agent. About the only counsel he could remember receiving was *the buck stops here, Son.* That line inevitably preceded a punishment; not that they'd ever laid a hand on him. Their idea of discipline involved polishing either the car or silverware, depending on the season. There was to be a moral lesson in it, he supposed, but one his parents imagined was self-explanatory, for they never enlightened him as to its meaning. It wasn't until years later, while in college, that he discovered that his father had stolen the buck-stops-here business from President Harry Truman. By then he'd long before figured out what a fraud his old man had been.

From his hotel room he could see the man stationed atop the hospital's highest building. The lookout appeared to be holding a two-way radio, although the binoculars didn't have quite enough magnification to clarify that point. By the time of the afternoon rush hour, the man had failed to identify anything else significant, so he went down to the front desk to request a room lower than the seventh floor, which was all the higher a fire department's hook and ladder could reach in an emergency. One of his competitors had once toasted the top five stories of a building to get at a stoolie, and ever since then the man had been careful about his elevation. While at the desk, he also rented an innocuous compact in which to cruise past Jackson General for a closer look.

He shot through the hospital's main campus, but avoided the

warehouse where he'd abandoned his friend, the portable rocket launcher, to the interrogation of forensic experts. The scene of old failures never did anything to buck up morale. Since the DEA knew he was on site now there should be some intense deployments. He'd have to come up with something innovative this time, or no, that's exactly what they'd expect. This time he'd choose a straightforward, simple approach that would later on make them curse themselves for overlooking the obvious.

A mile beyond the hospital, he pulled into the busy lot of a discount liquor store, closed his eyes, and replayed, frame by frame, what his mind's eye had recorded. He made two sedans, both Chevys, one positioned at each end of the hospital and each holding a casually dressed man who was too alert to the activity on the street. Without a hitch he had identified the opposing team's defensive formation, which made him smile, but then get down on himself for congratulations over nothing, really. He wouldn't have needed this sudden-death period if regulation playing time hadn't ended in a tie.

He recalled the thump of his car's tires over three manhole covers; the vibrations from below made him pan his inner eye upward to a cloudy sky. It occurred to him there was no obvious way to cross from one building to the other, save outdoors, which apparently his old friends from the DEA had refused to allow their soprano to do. So that meant there must be tunnels. He punched the car dash, cracking something but refusing to investigate whether it was his bone or the car's plastic. The tunnel oversight didn't matter. What counted was the discipline to overcome. Eyes still closed, he saw a taxi stand with two blue-and-whites and one Premier cab idling. He froze those frames, recalling every detail he could about the cabs. The Premier cab was larger, cleaner, and had whitewalls, which was enough to tip the scales.

Parking five blocks away from the hospital, he phoned the Premier dispatcher to request a ride. Within minutes he was picked up by a tired cabbie who should have been given a gold watch a decade ago. An oversized chauffeur's cap rode the driver's ears; his unzipped windbreaker revealed a black tie keeping his withered neck warm.

"Where to, Captain?"

"How's business?" the man asked.

Raising his eyes to the rearview mirror, the cabbie flicked down the lever on his meter and said, "Business stinks. Where to?"

From the backseat the man leaned toward the cabbie's hearing aid to say, "How'd you like to make three hundred a day for a week?"

"Do I get to keep my pants on?"

"If that's what turns you on," the man said, fanning fifteen hundred-dollar bills and holding them up for show and tell. "It could be a sweet deal."

"That funny money?"

Without comment, the man dropped the bills on the front seat, allowing the cabbie to ripple the stack by his floppy ear, sniff it with his long nose, even taste the corner of the top bill with the tip of his purplish tongue.

"They're your friends," the man said.

"Buddy, the last friend I had ran off with my wife." Rubbing a flat thumb over the edge of the bills, the cabbie pridefully said, "I ain't driving no ladies of the evening around. No floating dice either. Nix on drugs. And the last time I killed somebody, both of us was in uniforms."

"None of the above. All I want to do is drive your cab for a few days. You sit at the hospital, right?"

"Sure. It ain't so cutthroat as down by the convention hotels. Bunch a goddamn hotdogs driving down there."

"You sit the whole day at the hospital?"

"It's been known to happen, and I can tell you it ain't how I envisioned spending my golden years."

"OK then, I think we're in business."

"Not until you tell me what's going on, we're not."

"Divorce work," the man said. "I got a doctor's wife who thinks her neurosurgeon's spreading it around. There's children involved, so she wants the guy cold before filing. I've had an operative covering the doc's castle for two weeks, but nothing, so we figure it's shaking down here. And from what I've seen, anybody coming or going from surgery passes by your taxi stand."

"That's the godawful truth," said the cabbie. "So you're going to pay me fifteen hundred so's you can sit in my cab and watch? That's a lot of dough."

"Not to the medical profession. You and I both know it."

That almost clinched it. The old man said thoughtfully, "How do I know you won't just drive off and I never see these wheels again? I'd have a hard time explaining that one to the goddamn college educated dispatcher."

Pulling out his wallet, the man selected a phony out-of-state private investigator license and dropped it over the front seat. "You can hang onto that for collateral."

The driver picked up the ID and held it close enough to his nose to cast some doubt on his ability to see anything smaller than a semi coming at him. "This says California."

"That's where the wife is. She's just taken some high-powered job out there. She and Dr. Dick are supposed to be trying out one of these commuter relationships."

"Sounds pretty goddamn greedy to me."

"That about sums it up," the man agreed.

"Anything else I can rent you?" the driver asked, breaking into a morose grin visible in the rearview.

"No. But you can answer a few questions."

"It's your money."

"How long's your shift?"

"Twelve to sixteen hours. Depends on the day, 'cause it's all commissions."

"But you name the hours?"

"Mister, they'd let me live in this thing if I wanted to."

"What happens when your shift ends?"

"I drive to the garage, park it, and ride the goddamn bus home."

"So OK. At the end of each day I turn the cab back over to you and you take it to the garage. Right?"

"That's about it, except for the three hundred you pay me."

"That's all up front," the man said, "with a nice bonus at the end. Write your phone number down on something, so I can get ahold of you when I'm calling it quits for a day."

The driver pulled a take-out ribs menu from behind his sun visor and lifted a pencil stub out of his ashtray.

"What time you usually start your day?" the man asked.

"In the goddamn dark for the airport runs."

"When do you land at the hospital?"

"By nine."

"So pick me up at this corner at eight-thirty tomorrow morning. I don't think my neurosurgeon's into anything but people's heads before then."

Of course there was always the outside chance that the cabbie was working as a stringer for the DEA, although that was probably more the result of clinical paranoia than useful paranoia. But when they parted company, the man carefully tailed his catch to a matchbox-sized home that had a knocked-over birdbath out front. The taxi driver didn't try to communicate with anyone out of the ordinary and appeared to live alone, which would make things considerably easier later on.

# NINE

OVERNIGHT A NEW ARCTIC FRONT HAD settled in behind Miss Pepperidge's eyes, and the Little Admiral himself made a point of stepping to his door when Jan greeted his secretary good morning. Judging from the way his shirtsleeves were rolled back to the elbow, Jan guessed he had been polishing the gangplank he kept in his private water closet. Without speaking, he closed his door.

Apparently they'd been informed of the new chain of command.

Rather than waste time trying to mend bridges beyond repair, she went right to work, first placing a call to the beeper number Agent Windish had provided and leaving her extension number. After that, she pulled out the on-call list to have another squint at possible volunteers. The light of a new day didn't improve her prospects. Since picking an assistant on the graveyard shift presented the least problem, she started there. Jackson Martin was the only one from that time slot who would even consider cooperating without her having to pull rank, which she preferred to avoid if at all possible. There were too many ways to sabotage orders to make her want to draft someone against his or her will.

She called Jackson at home, hoping to catch him before he turned in for the day; maybe he'd even be groggy. She'd take whatever edge she could get, for her only real claim on Jackson was the fact that they'd been outcasts together on the graveyard shift for two, nearly three, years. He'd been the token black, Jan the token single mother of four. They hadn't been bosom buddies, but at least they'd developed a mutual respect. She hoped to play on that, among other things. Jackson Martin's nickname in the department was Action Jackson, not because he was quick to use his fists but because he had no patience for the county bureaucracy they all sank in. She intended to use that to advantage too. When he answered, Jan identified herself and got right to her leverage points.

"How'd you like to do something that will stick in everyone's craw?"

"Being a fish bone's my favorite thing."

"You'll have to pull OT."

"Fish bones usually do."

"Can you come back in this morning?"

"Who said I needed sleep?" Jackson asked with a snort. "But maybe you better tell me what's shaking before I take my pajamas off."

"You wear Pj's?"

"Just a cape and cowl. In case Gotham needs me."

"Gotham needs you," Jan assured him and explained what the assignment would be. Quick to pick up on the fact that the Little Admiral had been cut out of the loop, Jackson signed up with a low chuckle. Mutinous talk was forever circulating in Security's forecastle.

She knew that selling the assignment to someone from the evening shift wouldn't be so simple. She had absolutely no rapport with that shift's supervisor, Victor Wheaton, who thought equality in the workplace meant that every woman got an equal opportunity at undoing his zipper. His chauvinism had seeped downward to his men, who included Ginger. As far as Jan could tell, Ginger saw sex as a tool—a power tool—and had no trouble dealing with Victor

Wheaton, nor, whenever she and Studly had been on the outs, with Wheaton's zipper.

After Jan had twice ruled out the entire crew for one excellent reason or another, she forced herself to narrow the field to those who had some buttons she might be able to push. That left her with two non-candidates, as she found herself thinking of them. First was Stanley Charais, who once had embarrassed both himself and Jan by making a pass at her. Second was Jerry Cody, who could talk himself into almost anything if he thought his honor had been slighted. She was trying to decide which bullet to bite first when the phone rang and interrupted her concentration.

"You're ready, Officer Gallagher?"

No introductions, but the whirlwind could only belong to Agent Windish.

"Close," Jan lied.

"Good. Bring your people to MICU four when you're set for a briefing."

And he was gone, leaving Jan with the phone in hand. She took the plunge then, choosing Jerry Cody first because she knew what a handful she got with Stanley. An answering machine came on the line, repeated the number she'd just entered, and closed by saying, "You know what the beep's for." She was debating whether to leave a message when Cody picked up the receiver in person.

"This better not be about that medical deduction I claimed," Cody said without even a hello.

"It's not," said Jan. "At least not that I know of."

"This doesn't sound like my tax accountant," Cody said, turning suspicious.

"That's because it's Jan Gallagher down at the hospital."

"Jan Gallagher," he said, sounding convinced that someone was pulling a prank. "To what do I owe the honor?"

"To the fact that you've been known to think for yourself on rare occasions."

"If this is some kind of joke . . ."

"I'm recruiting someone off your shift for a special assignment," Jan said. "If you're not up for it, just say so."

"I've heard all about your sucking up to the DEA."

At least now he was taking her seriously, although his response left Jan momentarily at a loss for words as she marveled at the speed of gossip within Security. Gathering herself, she forged ahead with an explanation of what she needed. At the end of her spiel there was a longish pause. She could hear a sports radio talk show blathering on in the background.

"Gallagher, did Kennedy put you up to this?"

"I'm on the level. Are you interested?"

"Who else would I be working with?"

Knowing that the real answer would put him off, she said, "Undetermined."

"Why'd they pick you?"

"It was a popularity contest."

"More likely they couldn't get anyone else."

She could feel herself losing him, so went for broke. "Put your pants on backwards for a change, Cody. Live dangerously."

It took him a moment to sort that out, but when he did, his answer sounded final. "Ho. Ho. Ho."

Jan found herself alone with her phone again.

The call to Stanley Charais didn't take anywhere near as long.

"This is Jan Gallagher, Stanley."

"Too late," he said, and hung up.

He'd probably been saving that one since she'd had to slap his face.

A half hour later she was still staring at her phone's keypad, replaying her options, when her extension rang again. Without thinking, she snatched it up and snapped, "Yes?"

"This Gallagher?" It was a woman's voice, strained and demanding.

"Yes."

"This is Ginger. And I was just talking to Kennedy, who heard from Cody, if you get my drift. What's this business about you and the DEA?"

"I don't know if that's anything for you to worry about," Jan said.

"Gallagher," Ginger said with the kind of brassiness that was her trademark but today sounded forced, "let's not beat around the bush. OK? I hear you're signing people up to help protect Madame X and I'm volunteering."

Jan shifted her vision to the cubicle's blue-cloth partition without knowing what to say.

"You hear me?" Ginger said. "I'm volunteering."

"Isn't there a funeral you'll want to be attending?" Jan softly asked.

"Not going."

Without comment, Jan listened to Ginger breathe a moment.

"Tell me this, Gallagher. Where you going to get a better offer? You and I both know that nobody on my shift can stand you, but at least I'll be honest with you. I think you know you can count on that."

"Have you been drinking?"

"That was yesterday. Today I need to do something or go nuts."

Jan took one last look at the call-in list before pushing it away in frustration and saying, "All right. But if it looks like you can't handle it, you're out."

"I'll handle it," Ginger promised, actually sounding thankful. "You don't have to worry about that."

Jan chose not to comment about her worries.

To avoid any scenes with the Little Admiral, she waited for Jackson and Ginger in the lobby outside administration's wing. The lobby had three service windows—cashier, outpatient pharmacy, and the service league—in front of which fifteen to twenty people lounged about on patched furniture, tapping their feet, chasing children, or looking into empty wallets. Everyone was waiting to be called up by a pharmacist; no one bothered with the other windows.

Jackson Martin arrived first, all two hundred and thirty "black" pounds of him, as he liked to say. Packing that much muscle into a six-foot frame called for industry, of which he had plenty—another good reason to have him on the team. He stood beside Jan at parade rest, smiling furtively, when she informed him they were waiting for Ginger Foley.

"You really know how to throw a party, Gallagher."

"She volunteered."

Jackson whistled lowly, imitating a plummeting bomb.

"I figured this might keep her mind off what's happened," Jan said. "You going to have any trouble working with her?"

"Not so long as we're on different shifts."

"Then we're set," Jan said, "except for one thing. I want you to tell me if you notice—or hear—about Ginger doing anything, ah, inappropriate . . ."

"I see her doing any handsprings, you'll be the first to know."

"Thanks," Jan said, without mustering much enthusiasm.

Minutes later Ginger arrived, looking freshly scrubbed—too scrubbed—and revved up with something, maybe coffee, maybe a handful of her crash-diet pills, which she took to avoid getting meaty. It took a close look to find her eye whites amongst all the red, and she was blinking enough to make it likely she'd resorted to eye drops. She popped a white Life Saver in her mouth, but instead of sucking on the mint candy, ground it up. One other thing, she was real upbeat.

"Let's go get 'em, guys."

Jackson glanced at Jan and coughed behind a hand.

"First some ground rules," Jan said, silencing Jackson with a look. "One, any time either one of you wants out of this, speak up. We already know how bad it can get. Understood?"

Both Ginger and Jackson impatiently rolled their eyes and nodded.

"Two, you clear everything through me."

"How much everything?" Jackson said. Ginger laughed a beat late and a decibel too loud at his wisecrack.

"Everything within reason," Jan said without lightening up. "We're supposed to help these guys with whatever they need from the hospital. Protecting this patient, that's their job, and I don't want us involved in it. Keep that in mind."

More nodding, serious now.

"Third, when the Little Admiral pulls you aside and wants to know what's going on in the fourth MICU, you refer him to me."

"My pleasure," said Jackson.

Ginger, however, bit down on a new mint and said, "How many rules there going to be?"

"Four. You with me on three?"

"Unless I tell you otherwise," Ginger said, glancing away.

"Good," Jan said, starting toward the elevator banks. "Let's go then."

"Wait a minute," Ginger said. "What's rule number four?"

"I haven't decided yet," Jan said over her shoulder. Stepping on the elevator, she turned, saw they were both getting on behind her, and let her breath out slowly.

# TEN

In the morning he swapped places with the cabbie, taking the old man's short-brimmed cap, windbreaker, and narrow tie, because, as the driver put it, "The goddamn company wants us to make every son of a bitch feel like he's some goddamn Rockefeller."

Overnight the sky had shed its clouds and now shined a blue brilliant enough to give a DEA agent hope. The thought pleased him. As much for the cabbie's benefit as his own, the man slipped on a pair of dark sunglasses, affixed a thick mustache to his upper lip, and merged with traffic after properly signaling. Once settled in at the taxi stand on Wabash Street, sandwiched between Old General and New, he slouched in his seat like an honest-to-goodness cabbie doing a holding action on boredom. Within the first minute he'd checked his wristwatch twice.

At first glance the medical facility around him appeared to be carrying out its normal business of loading gurneys, filling wheelchairs, and accepting flowers, but the man hadn't reached the pinnacle of his profession by relying on first impressions. For starters, the DEA's two Chevy sedans remained posted at opposite ends of the complex in the exact same spots as the day before. A real lack of imagination there. He also duly noted that hospital security guards were screening people at the main entrance. That was a new wrinkle. When he'd first cased Jackson General two weeks before, security hadn't been so tight. But beyond the presence of these lookouts, he caught no contraindications for his operation. That, he knew, was a lie. Other obstacles awaited him. He simply couldn't see them. With that in mind, he sat still, intending to grow accustomed to the lay of the land before making any moves.

It wasn't a handsome land. The trash clotting the street gutters may not have contained discarded syringes and old dressings, but it felt that way. To his right, a seven-story Methuselah had all the pitted, hollow-eyed appeal of a smallpox survivor. Across Wabash Street stood a slightly newer five-story part of the hospital with the charm of a cardboard box. Down the street, where Twentieth intersected Wabash, was the only new structure in sight, the front of the parking ramp, which he refused to look at. Those odd corners or entrances of the hospital's buildings that had been dolled up with tinted glass or pneumatic doors stood out like eye lifts and chin tucks on a cadaver. The plain truth was: people came there to avoid pain and death. That was all. Amused by the futility of such avoidance, the man felt right at home on that street. He believed that he understood the battles being waged around him much better than anyone else could. He was intimately familiar with how stubbornly humankind resisted the most inevitable part of their lives—its end.

Several times patients or visitors of patients rapped on the passenger window to secure his services as a taxi driver. No matter how lame or scarred they were, he attended to them as though he was related to Mother Teresa, although he referred them to other cabs if they required more than the shortest of rides. The three times he did accept a fare, he collected nearly fifteen dollars in tips.

After each trip, but before hurrying back to the hospital, he stopped to telephone Jackson General's information number to request the extension of a patient. The first time he asked for a John Smith. No such patient in-house. Did he have the right hospital? Maybe not. Second time out, he tried the name Robert Smith. Still no luck. Third time, Mary Jones. Did he mean Marilyn Jones? He did indeed. Could they tell him her condition? He would have to speak to her nurse for that. If they would tell him what station she was on, he would do exactly that. Postcoronary recovery unit, which was on the third floor in the new building, the one on the west side of Wabash, in case he couldn't tell which old building was newest. Thank you so much. We're here to help you, sir.

Armed with the name of one of Jackson General's paying customers, he searched out a flower shop to buy her a get-well bouquet, a nice spray of daisies and baby's breath, for which he asked the florist to write a heartfelt message and sign it *Love Elmer.* Not that this was his name nor even close to it. Actually, ever since learning from a DEA agent he'd captured that his code name was the Hammer, he'd disassociated himself from his Christian name and stepped into the realm of the mythic, insisting that everyone call him the Hammer. He even perfected a crazed chortle to cue his associates in that he was serious about it, and went so far as to always refer to himself in the third person. Talking about himself that way made him feel much larger than life, which of course he was.

Placing the wrapped arrangement in the cab's trunk, he returned to the taxi stand to see if he would have an opportunity to lighten Marilyn Jones's day or whether he would have to wait. He wasn't opposed to waiting, but he wanted to be prepared if an unforeseen chance arose. He prided himself on being an opportunist, a trait he ascribed to all successful figures.

There was a side to being a sportsman that was too often ignored but without which he would have been just another bopper for hire, getting calls from real estate developers who were tired of their wives and from wives tired of their developers. The people who could afford to pay cash for his services, they weren't just paying for a bullet out of nowhere; they were paying to send a message. That's why his DEA handle was so perfect. Drug lords watched more movies than teenagers, and wanting to live up to their movieland reputations, they were always on the lookout for something that felt Hollywoodish, something like a man named the Hammer. So he kept show biz in mind whenever he went about his work. Always, he was on the alert for a special twist that would make his clients feel good about paying top dollar. As he sat at the taxi stand, he checked his wristwatch and hatched ways to get rid of the old boy he was renting the cab from. Since everything else about this outing would probably require a straightforward, no frills approach, he craved something exotic there.

# ELEVEN

THE MICU RESERVED FOR CARMEN ROMERO-MUEHLEN was located on the fourth floor of New General, which was only new if compared to the Old General. To get there from outside the administrative offices required a ride to the basement and a long walk through an eternally-lit tunnel to reach another elevator bank. On the way, their heels did all the talking as Jan and her helpers walked three abreast, just like the musketeers, except that Jan was a half step ahead of the other two. The way staff suspiciously sidestepped them; they might have been wearing plumes in their hats, if they'd been wearing hats.

When the New General's elevator doors opened on four, they were greeted by Art Glass, a day-shift security guard who took one look at them and mentioned the names of three musketeers other than the crew Jan had in mind.

"Larry, Curly, and Moe, what's shakin'?"

At least Jan took some encouragement from the way Ginger reacted normally.

"Fuck off, Glass."

He tried some funny stuff when they couldn't produce a pass, but eventually tired of it and waved them on. His presence meant that the Little Admiral still had a hand in providing security, which forced Jan to downsize the extent of her authority.

When Jan rounded the last corner to their destination, she found a pair of metal linen carts blockading the hallway in a staggered line. Two men looking uncomfortable in blue scrubs stood behind the carts, and came to attention as Jan appeared. She recognized the curly redhead manning the first cart; he'd been present in the televised shots of the helipad. She'd never seen the second man, who had a football player's squatness and melancholy scowl.

Beyond the two carts lay the entrance to MICU Four, which had been shut down for over a year owing to a drop in the hospital's census. After the MICU's door, the hallway crooked again to the right, where it dead-ended in an out-of-sight stairwell and service elevator. The DEA men didn't appear to have set up any precautions for someone approaching from that direction, and Jan made a mental note of it. But even if their backside was uncovered, they were vigilant about the front door. The fact that Jan, Ginger, and Jackson all wore hospital security uniforms, complete with badges, brass name tags, and photo IDs meant nothing to them. The man behind the second cart reached with both hands for something in front of him—probably not a towel—and the lead man held up his hand for them to stop.

"Hold it right there," the redhead said with a soft Texan accent, "and tell me what we can do for you."

"We're supposed to see Agent Windish," Jan informed him.

Lifting a clipboard, the lead man ran his eyes down a list. "You're Gallagher and friends?"

"Sort of," Jan said.

"If that's supposed to be funny," the redhead said, challenging her with a stare, "then I'm not sure you're in the right place. There's nothing funny going on around here."

"I was trying to be accurate," Jan replied, glad that she hadn't told him they were to see Cardinal Richelieu. "We're not exactly friends."

The agent weighed that a moment before saying to his partner, "Checks."

Jackson whispered out of the side of his mouth to Jan, "You going to tell them about your rules?"

"What was that?" the redhead demanded, not close enough to have heard the crack.

"He was wondering," Jan said, "why you're standing there with your backsides exposed."

"Because there's nothing to worry about behind us. We've got a man back there too. Now I want you to come forward one at a time so I can run this wand over you." He held up a metal detector. "The only thing metal beyond this point is inside our boss's head."

"I thought you said there was nothing funny around here," Jan said.

"Who's being funny?" the agent answered, impatiently waving her ahead with his hand.

Jan went first, allowing the agent to pass the detector over all the crevices of her body. When he asked her to turn around, she found herself facing a smirking Jackson and blank-faced Ginger. From up close she could see how sun chapped the agent's ruddy face was. He wore a V-necked T-shirt and cowboy boots under the hospital scrubs. Freckles dotted the back of his hands. When done he grunted "next," and Jan moved ahead, past the second agent to the MICU's entrance, where she held up, waiting for the other two. Jackson stepped forward and turned around before the agent ordered it. Lastly came Ginger, who stared straight ahead as if afraid of an electrical shock. She ignored the second agent entirely, which was so out of character—football players being something of a hobby for her—that Jan watched her a moment but said nothing.

Inside the fourth MICU everything was so dim that Jan had to pause to get her bearings. She heard a man and woman arguing about who was more faithless and after an instant recognized the voices were coming from a TV, an early afternoon soap. At the same time, she could smell that scrubbed, tangy scent that was the combined vapors of disinfectant, rubbing alcohol, and the faint trail of atoms left behind by souls bound for parts unknown.

As her eyes adjusted she saw that the large room before her had a vacant commons area with four empty bays, each capable of being separated by floor-to-ceiling drapes that were presently pulled back, leaving everything wide open. Blinds were drawn over the windows to the outside, and other than a low-watt reading lamp over an empty charting desk, no lights were on.

The TV voices drew her attention to the left and an isolation room whose nearest wall was glass. Inside the room, two nurses were bent over a patient whose face was concealed by the nearest RN but whose thin arms were braceleted with white tape and harpooned with IVs. Aside from a directional overhead light, the only thing illuminating the room was the TV, which was positioned barely inside the door, on a shelf just below the ceiling. The flickering light created a vaguely strobe-like effect and made the surgical caps, masks, and gloves that everyone wore seem all the more other-worldly.

Before Jan could stop her, Ginger drifted past, toward the isolation room. Her approach drew the attention of a man in extra-extra large scrubs who towered above the foot of the patient's bed. His massive arms were dark as terra-cotta, his shoulder-length hair was black as a Navaho's. A surgical mask cloaked all his features but his brooding eyes, which ogled Ginger's full figure so closely that even Jan felt a tug on her brassiere clasp. Coming to a stop ten feet shy of the glass wall, Ginger appeared oblivious to her admirer as she cast a bitter gaze at the patient.

Jackson stepped beside Jan to lowly say, "You wanted to know if Ginger did anything unusual?"

"Give her a minute," Jan said.

A few seconds later the patient arched her back in pain and called out a name in Spanish, causing the man at the foot of the bed to reach down and touch her foot with a lumpish hand. The spell broken, Ginger spun about to rejoin Jan.

On the other side of the unit was a second isolation room that had been turned into a dormitory. Three folding cots filled one corner; a low, round table held two telephones, an open box of sugar cubes, and an assortment of empty paper coffee cups. No pennants or bikini posters wallpapered the interior, but there were hospital floor plans taped over the glass windows that closed in the room.

Facing the coffee table were several straight-back chairs, one of them more than filled by Agent Windish who was currently reaming out someone named Norby over the phone. He waved Jan and her crew forward while trumpeting into the phone, "Norby, it damn well better be fixed," and hanging up. Addressing Jan and the others, he turned congenial. "Have a seat, people. It may be your last chance." When he smiled broadly to show them he was joking, Jan noticed that his parents hadn't wasted any money on orthodontists.

Thanks to a little shove from Jackson, Ginger led the way, stubbing her foot against the leg of a chair. Until that moment the only awkward thing that Jan had ever witnessed the woman do was pretend to be liberated. Jackson sat without taking his eyes off the agent. Jan was left the chair nearest Agent Windish, who hadn't changed out of the clothes he'd worn when she'd met him the day before. He hadn't shaved either, and his hair hung limply to the side, a strand of it repeatedly falling across his forehead. That was good because it gave his hands something to do other than roll and unroll his unnaturally green tie.

With everyone seated, the agent took a long, measured once-over of each of them, as if calculating his chances. The table may have been round, but this wasn't Camelot, the agent wasn't Arthur, Jan wasn't Guinevere, and so on down the line to Lancelot, who was missing too, although Windish's stiff-necked posture, loony grin, and fidgeting fingers all said there were still some dragons worth slaying. It didn't feel like a dusted-off isolation unit either. What it felt like to Jan was a sales seminar, as if they'd been assembled to be convinced that Camelot still had a glow. Without warning, the agent sprang up, pumped each of their hands energetically, and informed them they were about to embark on the chance of a lifetime, a historic opportunity, the point in the war on drugs at which it would eventually be said the tide began to turn. Releasing Ginger's hand, he began to pace back and forth. Other generalities flew.

To Jan's left Jackson watched the agent's canned speech by ticking his eyes back and forth. Ginger didn't move even that much; her eyes had settled in on the table before them.

"We've got the picture," Jan said when the agent paused for a breath. "What I think you should do is tell these two about the dangers."

"Like who's after your patient," Jackson said.

The agent momentarily stood with a hand still raised in the air from the point he'd been making before Jan's interruption. Lowering his arm, he was about to rebut, but stopped himself short and stole a sideways glance at Jan as if cautioning himself to show restraint. He needed practice. He paced for a minute, his hands tucked in at his belt, eyes studying the floor, before reaching what had all the trappings of an irrevocable decision.

"You're absolutely right," the agent said, wagging his large head seriously. "If you're going to help us, you need to know what's going on." He didn't take his eyes off Jan while delivering this testimonial, and he didn't blink as he went on to say, "They've called in the Hammer."

"The Hammer?" Jan said, thinking maybe she'd misheard him.

"That's the code name we've assigned him," Agent Windish confirmed. "He's a mechanic for the cartels."

"What kind of name is that?" Jan asked.

"That's not something you need to know," Windish said. "But I can tell you he's been solving cartel feuds for nearly ten years, so if they've called him in, they're desperate to get at our client. That's good. It means we're on to something. Other questions?"

"Who's this *they?*" Jackson asked.

"The people after our patient."

"So who's our patient?" Jan asked.

"A player," the agent grimly said.

"For which league?" Jackson said.

The agent turned his head toward Jackson to say, "You don't sound like you're with the program."

Before Jackson could answer, Jan intervened, saying, "Maybe you better tell him about the cosmic nature of your struggle."

For a moment the cosmic struggle in question seized the agent's chunky face. Lightness won out as he managed a smile and said, "You'll have to forgive me. I've had this on my mind for a long time. Let's leave it at this: I give you my word that your risk is minimal. We'll be dealing with all the heavy-duty stuff, but if you still have any doubts about signing up . . ."

When no one responded immediately, Ginger snapped to as if they were waiting for her to speak and determinedly said, "I won't miss him."

Jackson coughed to cover up a guffaw, and Jan had to look away herself. But the agent assumed she was referring to the Hammer and said, "That's the spirit."

"You might help matters," Jan said, recovering, "if you told us what you know about this Hammer."

"Jan," the agent said, "whatever I released to you, feel free to pass on. Keeping in mind that it's all strictly confidential. Other questions?"

Jackson had one. "What'd he use on our ambulance?"

"Jan will fill you in on that too," the agent said. "Now are we all one, big happy family?"

Jan shifted uneasily on her chair.

"All right then," Agent Windish said. "I want you to all solemnly pledge to never reveal anything you learn while assisting us."

They all did. Ginger even raised her hand.

# TWELVE

EACH MORNING BEFORE ARRIVING AT THE taxi stand, the Hammer checked in with his answering service and then phoned patient information to make sure Marilyn Jones remained hospitalized at Jackson General. Once assured that she did, he drove to a new florist for a fresh get-well bouquet. For two days he had no occasion to visit the ailing Ms. Jones, but shortly before lunch on day three the unforeseen arrived.

"Say *ah*," he murmured to himself, the surroundings putting him in mind of a medical examination.

Out of the main entrance across the way came a man and woman. He didn't know the blond woman, although he thought it possible she was one of the hospital security guards out of uniform. The slight forward tilt of her busty figure struck him as familiar, but her identity really didn't matter. He knew the man.

"This won't hurt a bit," the Hammer promised himself.

Manos, they called the man now leaving the hospital. He was Carmen Romero-Muehlen's constant bodyguard, a man who remained unswayed by all modern technologies of death and hybrids of martial arts. For him there remained but one satisfactory way to kill—with the hands fastened around the neck. The technique had become his calling card, earning him the street name of Manos, which translated into English as *hands*. In addition to his indestructible mitts, the rest of him had the mass of a robot and roughly the same range of facial expression. His glossy, black hair said Indian, but his features hinted at a genealogy modified by a few Spanish rapes.

"Do you have a history of death in your family?" the Hammer said to himself as he started his cab.

Several years ago, before Carmen had developed liver dysfunction, she'd hired the Hammer to take care of some nagging distribution problems. There wasn't any central personnel office when working for the *contrabandistas;* everything was second or third cousins passing his name along, and then phone calls, always in the middle of the night, with instructions. Then more phone calls in the middle of later nights with expanded instructions in low, urgent, consumed voices. Everything had to be done yesterday with much letting of blood. Always the blood. The Hammer loved that fire, but over the years had become fatigued by it too. In comparison, Carmen Romero-Muehlen had seemed a breath of fresh air. First, a woman in a man's world. That in itself had been appealing, for an Anglo like the Hammer had also been something of an outsider in that world. Then, despite her first cousin's rank in the cartel, it became clear she'd reached her position owing to her abilities. Could they find anyone else who could so successfully and unobtrusively handle their product distribution in North America? Calm, methodical, a scholarship student with a degree in business administration at a Big Ten university—she was nearly perfect for the job. So nearly perfect that the Hammer had been lulled into breaking one of his cardinal rules, namely, working alone.

Hopeful that her bodyguard might expand his repertoire, Carmen had paid extra to have Manos accompany the Hammer on his rounds. Unfortunately, the bodyguard proved to be a less than satisfactory pupil. He had too much pride in his own method to learn any new ones. During their sweep up the Texas gulf coast, Manos personally caved in the windpipes of three entrepreneurs with visions of a larger piece of the rock. One of the strangulations occurred after the upstart had pumped two small-caliber shells at point-blank range into the bodyguard's torso. Manos had twice grunted and broken into a light sweat on his brow but never loosened his grip for an instant. In a chest that large, vital organs had plenty of room to hide. Later, when the Hammer had had to explain that his tutorials had been a failure, Carmen gave her bodyguard such a tongue-lashing that Manos dropped to his knees to tearfully hug her legs. With pride, Carmen had explained, "He's a traditionalist."

The Hammer had nodded as if it made sense to him. One thing the sight of Manos on his knees had planted in his head—the bodyguard's fealty to his mistress was absolute, which meant the number of fatalities in the current operation had just doubled. He couldn't get close enough to dispatch Carmen without including Manos. It had become a package deal.

When Manos and the blond started across the street toward the taxi stand, the Hammer pretended to receive a radio call, averted his head, and drove away before they could unlatch the rear door. A block later he pulled over to wait for the cab that did pick them up. The tail job was an easy one, with no threat of being spotted by the passengers, who were too busy pawing one another to notice anyone weaving through traffic behind them. Roughly a mile later, the blue-and-white pulled curbside, and the woman led Manos inside an upscale apartment building. The Hammer immediately cut across traffic to turn left and double back to the hospital. With Manos occupied, could there be a better time to reconnoiter exactly where Carmen was laid up?

Pulling into a patient-pickup drive, he parked, unlocked the trunk, and lifted out his wrapped bouquet. To the flowers, he said, "No talking."

At the front entrance he was halted by a sway-backed security guard whose photo ID read L. KENNEDY and whose face had as much expression as G. Washington on a well-worn dollar bill.

"Destination?"

"Visiting an old friend," the Hammer answered, cooperative as he imagined any honest citizen would be, which was to say, not entirely, a bit nettled by the delay.

"Patient name?"

"Is there something wrong, Officer?"

"It's all routine," the guard said, becoming slightly more interested in him.

"I wasn't stopped like this last time."

"We're initiating a new procedure."

"I see," the Hammer said, standoffish but dropping all combativeness. "I'm visiting Marilyn Jones. I'm taking her some flowers."

"Mind if I look?"

Leaning over, the guard read the name written on the rose-bordered card attached to the waxy paper. His red nose sniffed deeply as he confessed that he ought to buy his own dear missus a bouquet just for the hell of it. Off a stool behind him, he lifted a computer printout that contained an alphabetical census listing. Quickly flipping pages, he ran a square fingernail down the columns until locating Marilyn Jones's name. Satisfied, he printed PCRC on the bottom of a pink sheet of note-sized paper that had VISITOR PASS across the top and the current date stamped beneath the heading.

"Take the elevator to the third floor," the guard said, pointing.

The Hammer thanked him and moved along, joining two old bats in full-length fur coats. True to the guard's word, the third floor held the postcoronary recovery unit, as a backlit panel inside the elevator told him, but of more interest to him were the medical intensive-care units listed on the fourth floor. Having done his homework, he knew that anyone sick enough to be flown in for a liver transplant would most likely need more than an ordinary floor bed.

Since the two octogenarians in fur were headed to the fourth floor themselves, to visit an ungrateful nephew leading a life of debauchery, the Hammer elected to tag along. Given his cabbie's uniform, he stayed quietly in the background, acting as if he was carrying flowers for the elderly crusaders traveling up with him. The two ladies paid no more attention to him than they would have an umbrella stand.

"Why couldn't he be a simple drunk like his father before him?" asked the taller of the two.

"You know how young people are," said the other.

They went on at greater length about the weakness of their nephew's character, but the Hammer was too busy memorizing the stations listed for each floor to pay close attention. He knew he'd struck pay dirt as soon as the fourth-floor doors opened to a pair of hospital guards, one a slight, black-haired woman, the other a tall, thin balding man. They stood three feet apart, jawing woodenly about something until the doors parted and they each put on their public faces. As the man greeted the old ladies and the Hammer with a request for their visitor's passes, the woman guard stepped around them and on to the elevator. The old ladies were flattered by the male guard's attention, and while they commented on his helpfulness, as if he'd been stationed there solely for their benefit, the Hammer tried to blend into their entourage by following obediently behind them with the flowers. That was a washout. Gesturing for his pass, the guard dispatched him down to three, where PCRC could be found.

Acting grateful for the correction, the Hammer stepped back aboard the elevator, being held open for him by the woman guard, whose name tag read J. GALLAGHER. Pay attention to the details, he always told himself. She stared so fiercely at the closing chrome doors that he saw an opportunity and went with it. Punching the button for three, he said, "He being a jerk?"

Since they were the only passengers, she couldn't very well ignore him, but the smile she flashed faded quickly.

"Pardon?"

"That guy, was he being a jerk?"

"Let's say he wasn't being fully cooperative."

"That's a mistake I wouldn't make," the Hammer predicted. The woman studied him quizzically, the intelligence in her eyes warning him that he was working too hard.

"I'm sure you don't make many," she said as the third-floor doors opened.

He knew it was a dig and knew he should let it pass, but couldn't resist giving her something to think about.

"So far only one," he said, stepping off the elevator where—surprise—there was no security guard waiting to greet him.

Wanting to keep his face's exposure to a minimum, he raised a hand in parting and walked away without a backward glance.

As he followed the arrows to the PCRC unit, it occurred to him that he could be strolling a floor below Carmen's bed, not that such proximity did him much good. Thanks to modern cement construction methods, only a bomb heavy enough to knock out the entire wing would guarantee him of a hit on the above target. Getting that much explosive into position wouldn't be easy, even if he'd wanted to. Besides which, gone forever were the days when blowing up an entire building pleased his sense of aesthetics. The exuberance of youth had been replaced by an appreciation of craftsmanship. With Marilyn Jones out of her room for tests, he laid the bouquet across her pillow and quietly left.

Back at the taxi stand he was calculating ways to narrow his target area when part of the solution arrived in a cab that unloaded Manos and the blond woman. They were back far too soon for their nooner to have been a success for anyone but a premature ejaculator. The massive bodyguard held the door open for his companion, who refused the courtesy, instead climbing out the opposite side. As soon as the woman cleared the car door, she angrily shouldered a carry-all bag, lifted a lunch cooler, and headed away from Manos without a good-bye. Encouraging. She went directly to an employee-only entrance, causing Manos to lift his chin and bray. Pausing, the woman gave a feisty toss of her head before disappearing inside. Once alone,

Manos threw money at the cabbie, slammed shut his door, and stormed the hospital's main entrance.

The bodyguard could wait. At present the Hammer was more intrigued by the woman, for surely she would know what room Manos was attached to.

# THIRTEEN

AFTER CARMEN ROMERO-MUEHLEN'S ARRIVAL, JAN RICOCHETED around General Jack for days. In Agent George Windish's mind disaster loomed barely a half second ahead, and as he whirled everywhere to prevent the next catastrophe, his backdraft sucked Jan along. He clearly preferred his obedience blind, which meant Jan asked "why" entirely too much, yet for some reason they had no words over it. When could they have? They never stood still long enough to talk extensively. Yes-no conversations took place while rushing to catch an elevator or while three phone calls were on hold or in between mouthfuls of cold food brought up from the cafeteria.

By eight on Jan's first morning on duty, Agent Windish had ordered her to secure a new color TV for the patient, one that had a clearer image than the current unit and one that also had no possibility of having been tampered with. That conversation took place during an elevator ride to the roof of Old General where Windish had spotted a man in a white lab coat staring down at the fourth MICU's windows. How Windish had managed this when the MICU's blinds were all drawn remained a mystery.

The man they captured turned out to be a first-year resident trying to steal a few minutes of solitude to calm his sleep-deprived nervous system. Since the hospital didn't entrust first-year doctors with keys, only with patients, his presence on the roof raised some thorny security questions. All rooftop doors were supposed to be locked thanks to a psych patient who thought he had sprouted wings. It took Jan nearly an hour to determine that housekeeping personnel were the culprits. They had blocked open the door to accommodate smoke breaks, which they had to take outside since a hospital-wide smoking ban had gone into effect. As for the first-year resident, he hadn't been staring at MICU Four but at space in general, rethinking his commitment to the health care profession. Jan spent a half hour tracking down the chief of medicine to obtain a positive identification of him. After that, Windish placed a lookout atop Old General and ordered him to check in via radio at fifteen minute intervals.

Not much later a parent attempted to bring a seven-foot toy giraffe to his ailing son; he made the mistake of boarding the same elevator car as Windish. The giraffe remained impounded until Jan delivered it to Radiology for an X ray of its insides, which proved to contain nothing but cotton batting and a wooden broomstick to strengthen its neck.

By the time Jan had returned the stuffed animal to the fuming father, her beeper had twice been set off by Agent Windish, who had discovered that Carmen Romero-Muehlen, their patient, was receiving oxygen through a small plastic tube. This nasal cannula was connected to a wall outlet that was hooked into an infrastructure delivery system whose conduit was vulnerable to acts of terrorism at so many points that the DEA agent could hardly catch his breath.

Since the medical staff refused to back off from administering the oxygen mixture to their patient, the source of the gas had to be switched to portable tanks that could be tested before they were hooked up. Then, having raised the spectre of poisonous gas, Agent Windish had trouble finding volunteers to personally sample the contents of any new tanks, and he refused to accept the staff's pledge that all tanks were meticulously certified before delivery.

The result?

Jan was dispatched to a pet store for a pair of canaries and to the newborn intensive care unit for an isolette, a clear plastic incubator that protected premature infants. The birds were transferred to the high-tech bassinet, which could be sealed off, and were privileged to receive the first giddy whiffs from each tank now used in the unit. It certainly boosted their musicality.

The birds survived, but one of the nurses didn't. An animal activist, she objected to using her fellow creatures in such a reckless fashion. Jan got the nod to reason with the RN, but the woman proved intractable and had to be replaced.

All this swept Jan up to lunch of day one. Thank God Agent Windish didn't have time for a mid-morning coffee break. The added jolt of caffeine might have put him into a high orbit—and Jan not far behind.

Nor was Special Agent George the only bull in the china shop. Soon after Ginger started her first shift at three-thirty, it became obvious that the patient's private bodyguard had a Hollywood-fueled thirst for blonds. Worse, Ginger began to act ready for diversions. Her attention span was zilch, and she was still popping breath mints. Windish did a doubletake of the lovebirds, pulled Jan aside, and ordered the romance nipped in the bud. A day later when for some unknown reason the dalliance self-destructed after the pair stepped out for lunch, Windish actually patted Jan on the back for a job well done. In truth, she'd had no more luck guiding Ginger away from the bodyguard than she'd had in prying anything out of her mother about her navy man.

Her evenings at home were considerably abbreviated owing to Agent Windish's whims. By the time she dragged herself in the kitchen door, she found supper long finished and those girls who were home, usually the youngest two, Katie and Tess, parked on the living room carpet in front of the TV console, homework spread out all around them. With their Walkman headphones on, they appeared to be taking dictation whenever they scribbled something in their school notebooks, but Jan didn't interfere in their study habits, not so long as they pulled passing grades, which they all did except for Leah, the oldest, who was a senior and failing in four out of five classes. The one subject Leah breezed through was precollege calculus, proving how hard she had to work for the *F*s in all her other courses. Jan had butted heads with Leah for years about being an underachiever and was convinced that the contest of wills had triggered her eldest daughter's rebelliousness. That was why she let the younger girls study however they wanted. So far the new approach seemed to be working.

Although it was a mystery how the girls could have the TV going, their Walkmans cranking, and still retain anything from the open books before them, what Jan truly couldn't understand was how they managed to track all that and still hear the telephone ringing. But they could. And the phone rang often.

If a daughter was tying up the phone, she was either in the kitchen or else in Jan and Claire's bedroom, where she propped her feet against the wall above the headboards. As of yet, those were the only extensions in the house. Phone calls were limited to fifteen minutes, which was one house rule Jan didn't have to enforce. The girls policed themselves on that point. Whoever was waiting for a call wound up the kitchen timer and set it beside the extension in use.

The unusual thing about this string of evenings was that when Jan arrived home, often as not it was Claire on the phone. The older girls would be out—Amy at some extracurricular school activity; Leah probably at a mall—the younger girls would be studying, and Claire would be gabbing, not with her new beau but with one of the ladies she'd recently met at the community center. Jan knew it wasn't the navy man on the other end because what sailor would spend his evenings discussing flea markets, casseroles, and mastectomies.

Nevertheless, the fact that Claire was on the phone at all marked a change from her usual darning and washing chores, which she dragged out through the day and into the night so that everyone would know how much she was doing for them. At least whatever had Claire so agitated but a few days before had passed. In fact, she was chatting like a schoolgirl. Maybe Jan's daughters were a positive influence on her after all. Before Claire had combined her household with Jan's, she'd verged on becoming an eccentric, somewhat bitter, recluse. Now she appeared to be coming out of her shell.

Jan was more than willing to make herself a sandwich and tune out Claire's conversations. When the girls complained that their grandmother had run way over her allotted fifteen minutes, Jan told them age had its privileges. Tess mentioned that age eight didn't have many.

The one night Jan did have enough pep to bring up her mother's previous bad mood, Claire had been evasive.

"Did you want to talk about whatever was bothering you the other day?" Jan had asked.

"Was something bothering me?" Claire was seated at her vanity wearing a frilly nightgown the girls had given her for Christmas two years ago and which had remained in its box until now. Her hair was in curlers and she was idly trying on earrings.

"Weren't you the one who taught me to always be honest?" Jan asked.

"That must have been your father."

Jan leaned over her mother's jewelry box, selected a pair of silver button clip-ons, and held them up to Claire's ears. Claire shook her head no.

"Rumor has it you're stepping out," Jan said, returning to her bed.

"A woman my age?" Claire said, pretending to be scandalized.

"I think it's great," Jan offered.

"You would."

"There any chance of meeting the gentleman in question? Or are you too embarrassed of us?"

"I'd say," Claire primly responded, "that you're reading far more into this than is there."

"At any rate, I'm glad your mood's improved."

"Hmmph," Claire answered, not about to be rushed into anything. Fastening on a pair of red coral earrings, she climbed in bed herself and turned out the light without a word about why she needed jewelry in her sleep.

After several minutes of listening to rustlings from the girls' rooms, Jan had nearly dozed off herself when Claire said with perfect clarity.

"I haven't that many years left, you know."

Jan had to blink before certain it wasn't a voice out of a dream. "Is that what's been bothering you?"

"Something else," Claire said, sounding preoccupied.

When Jan checked, she saw her mother lying on her back, hands folded across her chest, eyes open.

"Did you want to tell me?" Jan asked, uncertain that she wanted to hear.

"Not particularly," Claire said after a moment. "But that's the point, I guess. That's the way it is when a person makes a mistake this big. They usually don't want to talk about it, I mean."

"A mistake," Jan said, nearly reaching out to turn on the light but sensing that she shouldn't, that it would scare her mother away from whatever was weighing so heavily on her mind. Claire answered in a voice that seemed older and sadly wiser than Jan imagined possible from her mother.

"All my life," said Claire, "I tried to do what was expected of me, by my parents, your father, you and your brothers, neighbors I barely knew. You name it. Hardly a day went by that I didn't spend hours worrying what someone thought of me. And look where it's gotten me. I wouldn't know what I wanted if it jumped up and bit me on the nose. Just once I'd like to do something for myself, something nobody expected."

"Is there something you want to do?"

"I don't know," Claire said in a tortured way.

"I thought you'd been doing pretty good lately. Getting out and seeing people, making new friends."

"That's the worst part of it," Claire said. "It's showed me how much I've missed."

"Maybe it's not as bad as . . ."

"I'm trying to tell you something I've learned," Claire crossly said, cutting her off. "Would you let me do that?"

Jan closed her mouth. After gathering her thoughts, Claire continued on in a stilted voice.

"I know you're better at standing up for yourself than I ever was, and that's what I've been wanting to tell you. You were right to do that, and I've been wrong to tell you different all these years. I can see that now." The pitch of her voice rose. "And don't think that I'm saying you haven't made any mistakes. I'm just saying that I shouldn't have been pretending you didn't accomplish some important things, with your job and all." When Jan didn't comment, Claire sighed and went on, "I was jealous, I guess. Or maybe it was something else, I don't know." Another sigh. "I'm saying I was wrong, and I'm sorry."

The furnace briefly kicked on in the basement and they both listened to it. When it shut down, they waited for something else to listen to but nothing presented itself.

"Mom," Jan said, "I don't think we're as different as you like to believe."

"Go to sleep now."

"Who taught me to be so stubborn?"

"I'm not going to argue with you about it," Claire warned. "Go to sleep."

Taking her own advice, Claire was soon slumbering peacefully, as though a great slab of guilt had been lifted from her. Jan lay awake long into the night though, making a list of similarities between herself and her mother. In the morning neither said a word about their conversation.

Through all of the activity at the hospital, she caught repeated glimpses of the Little Admiral's squat, impenetrable shadow hovering on the sidelines. When someone rifled her desk, no doubt in search of news of Agent Windish, she reported the incident to Hodges who acted sympathetic enough to arouse suspicion. In response, she left a note on her desk that asked the searchers to please wash their hands before going through her belongings again. The next day she found the note crumpled into a tight ball.

So the days passed in manic splendor. After her purported success in nipping Ginger's fling with the bodyguard in the bud, Agent Windish insisted that Jan, and Jan alone, handle all transactions between the fourth MICU and the rest of the hospital. Ginger and Jackson were to be safety valves only. Flattering as this was, the end result was aching feet and even longer hours away from home.

Any spare moments were taken up with earnest prayers that a liver would soon be found for their patient, found before the state of grace at home turned to smoke. Divine intervention seemed the only way out from between the rock and hard place where she was caught, or rather, considering the physiques of the joint chiefs, Hodges and Windish, maybe it would be more accurate to say she was caught between a soft and a softer place. Her sole consolation was that she hadn't opened her *Webster's Collegiate* in days.

# FOURTEEN

HALFWAY THROUGH THE EVENING THE HAMMER again caught sight of the blond who'd gone off with Manos. Dressed in a security guard's uniform, she stepped outside the main entrance for a cigarette break. She was a healthy-looking thing, particularly with the snug fit of her clothes. The task ahead of him was shaping up to be no chore, although he could have done without the taste of nicotine her mouth would carry. He was about to cross the street to tell her that he was an officer in the surgeon general's cigarette police and wanted to know what kind of example she thought she was setting for the other beautiful women of the city—he'd had success with that line before—when a second security guard joined her under the flood-lights near the entrance.

The second guard was J. Gallagher, the woman he'd come on to earlier in the elevator. She laid a hand on the taller blond's shoulder and leaned close to say something. Whatever motherly advice J. Gallagher was sharing, it didn't play well. The blond brushed the hand away and turned toward the street, paying more attention to traffic than whatever was being said. J. Gallagher kept talking any-way. Suddenly, without saying a word, the blond flicked her ciggy onto the drive and strode back inside, leaving J. Gallagher curbside. The Hammer found himself chuckling.

Near midnight, when the blond's shift should be ending, he finagled his way to the head of the taxistand on the off-chance she wanted a lift home. But it wasn't to be that easy. Dressed in a baggy sweater and tights, she burst out the employee entrance, perhaps fleeing more advice from J. Gallagher, and hiked away from the hospital on foot. As soon as she'd turned the corner, the Hammer crept into traffic to follow until nearly two blocks later when the journey ended at a hole-in-the-wall bar named the Strong Arm.

Parking, he shed his mustache along with the rest of his cabbie uniform, and entered the bar, a loud, poorly-lit pit half full of paramedics and nursing assistants and sprinkled with career drunks. The blond wasn't hard to locate. She sat at the back side of the bar, alone, four shot glasses of clear liquor lined up before her. As he edged his way past a pool table to reach an empty stool beside her, she gunned the second shot, her only reaction a slight sucking in of her cheeks.

From up close she had a magnetism about her that emanated from her blond hair, which was extremely full and kinky but tied into a bushy ponytail. With her locks pulled back, her face appeared narrow and somewhat sharp, particularly around her brow and nose. She paid no attention to him when he removed the lunch cooler and tote bag on the stool beside her. Sitting down, he said, "It doesn't look as though I can buy you a drink."

No answer. If anything, she blocked him out even farther.

He said, "All men are bastards, aren't they?"

"I've a black belt in judo," she said in a monotone.

"Is that a promise?"

She turned toward him as if not hearing him quite right. "And a brown belt in karate."

"Those sound like belts I'd like to see."

"You some kind of pervert?" she asked, maybe intrigued.

"Not that I know of."

"I usually don't let strange men hit on me in bars."

"How about laundromats?"

"What?"

"Do you let strange men hit on you in laundromats? There's one across the street."

After sizing him up for a moment, she cupped a red-blooded hand over his nearest biceps and leaned close to confide, "I like your attitude."

Her name was Ginger. He introduced himself as Duke, a name that in his experience usually amused but also intrigued women. She answered that with the man luck she'd been having, she didn't really care what he called himself so long as he kept breathing.

"You look like a veteran of some war," she said after drinks three and four. "That's good. I like a man with combat experience."

But history wasn't her strong suit. She had no idea whether he would have served in Korea or Kuwait, nor did it seem to matter. What mattered was that she claimed to like the way he dressed, kind of funky, baggy clothes, hair short and bristly, with a widow's peak, and a fanny pack around his waist, as if he'd arrived on a bicycle.

"How dangerous can a cyclist be?" she asked after he bought her shots five and six of tequila. With a slur, she admitted to craving a little mystery in her men. She also liked the way he suggested they get something to eat, at her place.

"You're making me hungry," he had said.

"I like a man with an appetite."

"You know what they say about Chinese food?"

"Avoid the eggs?"

He shook his head in the negative, a hard gleam to his eyes, which were golden, like a jungle cat's, or at least that was how he liked to imagine them. Her hand was resting on his shoulder; had been for quite some time.

"They say it's best raw," he said. "Your place got a table?"

He ordered up a taxi, didn't offer to carry her bags, and acted sure enough of himself to help her overcome any doubts. On the way to her apartment he dodged most of her questions, admitting only to being in town on business, an answer that amused her.

"Married," she said, as if she'd suspected as much.

She mentioned her job at the hospital but mostly the last half of the ride was silent. Her eyes seemed a little teary, so he squeezed her knee.

At her apartment building, he watched her punch in the front door's security code and let her lean against him during the elevator ride up. Her efficiency apartment looked as though worked over by bargain shoppers, clothes draped everywhere, shoes scattered across the floor, perfumes hanging in the air. In one corner she appeared to be reconstructing the Leaning Tower of Pisa with pizza boxes. She acted too tipsy to notice the disarray, and when she opened a window, he suspected it was more to sober herself than freshen the air.

He ordered half the entries off a take-out Chinese menu, telling her, "No weight to that food." Rather than stroll three blocks to the restaurant, he paid for a cabdriver to do the pickup and delivery honors. When the egg rolls arrived, he gave her a hundred and sent her down to the front lobby to deal with the cabbie, claiming he had to use the bathroom, but actually wanting to limit the number of people who saw his face. She balked but he joshed her out of it by pointing out that he was trusting her with the change. One look at the explosion of female articles in the bathroom drove him back to the kitchen. To occupy himself, he poked through cupboards and drawers. On a hook above the two clean dishes in the place, he found a key that fit the apartment's front door and which he promptly pocketed on general principle.

Once their banquet was spread out, he sampled the cartons as if more interested in them than her. That added to the suspense, which he knew would be another point in his favor.

"I don't usually one-night, you know."

"Hmm," he said. "Try the subgum. Nicely spiced."

"So I don't want you making any big deal out of this."

"You and your boyfriend have a fight?" he asked, poking around in another carton.

"No boyfriend," she said defensively.

"There should be."

"Say," she said, jumping at a chance to change the subject, "you're a charmer when I least expect it."

"A-hmm." His mouth was full of something crunchy.

"Aren't you at all curious about me?" she asked.

"You want to be appreciated, that it?"

"You don't have to make it sound like work."

"Hmm." He moved on to the next carton, stirring the contents and after a moment asking, "So what's it like working at that hospital?"

"Mostly boring," she said. "And pecky."

"Pecky?" he said, using chopsticks to push the red peppers to one side of his plate.

"They've all got beaks down at the county."

He silently made an *ah* shape with his lips, sampled some fried rice, and asked with his mouth full, "So why stay?"

"I won't be for long," she assured him. "As soon as I pass the city's cop test, I'm out of there."

He chewed and watched her without comment, unless you counted a burp, which he didn't bother to apologize for. Those Tarzan eyes of his made her giddy as a teen, absolutely talkative, almost girlish, in a nice raging-hormone way.

"But until then it's an OK place to work," she said, trying to sell herself more than him. "Kind of exciting even."

"How exciting?" He dipped a piece of pork in the sweet-sour sauce.

"Different kinds of rushes," she said offhandedly while loosening her ponytail and fluffing her hair out. "Right now they've got me guarding this scaggy old broad who's on some kind of witness protection trip."

"Tell me about it," he said, gazing so intently at her that she turned away embarrassed.

"Actually," she said, "I was right the first time. It's pretty goddamn boring. All I do is sit there eight hours a day, can't even leave for a smoke. Maybe I get to run one errand a night for some federal jerk who acts like everything between his ears is stamped *top secret* and he can't say a word because of it."

"What kind of errands?"

"All of a sudden you're awfully damn talkative."

"Foreplay," he said with a shrug. Then he didn't ask one more thing about it but occupied himself with lifting another piece of pork from the container. Overseas training allowed him to handle the chopsticks like a pro, which was a thing she mentioned. He flexed a spare muscle or two when sure she was looking. That got a boozy laugh.

"You're something else, Duke. You ever going to tell me your last name?"

"Duke," he said with a conspiratorial wink.

"Duke Duke. And I suppose you're in town for a prophylactics convention."

"Miz Ginger," he said with a bully's playfulness, "I don't think you trust me."

"Now we're getting somewhere," she said, having to steady herself with a hand on the back of her chair as she stood.

"I think you've got a whole thing about men in general," he told her.

"And I suppose you're going to tell me about it?"

"Why should I?" he said. "You already know all the answers but one."

"Which is?"

"What I see in you."

"You're wrong there," she said, tugging on his arm.

"We can leave it at that if you want," he said without letting her budge him.

She wove her way from the kitchen to the unmade bed near the living room window. He let her drape herself across the knotted bed covers in various seductive poses for a minute or two without paying any particular attention. He wasn't in any hurry to join her on that mess, that was for sure. His reluctance was driving her pretty near crazy. When he'd had his fill at the table, he rose and told her he had to brush his teeth.

"I don't have an extra brush," she petulantly said.

"Not to worry," he said, pulling an electric toothbrush out of his hip pack. She groaned and collapsed backwards with her sweater pulled halfway over her head. That didn't prevent him from stepping into the bathroom to floss and brush with his eyes closed, which beat looking at the ringed sink and splattered mirror. Appearing at her bedside, he unzipped his fanny pack again.

"What else have you got in there?" she asked in a husky voice. She'd undressed and gotten under the sheets.

"Coconut oil and helmets."

"Helmets?"

He showed her a pack of rubbers.

"Anything else to show me?" she asked.

He shoved her backwards and then they didn't talk for a long time.

Two hours before dawn he left her snoring. Considering the way she'd cried herself to sleep after their exertions, he didn't want to be around for breakfast. Besides, now that it appeared he was through driving his Premier taxicab, he had some unfinished business with the driver he'd bought off. It would be best to clear that up without delay.

From the woman's apartment he walked to a nearby taxi stand, climbed in a cab, and rode back to the Premier cab he'd left near the Strong Arm bar. It had been eating on him for three days now that he'd saved the salesman on the airplane from choking to death, and gradually he'd seen a way to balance it out. Pulling through an all-night chicken joint, he ordered up a crispy-fried breast at the drive-through window.

Parking, he cut out a good-sized chuck of white meat and taped a tiny NFL sticker to it, just as he did to every weapon he left behind at the scene of a crime. Early in his current career, his chief complaint about the press coverage had been that no reporter had picked up on how he left a calling card—an NFL sticker—at the scene of every job. Eventually, however, he recognized the press's omission was because the authorities were keeping the fact to themselves, to screen out copycats. Such an honor naturally made his relationship with law enforcement people seem more personal, and it definitely increased his diligence in keeping up his end of the bargain. When it came time to let them know his hand was behind a death, he never cheated and always left his mark at the scene. Never having done anyone in with a chicken breast before, he hoped the sticker stayed in place.

Letting himself into the cabbie's dismal little house, he noted that every room stank of cat piss and cigarette smoke. Since he didn't flush out any cats, he assumed they must have departed with the wife and friend. Lights were on in every room, including the bedroom where the cabbie had fallen asleep with a racing form across his sunken chest. A cigarette, ash all the way down to the filter, sat on the edge of the nightstand beside the bed. The old man slept with his mouth open; his purplish tongue lolled at the corner of his lips.

Just as the Hammer was about to finish off his day's work, the old guy shook his head no and made a rattle-whimper in his throat, as if fighting off a bad dream. The skin across his cheekbones tightened, as did the wattle under his chin. His teeth were in a drinking glass beside the bed. He farted. His eyes shifted under his veined eyelids as if searching for who had broke wind.

Fascinated, the Hammer held up for a moment, wondering if the old man wasn't going to go in his sleep, right while he watched. But then the cabbie's breathing calmed and his eyes quieted.

The Hammer then had a strange thought: *Maybe I shouldn't.*

It seemed obvious that the cabbie wasn't far away from going on his own. Besides, how much could he know?

The Hammer stared at the sleeping man for a full minute before coming to his senses, the popping the chunk of chicken in the man's open mouth, and finishing the job in a way that Manos would have approved of—with his gloved hands.

Later, on the way back to his hotel room, he really didn't know what to make of his hesitation. It'd never happened before, not even when gazing into his victim's terror-stricken eyes. He was relieved the moment had passed but bedeviled by it too. Too wired to sleep, he detoured to the city's bus depot to collect the luggage he'd shipped back from Las Vegas. The suitcase contained his portable armory, which he always sent by bus to his job locations, that way avoiding airport security systems. There were some meticulously packed military items inside the case that should prove helpful now that he'd found a delivery system. Back at his hotel he made sure to brush his teeth before turning in.

The next night, the Hammer positioned himself outside the Strong Arm bar when Ginger got off work. With a quart of tequila under his arm, they quickly retired to her place to try the other half of the Chinese take-out menu.

"You look tired," he commented while dishing out some chicken almond ding. "Too many errands?"

"Never even left the unit," she sullenly said.

"Not even for supper?" he asked, all sympathy.

"No way. I have to pack my meals in. The little princess I'm working under ordered me never to leave while on duty. They might need me. Don't ask me for what. It's a mystery."

"How's the patient holding up?" he asked, wanting to move her along.

"Who knows? She's all tubes and electrodes and hypos. I can tell you one thing about her though. To be going through what she's going through—she don't want to die. In a big way, she don't want to."

"What's she in for?" he asked, acting more concerned with his meal than her answer.

"Liver transplant. And death warmed over would look better than she does."

"How long's her treatment going to take?"

"Nobody's telling me," she said, steamed about it. "But I can predict one thing. Before she's fixed up, somebody else has to be all done using their liver. That's what they're waiting on. Somebody else has to die, in a drive-by or something. Gives me the willies thinking about it."

"Maybe you need something else to think about," he suggested, curling a hand around her waist.

At least that night she didn't cry herself to sleep and it appeared she'd spent some of the day cleaning the place, although not as much as she should have. Much as he longed for clean sheets, he stayed beside her all night. When she awoke in the morning he was right there beside her, ready to do her bidding, as he sinisterly put it. So much for the morning. Around noon they finished off last night's fried rice and chop suey, and then he offered to pack her lunch cooler while she took a bubble bath.

"You trying to make me into something I'm not?" she coyly asked.

"Just wanted to soften you up, Miss Ginger."

It was a routine she claimed she could grow to like. While she soaked, he made her a wicked tuna salad sandwich and asked if he should pack a traveler bottle of Chablis.

"Or do they check your bucket?"

"They know better than to bother me," she bragged from the bathtub.

"Then Chablis it is."

# PART TWO

# FIFTEEN

It started with the terminally bored voice of the hospital's public address announcer.

"Plan X, building B."

The announcer repeated the overhead message three times at shortly after 3:40 P.M. The evening shift was struggling to get a handle on everything dumped on them by the day shift. All over the hospital annoyed nurses exchanged blank looks, orderlies and X-ray techs did likewise, as did ward clerks and hospital messengers. In each instance, one member of every pair said something equivalent to, "What's Plan X?"

Even patients and visitors, who thanks to television medical dramas had the illusion of knowing what hospital codes were all about, were stumped. They were familiar with *Code Blues* for cardiac arrests and *Mr. Reds* for fires. But Plan X? Not only had they no idea, but it sounded ominous, like some kind of doomsday code, like something that went hand in hand with red flashing lights and people keeling over in hallways owing to unseen gases. Restless, they button-holed the nearest person sporting an employee picture ID and demanded to know what was going down. They didn't get any satisfaction from the employees, which only added to the frequently voiced complaint that not one person in the entire godforsaken place knew the difference between a bedpan and an eyedropper.

People checked out the window but saw no funnel cloud, and even though the city had never recorded a tremor in its entire history, they touched walls to assure themselves there was no earthquake. Over the radio there was no news of a train wreck or high-rise fire or jet airliner trying to land on a freeway during rush hour or any type of disaster that would send scores of survivors streaming toward General Jack.

Then they heard footsteps pounding down the hallways, and they leaned out doors or around corners to spy security guards tearing by. Now everyone assumed that the overhead was a special security code, which intrigued them even more. Of course there weren't any security guards around when they were really needed, like right now to answer questions about this code.

On the fourth floor of New General, particularly on the south wing, the staff was extremely edgy about any unfamiliar procedures. Anyone working there knew about the heavy security measures for the transplant patient sequestered at the far end of the wing. They had long since grown weary of being checked by a guard every time they got off the elevator, and had grown huffy about the way the mystery patient's nurses were spirited on and off the floor so that no one had a chance to talk to them. In response to the overhead announcements and the intrusion of running footsteps, small knots of MICU staff congregated in the hallway, looking sideways at one another and conferring in low voices while waiting to hear what the paunchy security guard working his way down the line would have to say.

What he had to say was this: "Evacuate the area."

The bastard wouldn't even tell them why.

# SIXTEEN

THE ONE PROBLEM WITH SEDUCING THE woman security guard had been that the Hammer couldn't wear gloves while he did it. On the afternoon that he'd packed a special lunch for her, they'd left her apartment together at 2:00, when she'd departed for work. She'd wanted to know if she would be seeing him when her shift was over, and he'd told her that he didn't think that would possible. Business was calling him out of town. When she'd kissed him as if he was shipping off to war, she held on long enough for passersby to pretend not to look.

"Brush those teeth," she had bravely said.

The comment caught him unprepared and he hadn't been able to think of a thing to say, which pleased her all the more as she turned away from him and started on to work.

Suddenly he grew tired of cities and spring. The days were getting longer and that bothered him too. He never slept well after March. The planting of red and yellow tulips repulsed him. Each April his mother had done the same thing; perhaps she still did. He hadn't been in touch with his parents since he'd gotten into trouble with the army and they'd refused to attend his court-martial.

After leaving the woman guard, he headed directly to a neighborhood drugstore he'd earlier noticed and purchased a box of heavy-duty plastic garbage bags, a plastic bucket, a pair of Playtex gloves, and a bottle of Pine Sol. He was almost to the checkout lane when he had second thoughts and went back to add a two-pack of paper towels, a spray bottle of glass cleaner, a pack of Dentyne, and three packages of panty hose to his shopping basket.

Within fifteen minutes he was back at the woman's apartment building, keying in her security code. In all the comings and goings from the building, he'd only once seen another resident and she had been so engrossed in a computer spread sheet that she'd let the elevator doors close in their faces without noticing their approach. He'd known it was a businesswoman because the legs sticking out below the printout wore nylons. This trip through the lobby was no different than any other. No one paid any attention to him.

If the building had been truly security conscious there would have been a closed-circuit TV system run by a private security company, but there was nothing of the sort. Just the keypad controlling the entry lock, and a paper boy with a baseball card could have taken care of that. Up on the eleventh floor, he took out the spare key that Ginger had so thoughtfully left on a hook in her kitchenette.

He estimated that he had a minimum of an hour and a half to do his work, and since wiping the place of his prints would require maybe an hour, he first indulged one of his vices and snooped through his victim's belongings. To start with, he found a sheet torn from a stenographer's pad taped to the side of the refrigerator. He'd never noticed it before and took the time to read it now. Dated March 31st, which made it roughly two weeks old, the sheet contained a list of ten resolutions Ginger had printed out in pencil.

1. No serious relationships for six months.
2. Return that fucking Studly's things.
3. Improve my language.
4. Study for the cop test.
5. Call Mother once a month. (Yuk.)

6. Clean this place once a week. (Yuk. Yuk.)
7. Balance my check book.
8.
9.
10.

The last three numbers were left blank. As far as he could tell the woman had as good a shot at living up to numbers eight, nine, and ten as any of the other items on the list. At least resolution number six would be taken care of before he left. He'd clean the place so well that the woman's mother wouldn't be embarrassed to come collect her daughter's belongings.

Inside the refrigerator's freezer, which was in bad need of defrosting, he found a year's supply of frozen peas and a can of orange juice concentrate with two hundred dollars in twenties spooled inside it. He returned the money. The three cupboards contained a partially-eaten box of every kind of breakfast cereal known to Madison Avenue. In the top drawer of her dresser he checked the labels of her undergarments and deduced her measurements as 38-32-38.

The bottom drawer of the dresser contained a family album that was a collection of pictures of a younger Ginger with a man who had to be her father. There was a strong resemblance around the nose and chin. The mother, who only showed up in two or three snapshots, must have been the family photographer. The pictures caught Ginger learning how to hit a baseball, holding up a full stringer of pan fish, knotting her father's hula-girl tie, and so on. The last page held a yellowed obituary for John Foley, a city police officer who'd died of a coronary at Jackson County Medical Center. He'd been fifty-two and was survived by a wife and two daughters. The second daughter was nowhere to be seen in the album, which explained why several photos had faces snipped away. He carefully replaced the album in the drawer.

The only reading material in the place was in the bathroom, a copy of the Arco course study for police trainees.

Nothing he found really interested him except maybe the empty ring box that had been sitting on the iron railing of the apartment's tiny balcony. A pair of high heels sat on the cement directly below the box.

Snapping on his plastic cleaning gloves, he went to work wiping surfaces, collecting take-out Chinese containers, and filling the laundry basket in the bathroom with clothes he found stuffed under cushions and behind doors. The closet floor contained a lightweight barbell set, and its shelves held two velvet-lined cases, a long one holding a Smith & Wesson Silhouette, whose ten-inch barrel reminded him of a job in New Orleans, the other case containing an S&W police special and a snapshot of her father teaching her to aim it. The back of the photo had written on it in a man's awkward printing, *Gingee, age twelve.* As his time in the apartment neared the hour mark, he found himself stopping periodically to listen for sirens.

His next-to-last business in the woman's apartment was to make the bed. Lastly, he picked up the garbage bag he'd filled with refuse and let himself out, taking the stairway down to the lobby to make sure no one saw him leave.

Five blocks away he saw a garbage truck pulling into an alley and followed to pitch his plastic bag in its back.

From there he walked another thirteen blocks, which put him within four blocks of Jackson General. If he stepped into the middle of the street, which he did when the light turned green, he could see the hospital. As of yet, there weren't any flocking fire trucks or squad cars. Returning to the sidewalk, he joined ten to twenty commuters standing behind a bus bench. The number of waiting people varied as buses arrived and departed from the corner. None of the people dressed in suits and ties talked to each other, but several of the blue collar workers carried on loud conversations, speaking up to be heard above the traffic. Mostly, they bitched about an upcoming increase in bus fares. The federal government had cut its funding of the city's mass transit system. It irked the Hammer to have to stand in the crowd and listen to such trivial conversation, but he didn't have any choice. The bus stop offered the best camouflage.

At 3:55, after ten minutes of inhaling bus fumes, he finally heard the sirens. Whether anyone else heard them, he had no idea. No one else acted as if they did. When two squad cars shot past, he had to stand on tiptoe to see them. The people around him barely turned their heads to watch; a number twenty-two E bus was pulling curbside and everyone was too busy jostling for position to care about sirens.

When four minutes passed without any fire trucks clanging by, the Hammer stomped out into the street to get another squint at the hospital. Everything looked normal. He was considering whether to board a bus and ride past the hospital to see the situation up close when he heard another siren and rocked back on his heels, relieved. He rejoined the crowd of commuters, and a half minute later a third squad car sped by. Rumbling behind it was a panel truck painted a camouflage green and pulling a small, enclosed trailer that had a DANGER EXPLOSIVES sign on its back doors. He shoved people out of the way to get a clear look at it.

# SEVENTEEN

EARLY IN THE AFTERNOON OF THE seventh day of the special assignment, Jan slipped away from the hospital after a mere six hours of being run ragged by Agent Windish and of dodging the Little Admiral. Every other day in that stretch she'd put in twelve hours, at a minimum, and the stress was beginning to show in the puffiness beneath her eyes and a rash that broke out under her arms. Occasionally she talked to herself. Nothing consequential got said. It was Agent Windish himself who decreed she take the rest of the afternoon and evening off. When she received an exceedingly well-timed dinner invitation from Detective Frank White but minutes later, she suspected a payback from one whiskery male to another. Strangely enough—and it did strike her as queer—she didn't mind. In some twisted way giving her the time off showed that Agent Windish was satisfied with her work, and she was still vain enough to take some pride in that, even if she refused to trust the man.

That evening Jan's beeper sounded just as Detective Frank White, in suit and tie, was pouring the wine. By that point in the meal he'd already cautioned her that tonight he hoped she'd just call him Frank, scratch the title of Detective, throw their last names to the wind. At 6:00 P.M. they sat in the candle-lit glow of Frank's turn-of-the-century dining room, which had to be the one dining room on the block with fine linen and crystal laid out. Synthesized Beatles tunes mizzled out of hidden speakers. With the host's voice all husky and intimate, forbidden fruit might have been the upcoming meal's main entree. If the name of Frank's cologne wasn't Rutting Season, it should have been. As the beeper tweedled, the detective stopped the wine stream and made a pained face.

"I know that's not mine," he said.

When Frank wrinkled up his nose, a raw boyishness shined through his droopy mustache, got past the scarred disk of skin on his chin, and somewhat diminished his six-three, two-twenty-pound tonnage. Such regressions were necessary if Jan was to overcome the fact that she found herself sitting across from yet another cop with a twinkle in his eye. Once again she found herself charmed, and was willing—almost—to reverse her decision to leave his place by 10:00 no matter what. Of course she realized she wasn't being totally honest with herself. She wasn't 100 percent behind that deadline. If she was, how could she explain the fact that she'd rushed home to squeeze into her moderately slinky black dress?—the little number that had a lace inset and slit skirt.

"I warned you I would be packing a beeper," Jan said.

"For what, a week now?"

Which was true. When she hadn't been driven crazy by Agent George Windish in person, she'd day and night been hooked up to the hospital's long-range paging system so that he could bedevil her at home.

"If it was your dispatcher calling," Jan said, "what would you do?"

"Pretend the batteries are dead."

She gazed thoughtfully at him while asking in a neutral voice, "What aren't you telling me about Agent Windish?"

Wincing, the detective retreated to his end of the table, poured himself a healthy glass of wine, and moodily deliberated over her question before saying, "And you think *I'm* persistent?"

So here she sat, trapped in a Cape Cod house so neat and

controlled that all of the hardwood furniture, braided rugs, and decorative antiques looked cemented in place. It made Jan want to tip something over. She found a part of herself yearning for the great outdoors, not that she was much of a camper, but the walls were closing in. Worse yet, another part of herself was thinking it was rather cozy.

"Maybe the question is," Jan said, turning it slowly over in her mind, "are we getting something started here, or not?"

"And the answer?"

After a sip of wine, she pushed herself away from the table, saying "Where's the phone?"

"Follow me, ma'am."

"Are you always such a perfect gentleman?" she asked. It was a point she was beginning to hold against him.

"Only until midnight," he said, waving for her to follow him into the hallway, where he pointed out a cherry-wood end table beneath the railing of the second-floor stairway. A black phone sat beside a stand-up photo of two teenagers whose present whereabouts were unknown—at least to Jan—but who looked as though they'd been marinating for years in perfect manners. The mother and wife who'd helped instill those manners had flown the coop, a story whose retelling Jan had been avoiding all evening. His wife had run away with a lover; the detective had previously laid bare that much. If he was searching for sympathy, he struck out with Jan though. From her vantage point of two failed marriages, she figured the guy was lucky it was only one lover.

As she dialed the hospital's long-range operator, she watched Frank through the kitchen doorway. He was arranging lemon slices and parsley sprigs atop two pink-salmon fillets. The kitchen itself, agleam with copper and stainless steel, looked as though the detective fancied himself a chef. That fit. Most cops had fantasies about being someone else. At the moment, though, Jan wasn't worried about policemen daydreams; she was remembering the stacked dishes in her own kitchen sink. Then the paging system operator answered, bringing her back to reality. As she waited to be transferred to the calling party, she found herself reluctantly admiring Detective Frank White's derriere as he bent over a spotless oven. Then all carnal thoughts flew right out of her mind as a deadly serious voice came on the the other end of the phone line.

"Security Administrator Hodges speaking."

That was unexpected. Normally an after-hours page meant that Windish had crushed somebody's toes and wanted Jan to do some corrective surgery. Grimacing, Jan turned her back to the kitchen doorway. "Gallagher here."

"You might want to see this," Eldon Hodges said. "We've found a bomb."

The tickled way he announced it, Jan could almost imagine him smiling, a thought that made her shiver.

Escaping the detective's romantic web, she promptly overshot the nearest freeway entrance. The feeling drained out of her hands as she gripped the steering wheel. She had a near brush with Death as she removed her gold-shell earrings and used tissue paper to blot off lipstick while hurtling down the interstate at speeds in excess of the legal limit. These days Death was wearing a mechanic's coveralls and driving a city bus whose destination sign read OUT OF SERVICE.

At the General she expected to find the top half of a building blown to dust, the streets cordoned off, and TV crews scrambling over the rubble in the race for the most advantageous camera angle. But the only thing out of the ordinary was an unmarked truck illegally parked near the Wabash entrance. The oversized van was the size of a bakery truck but painted an army-fatigue green, which didn't make it look like the kind of vehicle that delivered loaves of enriched bread. It did have the bulky shape and plating of a specially equipped bomb squad truck. At present it appeared empty.

Rather than report directly to Agent Windish, Jan lifted a carry-all bag out of her Pontiac's cluttered trunk and detoured to the women's locker room to change into her uniform. Showing up in an evening dress wouldn't bolster her credibility. Within minutes she was tucking in a shirttail while hustling to the elevators.

On the fourth floor she came face-to-face with Stanley Charais, who first gestured like a traffic cop for her to stop, then upon recognition reluctantly waved her forward and turned his peevish stare to his right, her left. Stanley was back to encouraging a mustache but the poor blond thing wasn't filling in any better than had his last effort, which meant he continued to look too young to be a security guard outside of a day-care center. Neither he nor Jan made mention of their recent phone conversation. They didn't have to; their stiff body language said it for them.

If something was happening in the direction he so theatrically pointed, Jan couldn't see it. All that lay that way was an abandoned hallway, one thoroughly lit by fluorescent lights. She studied the emptiness a moment before muffled voices drew her attention the other way. In the opposite direction, through the narrow glass slat of a fire door twenty yards behind her, she saw the put-upon expressions of several members of the hospital staff, each taking a turn at glaring through the window.

"What's going on?" Jan said.

"I'm not the one to tell you that," Stanley said, making the most of an opportunity to be uncooperative. As his blue eyes glared down the hall at nothing, he kept clenching his right fist as though trying to crack a pecan. No breaking sound could be heard.

"Maybe you could get me started," Jan suggested.

His obstinacy lasted a split second before rupturing. The urge to be the first to tell her was simply too great.

"Ginger brought a bomb into the mystery patient's room."

"Intentionally?"

"Now there's a brilliant thought," said Stanley.

"Then how?"

"That's a question you'll have to take up with the one and only Ginger."

"Maybe you'd be so kind as to tell me where she is?"

He made a that-away gesture toward the empty end of the hallway.

"Don't use your radio," he warned as she started away. "You might blow us all up."

"Still playing games?" she asked without looking back.

"That's per the bomb squad," he said. "If the thing's got some kind of electronic trigger on it, radio waves might set it off."

She didn't verbally respond to that, but did slip a hand down to her belt to check the two-way she'd picked up on the way to the fourth floor.

The deserted hallway was long and true, except at the very end where it jogged out of sight to the right. Around that corner lay the linen carts and fourth medical intensive care unit. With open fire doors every hundred feet, the hall in front of Jan looked like the product of two facing mirrors endlessly trading a reflection. Any lights in the stretch were on, and each empty patient room or office was open for viewing. As per Security's bomb-threat procedure, which Jan knew by heart after having twice rewritten it, someone had actually remembered to open doors and windows to help vent pressure if an explosion rocked the floor, but as to why the Venetian blinds in front of all the windows had been closed, Jan had no idea. She did note that an evening breeze periodically filled the blinds, then died away, leaving behind a cascading tinkle. Each time she heard the sound her reflex was to slow. She had only to think about Studly and the two dead paramedics to know how could quickly this could all vaporize. Every foot she set down might soon be missing, and she had the mandatory thought about whether she was wearing clean underwear. She also wondered how long her mother would survive at the mercy of four granddaughters, and she caught a fleeting glimpse of the hereafter—a Southern California swimming pool that held a gently bobbing water lily.

Approaching the end of the straight stretch, she heard faint voices around the hall's first crook. The prospect of facing people, particularly I-told-you-so kind of people like the Little Admiral, forced Jan to take herself in hand. Lifting her chin, she calmed her eyes and rounded the corner as if she'd taken the entire walk at a brisk pace.

Unfortunately, there was no one present to appreciate her courage. Facing her were the metal-lined linen carts that blocked off the hall, but no strong, silent types stood guard behind them. Through the unattended doorway to unit four came quarrelsome voices. Eavesdropping being what it was at the county—a survival trait—Jan practiced surviving.

"The bomb's been removed."

That flat statement came from the Little Admiral. Since Stanley hadn't known about the removal, they must have used the rear service elevator. Jan managed to open her fists; some of the compression left her neck.

"I'm not satisfied," said Agent Windish.

"The city's bomb squad has given the all clear."

"What if there're two bombs?"

"The bomb squad says there aren't."

"We're not convinced," Windish maintained.

"We've patients in critical condition waiting to be returned to their rooms," Eldon Hodges reminded him.

"Bring them back too soon and they could end up worse than critical."

Which effectively dead-ended the discussion and allowed Jan an opening to enter the unit without stepping directly into a crossfire.

The fourth unit had been as thoroughly evacuated as the rest of the wing, although the pair of canaries remained caged in a corner of the isolation room that had housed the patient, who had requested the birds be moved in for company. Where the DEA had stashed Carmen Romero-Muehlen for safekeeping, Jan had no idea, but she quickly guessed that the convoy of agents, nurses, and portable monitors had been the reason for all the closed blinds she'd seen in the hall. The agents she'd been working with all acted twice burned when it came to uncovered windows. Inside the unit there wasn't any ticking shoe box or long wires leading to a plunger or fanatic with sticks of dynamite and an alarm clock taped to his or her chest. Actually, it was completely still inside the unit. At the center of that dead calm stood three men, each looking as though they'd taken a bite out of the same wormy green apple.

The Little Admiral had fastened himself erectly to a folding chair. Behind him Agent George Windish paced, rubbing the back of his neck and silently shuffling his lips. The third swatch of manliness was dressed in a thick bodysuit that appeared fashioned out of the kind of quilted blankets found in a moving van. The reinforced helmet that he cradled in the crook of his right arm had a clear-plastic bubble visor and enough hoses connected to its back to qualify for Buck Rogers. His red, pinched face looked on the verge of a sneeze, and he'd propped himself tensely against a windowsill as if the angle helped hold in an *ah-choo*. No one bothered to introduce him, but it wasn't necessary. His name was Ric Myles, and Jan knew him from the days when he'd served on a special tactical police squad with her second husband. He was a small, compact man, and when Jan entered the room, he straightened and acted respectful, or at least politely deferential, which wasn't easy in his getup. Such behavior wasn't anything new. Three quarters of the men her ex served with acted the same way upon chance meetings with Jan. It only meant they figured she was available. She scowled at Ric, which made him more frisky.

"Better late than never," Hodges said by way of greeting. Long since cured of doing the gentlemanly thing when Jan entered a room, he remained seated.

The comment caused Ric to snicker silently, but Agent Windish disregarded them both and breathlessly plunged ahead with his own agenda.

"We're lucky to be standing here before you, Jan."

If possible, the brush with death had wound the DEA agent up even tighter. His tie was tucked into his shirt between the third and fourth buttons, his belt tongue hung out, and his expression was somewhere between seizure and ecstasy.

"Nonsense," said the Little Admiral.

Ric Myles eased back down on his window perch, willing to be entertained. Twenty feet away, Ginger sat on a folding chair placed barely inside the dormitory's doorway. Two adjustable track lights cast a cold glow on the top of her tousled blond hair and threw the left half of her face into shadows. Her long legs were stiffly extended, her arms crossed below the line of her breasts, and the half of her expression that could be seen looked soft as good marble. She made no indication of noticing Jan's entrance but concentrated on the Little Admiral as if attempting to boil blood.

"We need to know," Windish said, jabbing toward Ginger, "how an explosive device found its way into her lunch cooler."

"Have you tried asking?"

"Repeatedly."

"What if she doesn't know?" Jan asked, studying Ginger's unblinking stare.

"That's an imaginary," Windish said, jerking his head sideways to signal that she should step aside with him for a private conversation.

On a normal day he twitched his large head this way twenty to thirty times. Naturally, as Jan and the agent went into a huddle, the Little Admiral showed signs of life and rotated on his chair to keep them fully in sight.

Once they were alone, Windish whispered, "This is the moment that signifies. He's left us an enhanced opportunity."

"He? We're talking about the Hammer?" The name cropped up at least a dozen times a day in the agent's conversation.

"Inescapably," the agent said, talking in the stilted way he did whenever excited. "We must generate positive events from this opening."

"I'm not disagreeing."

"Your subordinate over there is. Do you realize that she is all that stands between us and positive affirmation?"

Jan glanced over her shoulder to see if that's where Ginger was standing. "How did you find the bomb?"

"A routine security check of her lunch cooler," Agent Windish said. "My man noticed an NFL sticker on the bottom of her Thermos. That's all that saved us."

"Are you making that up?" Jan asked.

"It's the Hammer's little vanity," Windish explained. "He always leaves one of those stickers on his weapons. Your officer claims to know nothing about it, and by the way, that little fact about the sticker isn't for public consumption."

Jan eyed Windish a moment before saying, "You're not buying her answer?"

"That device," Windish reported, "was intended to be delivered to this room we're standing in. It didn't have enough size to produce without that much proximity. So my question is this: Unless your woman told him, how would the Hammer know that she brought her lunch cooler up here everyday?"

"Maybe one of your men told him."

"I'm not ruling out anything," Windish vowed. "But the telemetry all points to your guard over there."

"So what do you want me to do?"

"Talk to her," the agent urged. "Woman to woman. Knowing the Hammer's patterns, there's little doubt she's being used here. It's essential that we know exactly what your guard knows." He paused to tiredly squeeze the bridge of his nose. With eyes closed, he added, "You've got to convince her that it's not exclusively for our benefit that she open up communication channels here."

"Oh?"

"If she's had contact with the Hammer and knows what he looks like . . . well, you can see the problem."

Unfortunately, Jan could see more than one problem. There was Ginger's problem, and then there was Jan's problem, which naturally included Ginger's since Jan had signed her up.

"So much for our being on the sidelines, huh?"

"A slight miscalculation," Windish muttered, glancing away.

"If I talk to her," Jan said. "I do it alone."

Windish opened his mouth to provide a half dozen or more reasons for why his assistance would be invaluable, but Jan cut him off.

"Listen," she said, "you come along and it will end up being a big confrontational thing."

"Go for it," he said after a moment of sour reflection.

Shaking her head in resignation, Jan went.

From up close, Jan could see that Ginger had shed a tear or two, but seemed to have pulled herself together enough to move beyond any feelings of remorse or vulnerability. The tears had dried and for the first time since Studly's death, Ginger appeared to have reverted to her normal self, which was part professional wrestler, part frontierswoman, and part jilted bride. She usually behaved as though she had at least three parts struggling inside her. Not knowing how else to proceed, Jan opted for a conversational approach.

"What do you think, Ginger?"

"That I need a drink," Ginger said, too busy glowering to entertain any deep thoughts.

"I'm supposed to talk to you woman to woman," Jan said. "Personally, I'm not sure we've got it in us."

"You want to know what Hodges said?" Ginger asked.

"Something immortal?"

"He says," Ginger said, screwing her face up and making her voice prissy, " 'I didn't hire her.' That's what he says when Agent Hotshot wants to know how I got my job. If he didn't hire me, I'd like to know who the hell did."

"Can we try to rise above it? Maybe jump to the part where you tell me what's going on here?"

She slid a second chair up to Ginger's and sat down beside her, facing the same way so that the three men were lined up in front of them, a bit like milk bottles in a carnival booth. The only bottle moving was Ric Myles who was unzipping his bodysuit.

"Those assholes out there think they can blame me for all this." Her eyes evasively skipped to Jan and automatically back to the three men outside the room. "But I don't know how my Thermos ended up packed with plastique or dynamite or whatever it was. My best bet is that somebody pulled a switch when I stopped at the Strong Arm for a pick-me-up."

"You've been under a lot of stress," Jan said.

"What's that supposed to mean?"

"Maybe you're forgetting something."

"You're saying something," Ginger gamely answered. "I can feel it."

"Tell me this," Jan said. "Have you made any new conquests lately?"

"I've been a dry well," Ginger spitefully said.

"What about the patient's bodyguard?"

"A lot less happened there than everyone wants to think."

"Tell me about it."

"There's nothing to tell, believe me. He made some crack about Studly and I showed him the door."

"This guy the agents call the Hammer," Jan said, leaning toward Ginger and keeping her voice low, "if he's using you, he's not going to be dumb enough to come right out and ask you to bring a bomb up here."

"If we're talking about a man," Ginger said, "he'd be dumb enough to try almost anything."

"Whoever's responsible," Jan said, smiling at Ginger's bravado despite herself, "didn't care that you might be around when the bomb went off."

"The thought's occurred."

"Has the thought occurred about what happens when he finds out the bomb didn't go off, you with it?"

"Huh?" Ginger said, coming up short on that exchange. Some of the angry color slipped from her cheeks.

"You can identify him," Jan said. "What's he going to do about that?"

"You're guessing," Ginger said, sounding more mad than afraid.

"Am I guessing right?" Jan persisted. "That's what I need to know."

"I'm on the record," Ginger said, back to staring at the men in front of them.

"And you're going to stick to that?"

"You want me to make something else up?" Ginger asked with a satisfied smirk.

"We're talking about a killer."

"I'll try to remember that. . . . if I ever meet him. So what are you going to tell the boys out there?"

"That somebody must have gotten at your cooler while you were in the Strong Arm. But I got to say, Ginger, I believe it even less than they do."

"Why's that?"

"Because I've been in that bar's powder room," Jan said, standing, "and nobody ever goes in there twice. One thing's for sure. You're all done up here. I just hope you're not planning on doing something foolish."

Ginger curled back her upper lip in a sneer and made a *shoo* motion with her fingers. Jan obliged her.

Returning to the three waiting men, Jan said, "Next?"

The Little Admiral didn't react, which was his specialty. Cold reds shot through Agent Windish's face and his mouth began to quiver, although no words tumbled out—yet. Ric Myles, who had stripped out of his padded suit, revealing a police uniform, paid no attention to her question as he neatly folded up his protective gear. A testiness remained in the air. Apparently the three of them were still trying to iron out who got to be alpha dog.

Once again Agent Windish was twitching his head to the side, seeking private audience with Jan, but before he could spur on further optimism and point her back toward Ginger with redoubled vigor, two of his minions swooped into the unit to report that they'd secured the coordinates above and below, discovering nothing. They'd also conducted a sweep of the perimeter, where the Hammer could have been waiting with a radio transmitter to trigger the device, but they'd found nothing more than a wife beater lying in wait for his missus who was getting stitched up. Apparently there was nothing to worry about, unless you were married to the wife beater, of course.

"Surprise, surprise." That contribution came from Ric Myles.

Rather than respond to the low blow, Agent Windish rallied his agents around him and they stepped to the side en masse.

As the DEA conspired in a cankerous hush that had the Little Admiral straining to catch stray phrases, Ric Myles stole up beside Jan to ask, "You work for these fools?"

"I'm not doing it for free," Jan said.

"It could prove extremely hazardous to your health."

"It already has," Jan lowly said, gesturing with her hand that they should step farther away. They moved to a shadowy corner without attracting attention. "I haven't had a decent night's sleep for a week."

"I'm not talking hazardous over the course of twenty years," Ric said, "like cigarettes, or something. I mean right here, today. Their little feud could do somebody in. Maybe you. And that fat one, Christ, he's a general menace to society. He could do a few dozen of us in and never even notice."

"Which fat one?" Jan asked, not trying to be funny, only wanting to be certain.

"The very fat one," he said, nodding at Windish, who continued to confer with his two agents. "The one who thinks he's the Gipper."

"What's he done now?"

"Only wanted me to disarm the sweet little thing they found up here," Ric said with a disparaging snort. "So they could analyze it. When I said nuts to that, he came down on me as if I was incompetent, as if I didn't know my crazy job."

"So what did you do?"

"Told him to defuse it himself. Whose hands are we talking about, anyway? That's when the little fat one jumped in. He's no prize either. If he'd had his way, I would have carried the goods out of here on my back. No time to bring a robot in and do it by the book."

"I see you're still standing," Jan observed.

"We agreed to do it my way."

"Tell me about the bomb," Jan said.

"Exploded it in an empty field. The boys in the lab will be

analyzing the leftovers, but I can tell you that whoever put that baby together knew what they were about. Probably used some jazzed up military plastique with a pressure trigger. If that Thermos cap had been unscrewed, everything would have been coming up roses around here." Touching her elbow, he added, "If you're stuck with these two, go slow or they'll use you up quick."

"Any other insights?"

"That'll about do it," he said with a playful love tap on her shoulder. "Unless you want to get together some time."

"Aren't you still with Wendi?"

"Sure, but you never cared for her anyway, did you? Hear anything from Karl?"

Karl was her second ex-husband.

"Not as much as I should," Jan said. "Particularly around the first of the month." Which was when child support was due.

"I heard he was seeing someone new."

"Maybe Wendi?" Jan helpfully suggested.

That hit closer to home than Ric liked but he recovered quickly by giving Jan another playful tap on the shoulder. "I'm out of here. Watch yourself with these two, hear?"

Jan gave him a chipper thumbs-up sign, but as soon as he turned away, she scowled. For a short, numb interval she watched everything around her with a more critical eye. Windish and Hodges had already begun trying to out-mister each other. Since the Battle of the Parking Ramp, as the shooting down of the ambulance was now widely known, the two of them had been competing at that game.

"You can end the evacuation now, Mr. Hodges."

"But Mr. Windish," the Little Admiral countered, "what about your special patient?"

"I think it's perfectly safe now, Mr. Hodges. My men will be returning her to our protective grid, which I think you'll have to agree functioned as intended."

"I wish I could agree, Mr. Windish. But that bomb did get all the way up here."

"Thanks to one of your guards, Mr. Hodges."

And so on, back and forth.

Within fifteen minutes a squad of DEA agents had whisked Carmen Romero-Muehlen, plus bodyguard, back into the fourth MICU. Pity that the patient was too weak and sickly to enjoy the homecoming. Her eyes were pinched shut in a way that said she was racing against nausea or pain or something grimmer. She couldn't have been much older than Jan, early forties, although her once handsome face already had the broken lines of a ruin. Nor was she any taller than Jan; her form under the blankets was barely longer than a child's.

Jan instinctively lifted a hand to her own head as the woman was wheeled past. Her hair was the same deep black as the patient's, a fact that sillily enough made her want to comfort the woman, although it was impossible to get close enough to touch her. Barring the way were two nurses, one on either side of the bed; a physician at the foot of the bed; the patient's personal bodyguard; and two agents flanking him. Overall the DEA agents in the unit had been fruitful and multiplied. They swarmed about, their increase in numbers serving only to draw attention to their vulnerability. The Hammer needed to get lucky but once, and if she was to believe Agent Windish, the assassin had been in business a long time.

The only person subtracted from the crowd was Ric Myles, whose presence lingered on in the speeded up, alert way everyone now hustled about their duties. Still squatting on his throne, Eldon Hodges watched events with a faster eye. Over in the opposite isolation room, Ginger was baiting a soft-spoken agent now assigned to interrogate her. He didn't appear to be wringing anything but estrogen out of his subject. From time to time he stepped away in frustration.

As soon as the patient was settled back in behind her glass wall, Agent Windish hiked up his polyester pants and told Jan, "Wait here." For Eldon Hodges's benefit, he added, "Stay put."

After delivering those edicts, he threw his considerable weight into the peculiar, stiff-legged gait he employed when in a full, five-alarm hurry, as compared to those times when he was only in a terrific hurry or those rare moments when he was merely in a hurry. Naturally, regardless of what state of hurry he found himself in, he never conferred with Jan concerning his destination, nor did he bestow that information upon the Little Admiral. He might have been rushing to the men's room or to a teleconference with the head of his agency. He attacked every task with the same bursting-bladder ferocity. Whatever he was up to didn't really matter to Jan. All that she cared about was that he was out of sight because for once she didn't intend to follow orders.

## EIGHTEEN

IF JAN HAD TAILED AGENT WINDISH for two minutes, she might have temporarily softened her opinion of the man, for he fled from the ICU to the hospital chapel where he kneeled before the small altar and crucifix, leaned his forehead against the wooden rail, and prayed. After a half minute, he stole a glance around the chapel and seeing that he was alone, slipped behind the altar to rub Jesus' toe.

The chapel was on the first floor in New General. Two right turns and a fire door later, Agent Windish had regained his full stride as he cruised through the main lobby and out the pneumatic doors that led into the night. Ignoring the cool air, he started without a coat down Wabash to Twentieth, where he turned right, heading for the warehouse from which the Hammer had made his first attempt on Carmen Romero-Muehlen. At the warehouse he let himself in the locked door next the closed community clinic on the first floor. With no working elevator handy, he had to mount an entire flight of stairs on his own locomotion. By the top he was grasping the handrail with both hands.

Second floor lighting was minimal, nothing more than bare bulbs that cast long shadows; a damp smell of cardboard filled the hallway, disturbed only by a faint trace of something acidic. He shook his head in disbelief upon detecting a whiff of coffee as he caught his breath. He knocked twice on the third door in, paused, knocked twice again. A light squeak of footsteps filtered out from inside.

"Yes?"

"No," Windish said, providing the appropriate response.

The door opened inward and a short, black man in a dark jogging suit with slats of pink under the arms admitted him into the large, unheated room where the Hammer had originally set up shop. With the forensics squad gone, the cement floor and iron girders were spotless. Other than the rocket launcher, they hadn't found anything more incriminating than a number of blond pubic hairs, which Windish suspected had been planted to mislead them about the Hammer's pigmentation.

Across the empty room sat a second man who was white, had graying hair, and was bundled against the night air in a bulky russet sweater. In front of him was a long folding table that supported a row of five stand-up tape recorders whose reels were all turning. He held a headset from the middle one to an ear and didn't react to Windish's entry in any way.

"Didn't I warn you about coffee?" Windish said to the man letting him in.

"Warn Norby," the short man answered, leaning out to check the hallway. Satisfied they were alone, he holstered an automatic, closed the door, and bolted it.

Windish stomped across the room without gaining Norby's attention and stood behind the seated man for nearly a minute of heavy breathing, but that was a washout too. Finally he reached over Norby's shoulder to lift the coffee cup out of his left hand. Norby never even raised his splotchy face upwards.

"Still pretending to be married?" Norby said, nodding at the wedding band on Windish's hand.

"What if the Hammer had decided to drop in?" Windish asked, holding up the cup. "He'd have smelled this from the top of the stairs. Maybe the street."

"Wouldn't make any difference."

"With him, the slightest edge could be all that keeps you alive."

"What gives with you and this guy?" Norby said. "You act like you dream about him or something."

"Maybe I do," Windish said.

"He ever doubled back before?"

"He's never missed before."

"That we know of," Norby corrected.

"We'll never get another shot at him like this one. Did you get the conversation between the women?"

"Every word of it," Norby said, offering the earphones to Windish, who waved them off.

"So how did the Hammer get the bomb in the lunch box?"

"No idea. She wouldn't tell Gallagher either."

"She knows," Windish said.

"She's playing with the devil," Norby agreed.

"So how do we find out?"

"Depends on how involved you think she is."

"A pawn."

"So why bother to find out at all?" Norby said. "Have you been thinking about Plan B?"

"You trying to undermine my confidence?"

"What I'm hearing here," Norby said, holding up the earphones, "you and this Gallagher aren't exactly best of friends."

"I'm working on it," Windish snapped. "Before this came down, I gave her the goddamn night off, didn't I?"

"Better work harder," Norby advised. "When your docs go in that corner of the unit where they think no one can hear them, they're saying fifty-fifty for Carmen. We lose her and we've got nothing more than Carmen's affidavit and this Hammer you're so fond of. And you got one thing right, we might never get a better shot at him than this."

"I'm making headway," Windish maintained. "Gallagher will pitch in if we need her."

"Hope so. May I have my cup back now?"

"The trouble with you spooks," Windish groused, keeping the coffee mug in hand, "is that you think you're invisible. I want the rest of your equipment moved over now. We're done playing this low key."

# NINETEEN

AFTER SPOTTING THE BOMB-SQUAD TRUCK, the Hammer stormed blindly away from the bus stop, gasping like a fish out of water, punching a man in the groin, and attempting to dent a stop sign with his bare fists. He managed a small dimple in the sign, right below the T but barely noticeable to the naked eye. Blood trickled down his knuckles.

He doubled back to Jackson General from several different directions, walking in a huge clover leaf, but discovered no gaping holes in the hospital's outer walls, no debris-strewn streets, no pandemonium or at least no more than usual. Since the woman security guard named Ginger was apparently still alive and knew his face, he never ventured nearer than two blocks to the hospital, but that was close enough to see that the place was running up Medicare bills same as usual.

As he walked, he muttered, causing people to stand clear on the sidewalk. That suited him fine. In fact, he liked to see them scatter; it eased some of the sting over having missed for a second time. After he'd cooled a bit, he held off a migraine by talking himself through his two tries for Carmen. Eventually he reached a conclusion: He'd been too far away both times. In his line of work that meant he'd been playing it too safe. For some unexplainable reason he'd been shying away from getting close to Carmen herself.

Why that might be he had no idea, but he didn't let that bother him. Over the years he'd twice been interviewed by shrinks, both of whom had described his behavior as antisocial but failed to clarify what that meant. One of the shrinks had visited him while he'd been in the stockade for busting the Dudley-do-right jaw of a West Point graduate during special forces training. That one had rubber-stamped his dishonorable discharge. The other doctor had come calling on behalf of the Hammer's college football coach, who grew edgy upon hearing of the Hammer's habit of sleeping while hanging upside-down from a bar—a ploy to spook his roommate who was on scholarship and competing for the same safety position. That doc had pronounced him sane enough to play football but not so sane that they had to keep him off the special teams. The doctor had been an alumnus.

Actually there had been one other shrink, met while he'd been earning his keep as a mercenary, but the Hammer wasn't sure she counted. Seeing as how her purse was stuffed with penicillin, he had a hunch all she really wanted was to get laid by every soldier of fortune she could locate. He'd taken her battery of tests, and in the end, maybe she'd come the closest to explaining his inner workings.

"Little boys playing with toy soldiers," she had said, referring to the mercenaries she had known. "You all want to be generals and think everyone's plotting against you."

"What sane man wouldn't?" he'd answered, and then they'd gone back to the missionary position in the Salvadoran hotel where she was conducting her interviews.

As he circled Jackson General, he searched for some inspiration on what to do next. At first nothing brilliant occurred to him. All right, he thought, maybe some old-fashioned *blam-blam-blam*. Shoot my way in. And out. Uncreative, but at least it should be bloody.

The trick, he decided, would be to get close before he opened fire. Taking a running start from the street with bullet belts crisscrossing his chest wasn't going to cut it. After a couple hours of aimless wandering, a chauffeur-driven limousine cruised past, calling to mind the two old bats in full-length fur coats, the ones visiting their debauched nephew in an intensive care unit on the same floor as Carmen. Pulling to a stop, he chuckled and double pumped a fist. This time he would be as close as Carmen's bedside. What he had in mind was the stuff of legends. They would be talking about this job on the street for years and years. He cut immediately for his hotel room to place a call to his current employer, who was eager for good news.

"Have you nailed that bitch yet?"

"Not long now," the Hammer promised.

"Make it painful if you can. Forget what she knows about our operation, which is pretty much everything. We're getting word that she's ripped us off for a million. I want to make sure she don't get a chance to spend any of it." His voice dropped to a hungry whisper. "How you going to do it? You figured that out yet?"

"That's why I'm calling. I need your help with something."

"Now hold on, man. I'm not paying like you was a baseball player or something to have to help you."

"This one will be painless," the Hammer assured him. "I need the name of a doctor."

"A doctor? Christ, that city you're in must be crawling with them."

"A doctor who can keep his mouth shut, if you follow my drift."

"Not exactly," the man said.

"That's all right," the Hammer patiently said. "You'll be pleased with the results. Believe me. Just get me a name. Someone who writes scripts and knows his business."

"I'll work on it. Call back tomorrow."

His second call was to Atlantic City where he got an answering machine.

"This is Randi," the recording said. "You know I've been dying to hear from you, so please leave a message."

The woman's voice sounded as though she'd been languishing away all day, waiting for someone to sweep her off her feet. In the background he could hear soft violin music. A pro from first to last, that Randi.

"This is the Hammer," he said after the beep. "I'd like to buy you a weekend vacation. I'll call you tomorrow to arrange the details. But leave this Friday and Saturday open. I'll make it worth your time."

# TWENTY

AFTER AGENT WINDISH LEFT JAN GALLAGHER and Eldon Hodges waiting in the fourth MICU, the Little Admiral ticked for all of five minutes before rising to his full five feet, eight-inch height and taking his own leave. "You appear to have everything under control, Gallagher."

Unable to think of a comeuppance, Jan had to satisfy herself with waving good-bye. Her only regret was that she hadn't disregarded Agent Windish's orders first. She allowed Hodges two minutes lead time before sneaking out of the unit herself. Informing one of the men now manning the linen wagons that she'd be back within the hour, she returned to the elevators where Stanley wanted to know if Ginger had confessed.

"Not yet," Jan said, stepping aside to make way for two orderlies coasting a bedridden patient down the hall. "Were you stationed here when she came on?"

"I rode up with her," Stanley admitted, shifting his eyes to the closed elevator door.

"You see the lunch cooler she was carrying?"

"Her little blue-and-white job?" His eyes darted to Jan and just as quickly away. "I saw it. The only thing dangerous in there would be her egg salad."

"What'd you two talk about on the way up here?"

"Nothing."

"Come on. She's in something deep here."

"I wouldn't know about that."

"The two of you still fighting about who called it quits first?"

Stanley and Ginger had been a brief item before Ginger's initial engagement to Studly.

"I wouldn't know about that either."

"You're a prize, Stanley. What were you fighting about?"

"How would I know? We're not talking."

"Did she say anything about seeing another man?"

"We still talking about Ginger?"

"I am."

"What makes you think there'd be only one guy?" Stanley asked, bitter as usual about past loves.

"My mistake," Jan said, pressing the elevator button.

By then it was 9:00. Outside the hospital it was dark as it ever got in that neighborhood, which, thanks to floodlights trained on the General's buildings, was a kind of twilight glow that made the complex seem somewhat supernatural. The sky was again thinly overcast, cool and damp, the night air clingy as a shroud. A horse-drawn carriage with a hunchback at the reins would have fit in nicely with the modest traffic on Wabash. A county ambulance went whistling and flashing down the one-way, causing maybe one out of three good citizens to pull over and make way. Given the setting, the rig could have been tearing out to collect spare body parts for Herr Doctor Modern Medicine. These days Frankenstein was old hat. Hands got sewn back on regularly; hearts were replaced without worldwide news coverage; dead bodies were routinely jolted back to life with electricity.

She never felt completely safe outside the General at night so kept her pace brisk as she crossed the street and covered the block and a half to the Strong Arm Bar, intending to check on Ginger's story. It was the kind of obvious detail that Agent Windish tended to overlook in his haste to deploy the technology and manpower at his disposal.

Having once or twice been hit upon while within the confines of the Strong Arm, she avoided the wavering paramedics, and pulled up to the draft pulls where Burt, who was the day and night bartender, also the owner, kept his right arm in shape. He wore a white apron, waxed the tips of his gray mustache, and held the entire medical profession in open disdain, which suited his patrons, most of them hospital employees, to a tee.

"What'll it be, Florence?"

Any woman on the premises was a Florence, as in Nightingale. Over on the jukebox, Florence Wynette sang about standing by your man, although none of the specimens in the vicinity looked worth the effort.

"Information," Jan said, leaning over the counter to be heard. "Was Ginger in here earlier today?"

"Today and every day this week," Burt said with a wink.

"You're positive?"

"That's what I am, all right."

"She alone?"

"She was talking to herself," he said. "That count?"

"Depends on if she was answering, I guess. What was the conversation about?"

"Never intrude on a private conversation," Burt gravely swore. "My sacred oath."

"Come on Burt, I'm trying to help her out of a jam."

"My heart goes out to you, Florence. But when she was in, I had a real sob story going down on stool three." He jerked a thumb toward the far end of the bar. "Couldn't hear a thing."

Reaching over the counter, Jan snagged an ice cube from a bin and told Burt to put it on her tab. He told her she didn't have one. They watched each other as if there was more to be said but neither of them quite knew how to say it. Burt pushed his cheek out with his tongue, which made him look thoughtful, sort of.

"Any strangers in here about the same time as her?" Jan asked.

"Usual deadbeats." A resigned shrug.

"She have her lunch cooler with her?"

He closed one eye as if trying to remember. "Blue-and-white plastic job?"

He nodded when she nodded, then waited sphinx-like for her next question.

"You see anyone messing with it while she went to the bathroom?"

"Nope. Never saw her go to the biffy."

"She been in with a man lately?"

"Some guy was pulling her chair out a couple days ago," he said, pleased that she'd asked the right question. "Kind of guy who's always bulging a muscle and waiting for some pipsqueak to look cross-eyed at him."

"He from the General?" Jan asked, leaning forward.

"Never seen him before."

She thanked him and turned to go.

"Say," Burt said, "what's all this buzz about your place of employment almost being a big hole in the ground? Some sawbones mix up the wrong chemicals?"

"Keep that to yourself," Jan said, "or we'll lose the public's confidence."

He solemnly raised his hand to indicate he did so pledge.

Back at the fourth floor Stanley pretended she was invisible. She was hoping for a similar reception down at the last MICU, but no such luck.

As she reached the end of the straight stretch of hall she encountered one of Agent Windish's fleet of hand-picked protégés lovingly setting up a closed-circuit camera on a tripod. All of the DEA agents gave the fleeting impression of having been chained to television sets as youths. Depending on which shows had been popular during their formative years, they had patterned themselves after different TV lawmen. One pair ambled around like Texas rangers, another button-down twosome spoke in the clipped code of "Hawaii Five-O," and one handsome, ponytailed duo had the glitter sleaze of "Miami Vice" rubbed all over them. What they all shared in common was a gung-ho sense of having joined a jihad against runny noses. The agent she now approached was nicknamed Sonny, and he managed with calculated scruffiness to wear his rumpled blue scrubs as if they were the latest in Parisian fashion. Rather than approach his blind side, she stopped several feet shy of his dirty-blond ponytail. Without checking over his silky shoulder, he said, "He's expecting you, Officer Gallagher."

No matter what TV series she was dealing with, all the agents got a kick out of these little superman stunts—eyes in the back of their head, that kind of thing—which Jan had learned to downplay by withholding a reaction.

"What's the gizmo for?" she asked.

"Perimeter extension," Sonny said while making a fine adjustment with a palm-sized screwdriver.

"Anything else I should know about?"

"Only that we think you're doing a super job."

She could see the gap between his front teeth as he delivered that compliment. The flattery had her glancing over her shoulder as she passed him, but she didn't catch him crossing his eyes at her back. The ingratiating way they kept heaping on praise for doing what any messenger boy could have, that was puzzling. In the end she assumed it was just another case of men not knowing how to work with a woman.

Around the corner, she found that the linen carts remained manned and this time dogged too. The other half of "Miami Vice," a lanky, unwashed agent called Bug—she steadfastly refused to ask why—was settling in a black Labrador and German shepherd. Bug's ponytail looked as though stolen from a sickly raccoon; his ear-stud was a tiny ruby that enhanced the glow in his brown eyes. Jan pulled up short when something rumbled in the muzzled shepherd's throat.

"It's cool," Bug said, a graduate of the Berlitz school of street talk. "Without a command he's a pussycat."

"Sounds more like a tiger."

"All show," Bug assured her while straining back on the beast's leash. "Mind if I try this one out on you?" Without waiting for her answer, he made a hand gesture that brought the Labrador's nose to life. As the dog sniffed Jan over, Bug confided, "The agent who normally handles them couldn't make it."

"Why would that be?" Jan asked without taking her eyes off the wet black nose at her knee.

"No can work with Windish," Bug happily said. "Part of the war within the drug war."

"That's a war I hadn't heard of."

"They were born in different agencies," Bug explained. "Windish came over from customs, but the trainer's from Hoover country. Fire and ice. Pity too, cause the only thing I can get this black one to smell is beef jerky, and the shepherd only barks at women."

"Takes after you?"

"I'm more a crooner, ma'am."

"I'm comforted."

"If comfort is what you want . . ." He smiled suavely and modestly glanced down at his long nails.

"It's not," Jan said.

"Pity," Bug said. " 'Cause it looks like you smell good." He nodded at the Labrador's wagging tail. Pulling the dog off, he waved Jan ahead after slowly running the metal detector over her. She refrained from commenting on the innuendo involved there.

Considering that she couldn't have been gone much more than a half hour, the level of activity inside the dimly-lit unit was unexpected. What light there was came from the fixtures in the patient's isolation room or flashlights held by people outside that room, people who appeared to be racing against the clock. Two of General Jack's brown-shirted maintenance men were working up a sweat bolting metal sheets over the outside windows. The whirring of their drill bits drowned out all conversation. Several DEA agents were uncoiling electrical cords and taping them in place on the floor. Other agents were slapping together metal racks in the bunk room and stuffing monitors on those racks and plugging cords into those monitors. One of the tubes was already on, casting a silverish, tinker-bell kind of glow on their activities. Most amazing of all, Ginger was involved too, measuring off distances with a tape and faithfully reporting feet and inches to the agent she was assisting. She was far too busy to acknowledge Jan's entrance.

Agent Windish had staked out a small patch of bare floor near the patient's glassed-in room and milled about there. In his right hand he gripped a compact walkie-talkie, in the other, a portable tape recorder. Rotating between broadcasting orders to his outposts and dictating notes to himself, he eagerly beckoned Jan to his side.

"We're on the verge," he said, so excited that he failed to mention her disappearance. Curling a hand around her shoulder without actually touching her, he rushed on, "We've never come this close to him before, so I'm calling in reinforcements and believe me, we'll get them. Our energies are focused. Our ideologies pure."

"What's that business out in the hall?" Jan asked.

"You don't catch . . ."

But something coming in over his earphone caused him to hold up a hand for quiet. After ten seconds of intense listening, he lifted the walkie-talkie to his mouth and said, "Not the depth charges, that was the last job, for Christ sakes. And find out what's the delay on those motion detectors." When he got back to Jan, he said, "Chain of command is always where the rub is. Where was I?"

"Cameras and dogs," she said, which drew a puzzled frown from him, so she added, "in the hall."

"Ah," he said, curling his arm around her again. Still no touchee. "You don't catch a pro like the Hammer with old-fashioned flypaper, that goes without saying. We're close, Jan. We've foiled him this time. Next outing we'll have him. That's my prediction."

"What about Ginger?" she asked, tensing up. The reaction was automatic whenever the agent used her first name in a familiar way.

"Precisely," Windish said, making a small motion of his head for her to join him in the absolute farthest corner of the room.

"Are you done questioning her?"

"For now," Agent Windish whispered with a chuckle of admiration once they were completely alone. "We didn't learn a thing. Not a thing. Amazing, isn't it?"

"You believe her?"

"Not at all," he confided.

"Then what's she still doing here?" Jan asked, her voice rising. "I told her she was gone."

"Sorry, Jan," he said, making a patting motion for her to keep her voice down, "but I had to countermand that order. Believe me, it's better to know where our leaks are."

"She's not a leak," Jan objected. "She's a mixed-up . . ." But she couldn't find the words to finish, besides which, Agent Windish was *shhhing* her.

"That's my operational matrix," Windish advised her. "Find the leaks, watch them. Actually, that's where you come in, Jan."

"What am I coming into?" she asked, leaning away from him. Her eyes narrowed and darkened.

"We're going to need a data trace on your subordinate."

"Let's break that down into English."

"A tail," Windish explained. "And you're the logical person to help us. That's all I'm asking. Lend a hand. You know the terrain and the subject, and we need whatever edge we can get. Trust that."

"You expect me to spy on one of my own?" Jan asked, her voice going hoarse.

"Think of it as protecting her. What I said about her being able to identify the Hammer, that's not a loose end he's going to leave lying around. There was a secretary in Reno . . ."

"Goddamn it," Jan said, waving him quiet. "How safe is this?"

"Believe me," Windish said, reaching out to touch her elbow, almost, "it's better than letting her wander around on her own until she decides to tell us what she knows."

"What if she really doesn't know anything?"

"She's involved whether she knows it or not," Windish said with a worldly shake of his head at her naïveté.

His expression was open and true-blue as an eagle scout's, which naturally made her pause. She'd seen him pull this honest-injun stuff whenever trying to wheedle something out of his men. What advantage he was currently after, other than what he'd already stated, she couldn't figure out, but the question did make her decide to stuff what little she'd learned at the Strong Arm. A moment passed before Windish earnestly informed her that if she didn't help, they'd follow Ginger anyway, for her own good, but it was thinking about some secretary in Reno that more than anything he'd said convinced Jan to cooperate, although of course he'd said that too.

She met with the two assigned agents in the hallway, back by the service elevator to prevent Ginger from seeing them congregate. With no place to sit, they stood awkwardly before the elevator as if waiting for it to open. The agents she was working with were Tommy and Henry, the button-down "Hawaii Five-O" pair, both in their thirties and dressed like management types who couldn't quite keep pace with the times. Their dark ties were knotted tightly, their suits bought before their waistlines had begun to spread. Tommy acted vigilant as a casino pit boss; Henry, uptight as someone in charge of a storage facility with a barbed-wire fence around it. They listened to her with such undivided attention that an Agent Windish directive had to be at the bottom of it. She detected resentment in their clipped answers and the way their eyes constantly glanced away from hers.

"I don't know anything about tailing someone," she confessed.

"True."

"So I'll let you handle it."

"Good."

"But Windish thought I might know something about Ginger that you might find useful."

"That's what he said."

Henry was doing all the talking, what there was of it. Tommy remained on the sidelines, no doubt saving himself for something insightful. Tommy had as much muscle as a coat hanger and poked out of his dated suit coat like one too, all elbows and shoulder bone jutting away from a round belly. Henry was softer, with a Graceland pompadour and rosy cheeks that shined through his perpetual five-o'clock shadow.

"So what do you want to know about her?" Jan asked.

She stumped them there. Tommy scratched behind a small ear, while Henry tugged at his frayed collar until tentatively saying, "Anything you think is important."

"She's not an easy woman to know," Jan said, realizing as she spoke that she'd thought more about Ginger over the preceding months than she cared to admit. The two of them were opposites in so many ways that it intrigued her. "Or at least not easy for another woman to know. She's one of those women more comfortable around men."

"Does she play around?" Henry asked, embarrassed about having to ask a woman such a question. He stared at Jan's feet as he spoke.

"She's been known to."

"With strangers?"

"If you're asking whether she could have hooked up with this Hammer, I suppose it's possible."

"Is she that dumb?"

"Not dumb," Jan flared. "She's just been jilted by her fiancé. He was one of the guys who went up with the ambulance."

The agents exchanged a surprised look but said nothing.

"At the time I thought she'd be highly motivated," Jan said in answer to their implied criticism. When they'd lowered their eyebrows, she said, "So how are we going to work this?"

"Shifts," said Henry.

"When do you want me involved?"

"Not tonight," Henry said, making it sound as though probably not tomorrow either.

"You really think it's important to keep an eye on her?"

"Yes."

Jan looked from Tommy to Henry and back. Tommy and Henry looked at one another and back to Jan. Around the corner either the

Labrador or German shepherd made a snuffling sound. She thought probably the Labrador.

"Why did Windish really send me out here?"

"Because you're part of the team," Henry automatically said.

"What part?"

Tommy and Henry looked at each other.

"An important part," Tommy said, speaking up for the first time. His statement leaned toward being a question.

They looked at each other some more until Jan gave up on learning anything and said, "You'll let me know if anything happens?"

"A given," Henry answered.

"Just beep me," she said, making sure they had her number. She left before Tommy felt obliged to say anything more. The thought of tailing Ginger left her depressed and—strangely enough—lonely. She swore at Agent George Windish, which made her feel slightly better, which made her feel foolish, which made her think she was feeling entirely too much. To remedy that, she stopped at a nursing station to phone Detective Frank White.

"That wine still chilled?"

"Ready and waiting."

"I'll be there in about forty-five minutes, an hour at the longest."

The drive to White's was a half hour, but she assumed it would take a while to change clothes and explain to her mother that she would be later than expected. She was wrong about that too. Claire chuckled and said that some days were like that, which left Jan staring thoughtfully at a hand-printed sign on the wall that said TIME CARDS DUE.

Back at the detective's nothing had changed, except the Beatles Muzak, flip side now. At her suggestion they adjourned to a sitting room that had an old RCA radio standing in the corner. He turned on a three-way floor light, low setting, and joined her on the crushed-velvet settee, keeping a respectful distance between them but looking hopeful.

"Was it a bomb?" he asked, handing her a glass of wine.

"You think I made it up?"

"No, no," he hastily said. "But usually a bomb threat is empty."

"Not this time. They found one."

"Sorry," he said, actually meaning it, which bugged her. Why should he be apologizing for something he had nothing to do with?

"Look Frank, maybe something's about to get started between us, so we better have us a talk."

"What topic?"

"George Windish."

He eased back on his cushion as if this might take a while.

"It may be my imagination," Jan said, "but I keep thinking that maybe you know something more about him, and after this bomb scare tonight, I'd say I've a right to it."

He sipped his wine.

"The trouble is," Jan went on, "if you don't tell me now, up front, you're going to think that maybe it's the reason I finally took an interest in you. And who knows, maybe you'd be right."

After another carefully measured sip of wine, he grinned sadly, saying, "This sounds pretty close to extortion."

"After what I've been through tonight, I need to be held, Frank, and I don't want you taking advantage of it."

He did a strange thing then. Jan didn't know if she would ever forget it. First, he leaned forward to set his wineglass on the coffee table before them. That wasn't so peculiar, merely fussy, as if setting the stage for something he didn't want to consider. He made sure a coaster was centered beneath the glass. Straightening, he solemnly extended both his arms, monstrous appendages, big around as a child's thigh, and pulled her so close to his breast that she could hear his heart beat. It sounded enormous. And then came the strange part.

He sobbed. Once.

Or at least that's how it sounded to Jan, nestled tightly against his chest, overcome by his cologne. When she leaned back to check his expression, his eyes were shut and he looked as though afraid to let go of her. Maybe he'd gasped rather than sobbed, but whatever the case, when he started talking, the throaty catch in his pipes made him sound fearful of losing something.

"I've been meaning to tell you this," he said, eyes still closed. "Don't know why I haven't. No," he said, sternly correcting himself, "that's not true either. I know why. I didn't want you to think less of me." He opened his eyes, took a breath. "Here goes. Back on that case I worked with Windish, we had a little accident."

"How little?" she asked, leaning away.

"One of his men got taken out."

"How far out?" she said, edging out of his arms.

"All the way," he told her. Folding his hands on his stomach, he said lowly, "Windish could have prevented it with a little common sense. We had one lead on the case, the girlfriend of the dead informant. She witnessed the murder but was too terrified to tell us anything. She knew what was hers if she did. Windish tried everything he could to budge her, couldn't. So he got inventive. He knew of a controlled leak in the prosecutor's office and used it to let the other side think the girl was going to testify. I guess he figured the bad guys would try something that would scare her into cooperating."

"You mean he set her up."

"Without her knowing," the detective confessed, adding in the same breath, "without my knowing either, for that matter. Windish just took it upon himself, didn't consult anyone. Leaked it and then positioned his men to save her from whoever showed up. But it didn't work like he thought. A gun got in through the basement, kicked her door down, and unloaded before Windish's boys could do a thing. The nearest one tried and got drilled. Blown apart might be a better way to put it."

"And the girlfriend?"

"Missing."

"So it wasn't just one of his men who got taken out?"

"I guess not."

"And you sent him to me," Jan said, a numbness flowing down the back of her neck.

"I figured it'd give you a reason to get in touch with me."

"Am I supposed to be flattered?"

"I can see how selfish it was," he said, staring at his antique radio, his eyes blinking a great deal. She tried to look elsewhere too but the tilt of his chin and stillness of his hands kept drawing her back to him.

"Don't get all weepy, Frank. I could have said no to the whole business."

"Weepy?" he said, offended.

"I still could say no."

His indignation passed. "But will you?"

"No," she said, her eyes hard on his. "If you want the truth, it's already occurred to me that Windish doesn't have the best judgment. And let me tell you one more thing, Detective Frank White. You don't get any points for being honest about it now."

"It's a little late?" Frank asked, moving closer to her. His lips loomed awfully damn close, as a matter of fact. Touching hers, as it were. As if this was his last chance to plead his case. How did he know to do it exactly the way that always made her tremble? A soft, nearly nonexistent kiss. No tongue. Barely a touch of the lips. It set something quivering deep inside her, made her realize that this contact, this physical press was what had been missing from her life.

Goddamn her mother and all those Gothic romance novels she left lying around the bathroom.

Even if this wasn't exactly the prince she'd been waiting for, he was here and he was now and she had her needs. Besides which, she didn't quite believe everything he'd told her. He still seemed to be holding something back, an impression that may have been nothing more than the current state of affairs between men and women, particularly divorced ones, but if he was keeping something back, she needed to know what. So even though it felt as if she was taking advantage of him by letting him take advantage of her, she said, "Where's the bedroom?"

Feeling cheap, she followed him upstairs. The trouble was, she didn't find anything more out, not about Special Agent George Windish anyway. The detective was such a perfect gentleman in bed, which was one place she did appreciate manners, that she went all tender and couldn't bring herself to press him any farther. She dozed off next to him, thinking that she liked the comfort of going to sleep this way, with their thighs touching, even better than the sex.

Sometime later she woke with a start, which woke him too. They were both on their backs, thighs still touching. After a moment, he said, "How was it for you?"

"Christ, Frank," she said, throwing off the covers to hunt up her clothes.

"Where are you going?"

"After what you told me tonight? To try and save somebody's life."

"I'm coming with you."

"I think you've done enough for one night, Frank."

She was dressed and out the door before the detective had time to think about what she'd said and quit grinning. Jan's ride to Ginger's was express lane all the way.

# TWENTY-ONE

COUNTING MANOS, THE HAMMER HAD TWO pieces of unfinished business. He wasn't going to get close to Carmen if that woman security guard got a look at his face and started shrieking. So how was he going to X her out? Waiting at her apartment didn't strike him as a winning game plan. By now she would have spilled everything she knew and even made up a few details on her own—who wouldn't have?—so she wasn't going to be roaming around the city unescorted. His problem was to find a way to get at her while she was being watched. To get a perspective on that, he returned to Jackson General, this time under the cover of darkness. If knowledge was power, he aimed to get himself some. It was but a ten-minute walk from his hotel, and aside from a nine-millimeter automatic, all that he took along was a pack of Dentyne and some panty hose, which he'd always found to be an extremely versatile item.

Two weeks before, during his original reconnaissance of the hospital, he'd watched a bundle of rags that happened to contain a wino check up and down the street several times before sneaking down the alley that ran beside St. Stanislaus, a domed church directly across Twenty-first Street from the Old General. His curiosity pricked, the

Hammer trailed the bum in time to catch sight of him slipping in a basement window that was obscured by bushes and a blue-robed statue of the Virgin Mary who seemed to beckon him onward. Since he was on a fact-finding mission, the Hammer accepted her invitation too. He never found the heated corner the vagrant crawled into, but he did discover a window leading to the church's roof, and from up there he had an unobstructed view of the main entrance of New General and a partial view of the employee entrance. A lit sign for the emergency room blocked 25 percent of the employee entrance, but even so it was just the vantage the Hammer wanted.

The roof had a flat, tarred section that ran in front of the large, stained-glass wheel window at the church's front. Crouching over, he wasn't visible to anyone from the street, which by 10:00 at night was basically empty of pedestrians, who generally knew better than to be out after dark in that neighborhood. Two people waited at the bus stop and it wouldn't have surprised him if they were armed. Except for pigeons on the ledges above him, he had the roof to himself. Thanks to bird droppings and the moisture hanging the air, the footing was treacherous; also, he could have done without the constant cooing, which reminded him of whispering voices second-guessing him. Down below, no bomb squad truck was any longer visible, but the DEA's pair of surveillance cars remained in place on Wabash, or at least the nearest one did and he assumed the other hadn't budged either, although he couldn't see it because Old General was in the way. At intervals he also caught glimpses of the lookout stationed on top of the Old General's roof, five stories higher than St. Stanislaus, but the man up there was interested in the doings on the street level, not on an old church roof where a man crouched in dark clothing.

With all that was not happening, he found himself thinking of his youth. Contrary to what the few people who had known his family might have thought, the central issue of his formative years hadn't been his parents' strict discipline. He had survived that, probably even benefitted from it. Those early trials had put into perspective football coaches who believed in rites of passage and the army's basic training. No, the central issue of his youth had been the hypocrisy of his parents, which he'd discovered when he'd been a sophomore in high school.

That year he'd been so scrawny that the only way he could have gotten on the football team would have been as a stowaway in somebody's shoulder pads, if his father would have permitted it, which he wouldn't have. There were too many character-building chores at home for him to have time for extracurricular activities. Besides, weighing in at ninety-nine pounds as he did, football wasn't high on his list of wanna-do's.

The day he learned the truth about his parents was a blustery one. A light rain fell diagonally, fallen leaves gathered in the gutters. The sky couldn't have been any grayer without it being night. Each Monday the Hammer—although of course he wasn't yet known by that name—was to report to his father's office after school to polish and dust everything in sight. His father was employed as an engineer for a small family-owned outfit named Scanner Switch, which made electrical switches for industrial use. Exactly what his father did remained a mystery, and not one that the young Hammer was necessarily eager to uncloak. The only thing he knew for sure about his father's work was that it required precision, a trait whose value he was only now beginning to appreciate.

At any rate, every Monday that fall he was required to bicycle from school to his father's place of employment. Rain was hardly an excuse and on the ride to the factory, which lay in an industrial park reclaimed from a cattail marsh, he had to twice take the ditch or be clipped by cars that wouldn't have seen him until too late even with their high beams on. Worst of all, he had to pedal by the high school's practice field. By his age nearly everyone had obtained their driver's license and thought bicycles fit only for children. As he sped past the football team some clod blew on a duck call, which drew hoots from everyone until the bearded line coach ordered them over to the blocking sled.

Not about to risk tracking up his father's office, the first thing the Hammer had to do at Scanner Switch was clean up his shoes. That, combined with delays from having been run off the road, put him far behind schedule, but to his immense relief, his father never said a word about it. Dear old Dad was too busy chewing out the shop foreman about the variance of contact points, or at least those were the words the Hammer recalled years later as he sat on the church roof unwrapping a fresh stick of gum.

Later, when his father stowed the Hammer's three-speed bike in the trunk of the family Volvo, the only auto manufacturer whose engineering his dad approved of, he had told his son, "You didn't dust my plaques."

"Sorry," the Hammer said, knowing better than to contradict the old man, although of course at the time he never dared think of him as the old man, that insubordination didn't come until many years later, or more accurately, that insubordination never came, at least not face-to-face.

"Tomorrow you'll come back and do them."

"Yes, sir."

"And when we get home you'll vacuum my car truck. I saw mud on your bike wheels."

"I planned on doing that," the Hammer said, and he had.

"No you didn't," his father said. "If you'd planned, you'd have cleaned the wheels before I put them in the trunk."

Even twenty years later he could remember the crisp conversation verbatim.

Then they drove far too fast, as was always the case with his father, who had total faith in his own reflexes and the engineering excellence of his car. By then it was a soupy dusk, and as they sped along the back road away from the factory, the very one the Hammer had earlier bicycled on, the windshield wipers were on high speed and the car's front wheels sprayed water against any sign or guardrail they passed. On a particularly tight curve just before the football field, their front left tire caught the lip of the shoulder, causing his father to overreact and crank hard on the steering wheel. They swerved across the oncoming lane and onto the opposite shoulder. A suitcase-sized white blur flashed in front of them. This was immediately followed by a pulpy thunk. The car bounced as though they'd taken a speed bump at sixty, although they were probably only going forty and should have been under twenty. The Hammer had never been sure but he always imagined that he'd actually seen a framed face disappear beneath the front grille of the car.

His father hit the brakes. The Hammer braced himself against the dash.

"What was that?" his father said, for the first time ever asking his son a question that he, himself, didn't already know the answer to.

They got out of the car, his father angry with the delay, and jogged the twenty yards back to the wreckage of a young football player crumpled beside the road. His protective pads were all cockeyed, his belly pressed the gravel shoulder, the front of his helmet was screwed around until it faced the raining sky. There was no need to check for a pulse.

The football player's name had been Chuck Kondrake, a second-string offensive tackle known for his practical jokes and most likely running down the road as punishment for a dab of red hot in a coach's jock, or some smart-ass answer to a question. The Hammer had a geography class with him and had never liked the clown, although of course that didn't matter now.

"Back to the car," his father finally ordered.

Once in the Volvo there was a brief moment when his father had stared ahead at the curving road and the young Hammer had stared at his father's profile. He'd never seen his old man so alive as at that moment. There was a flush to his father's normally pale cheeks and the rain had flattened his thin hair against his skull. He'd removed his wire-rim eyeglasses and absently plucked a tissue from the box on the dash to dry them. Thank God the box wasn't empty! It was the Hammer's job to keep it filled. He remembered holding his breath and wondering what would happen next, both that day and for the rest of his life, for even then he realized that a divide had been reached. Then another car went spraying by, laying on its horn but continuing on without stopping. Whatever strength had been building in his father's face broke and fled as the second car passed. Slamming the car into gear, he said, "Buckle up."

Squealing the Volvo around, his father raced back the way they'd just come, taking the long route home to avoid being connected to the hit-and-run.

"The young fool shouldn't have been there," his father said. "There's nothing to be gained," his father said. "Not a word to anyone," his father said, adding in afterthought, "especially not your mother."

And that had been the last either of them had ever said about the topic, although the next morning at the breakfast table the Hammer announced he was going to try out for the football team. His mother told him not to be silly, but his father refused to look up from his papers and finally commented, when pushed by his wife, "Let him bust his head open. We're insured."

Even though they didn't know the grieving family, his father insisted they all attend the funeral of one of the Hammer's classmates, informing his perplexed wife it would be a good life lesson for their son. His old man sounded particularly sincere as he gave the grieving family his condolences. That's what the Hammer was thinking about when the woman security guard named Ginger suddenly left the hospital by the employee entrance.

She scurried across Wabash Street to the taxi stand, dove into a blue-and-white, and drove off with the rear DEA car pulling into traffic behind her.

Retracing his steps off the roof and out of the church, he hailed a cab for a ride to Ginger's apartment, where a brief stop was enough to identify that the DEA agent following her had parked across the street from her building. Up on the eleventh floor, the woman's apartment was ablaze with lights. He would have loved to have been there when she discovered the cleaning job he'd done.

Satisfied that he knew the woman's whereabouts, he directed his cabbie to pull back into traffic. Ginger could wait. Right now she'd be all keyed up, wondering if she was safe, which she wasn't, but later on she'd let her guard down, out of exhaustion, if nothing else.

Besides, he needed time to consider how he wanted to do away with her. He'd reluctantly taken a liking to the woman. She might be a little bit crazy, not in his league, of course, but definitely deserving of some recognition.

Now it was time for some misdirection. Out of habit, he switched taxis before returning to Jackson General to wait in the shadows of a contract parking lot four blocks removed from the hospital. Employees used the private lot because it offered lower monthly rates than the county's ten-floor parking ramp. Two weeks ago he'd watched security guards escort nurses to cars in this lot at all hours of the night. This time he had to wait but a half hour before a short, slightly knock-kneed guard in a leather jacket with hospital insignia on the shoulders escorted a pair of nurses to their Toyotas. It would have been a simple matter to draw a gun on the guard and take away his employee ID, but the Hammer needed to let off some steam. Tugging a pair of panty hose over his face, he waited until the nurses pulled away and then stepped in front of the returning guard to say, "Ginger begged me not to bother you, but I told her you needed to be taught a lesson."

"Mister," the guard said, more annoyed than leery of a stranger, "what are you talking about?"

"You're breaking her heart."

The guard shook his head as if trying to dispel an apparition. Failing that, he unhitched his nightstick and patted it in his hand.

"That's not all I'll be breaking," the guard promised.

"You're Sean, right?"

"Who the fuck's Sean?" the guard said, straightening slightly.

That lowering of his defenses was opening enough. The Hammer feigned left, behind which he launched a front kick that flattened the guard, although the apparent thickness of the man's skull prevented a knockout. While the guard woozily checked his mouth for AWOL teeth, the Hammer pulled out a second pair of panty hose and trussed the fallen man up with them.

"Going to pulverize you," the guard thickly said.

The Hammer tied the man's hands behind his back with one leg of the hosiery.

"Little pieces," the guard threatened while groggily shaking his head.

After tying the guard's ankles with the other leg of the panty hose, the Hammer lifted the guard's wallet out of his back pocket and stuffed it in his mouth, although not before the guard managed to say, "Stomp you into . . ." The rest of what he said had a leathery accent. Rolling the guard onto his back, the Hammer removed a clip-on employee ID from the front of his uniform and patted him on both cheeks.

"Tell Ginger that Duke sends his love."

With that the Hammer prepared to leave, but as he pivoted away he heard keys jingling on the struggling guard's belt and stopped to collect them as well. Three blocks away he pitched his mask and the plastic employee ID in a storm sewer for safekeeping. The card itself was meaningless to his plans, its only value came in forcing the DEA to wrack their brains over why he wanted it, but the keys he kept. Those could possibly provide a way out once he delivered his gift to Carmen.

# TWENTY-TWO

FAST AS JAN DROVE TO GINGER'S, she couldn't outrace her thoughts, which at first were evenly distributed amongst excusing Frank White, cursing Special Agent George Windish, and blaming herself for all that had happened with Ginger. But the closer she drew to her destination, the more often she found herself forgetting those accusations and worrying instead about what might be awaiting her.

A block short of Ginger's building, she pulled over in front of a restaurant named Broccoli Amore to survey the scene and buy herself some time to figure out what she would tell Ginger. All the vegetable lovers had called it a night, as had nearly everyone else. After 2:00 A.M. the bars in the city were closed and the traffic thin. Occasionally a car or van pulled up to the main post office's late-night drop box, which was across the street from Ginger's. The only approach she could think of for Ginger was to resort to scare tactics. Since nothing Jan had ever said in the past had left Ginger quaking—exactly the opposite—she found herself searching for the DEA's surveillance car in hope that pointing it out would shock Ginger into cooperating.

Eventually she detected movement in a dark Chevy parked farther up Hargrove. Whenever a car pulled up to the PO's drop-off box, headlights played across the Chevy, causing a figure inside to slump in the driver's seat.

For several minutes she battled with herself over whether to storm up to Ginger's unannounced, or to check in with the surveillance car. In the end, she elected to pay her respects to the DEA first, which she had to admit was a standard county, cover-your-ass type move, but then for better or worse, she was after all a county employee. Everything beyond that was rationalizations, such as, what if something had happened that she should know about? Her next-to-last thought as she locked her car up was that she wasn't going to let them talk her out of anything. Her last thought was that she wished she was back in her uniform instead of an evening dress.

Jumpy as the agents were, she approached on foot, walking ten yards past Ginger's front entrance, which put her even with the Chevy. From there, she marched directly across Hargrove so that the agent could see her all the way. By the middle of the street she was certain it was Henry who remained on duty; the upward sweep of his hairstyle was a dead giveaway. He stayed slouched on his seat for nearly a half minute before cranking his window down.

"What?" he said.

His peevishness wasn't exactly the kind of forced camaraderie she'd come to expect, and it made her cautious.

"Checking on progress," she said, staying two steps removed from the car.

"Our progress is this," he said without bother to sit up. "She's still in her apartment."

Facing Ginger's building, Jan counted up eleven brick-and-glass floors and scanned the windows. "I don't see any lights."

"Hers went out at twelve-twenty. Believe me," he gloomily added, "she's still up there. If we're going to bare our souls, you better get in here. Surveillance works best when no one knows you're there."

When Henry rolled up his window, she stared at him a moment through the glass. He pretended not to notice, but when she crossed around to the passenger side, he did make her wait before unlocking the door. Inside, the red glow from a two-way radio under the dash lit up a portable chessboard opened on the plastic coin tray between the bucket seats. An automatic pistol lay next to the game, making Henry look like a poor loser. The interior stank of cigarettes, and she cracked her window. They were parked next to a row of spruce trees planted to obscure a municipal parking ramp adjoining the main post office. In the shadows, all that she could tell about the agent's expression was that he wore aftershave.

When the agent paid more attention to Ginger's building than to his guest, Jan kept a hand on the door and said, "You're hoping she'll lead you to to this Hammer, aren't you?"

He had no surly answer for that.

"I'm calling the game off," Jan said, cracking her door.

"She's perfectly safe," the agent said, his voice climbing. "No one followed her home."

"Who said he had to follow her?" Jan said with a short laugh of disbelief. "If you're right about anything, he already knows where she lives."

"There's something going on over here," Henry said, nodding toward Ginger's. "She's come down to the lobby twice and acts as if she's expecting someone."

"How's that?" Jan said, her lips suddenly dry.

"She steps up close to the lobby window and checks out the street. And I think she's been drinking."

"You can smell her breath from over here, I suppose."

"It's the way she's walking. Maybe Windish should explain."

"That'd no doubt be entertaining, but I'm not running back to the hospital."

"He can be here in minutes."

"You've got five," Jan said, knowing that the hospital had to be at least ten minutes away.

But the offer pacified Henry, who picked up his two-way and called for someone named Casper. Within seconds he got an answer from the Friendly Ghost.

"Ms. Gallagher has joined me," Henry said with some trepidation into the radio. "She's planning on visiting our Golden Goose and won't let me talk her out of it."

"Coming," was all Casper said.

After that exchange, Henry concentrated so faithfully on the lobby of Ginger's building that Jan silently joined him. She never got the satisfaction of saying his five minutes were up. Four minutes into their wait Special Agent George Windish, wide as ever, stiff-armed open the lobby's door and crossed Hargrove like a bolt of ectoplasm on a mission. Henry cast a superior look at her, but Jan refused to ask any questions.

Windish tapped on the rear driver's-side window, in code, of course, and squeezed himself into the backseat, breathing heavily. There they all sat, Jan and Henry quarter turned on their seats like bookends, Windish filling up the backseat like an unabridged Nero Wolfe. As tea parties go, it was a glum one. Henry resituated himself to face Ginger's building, which left Jan and Windish as much privacy as they would get.

"She's sitting up there in the dark," Windish said, "with a pistol in her hand."

"I would be too," Jan said, refusing to act alarmed. "And how do you know that?"

Windish lifted a stethoscope out of his coat pocket and held it up for her inspection. "Talking to herself. Drinking too. Maybe you should pay your respects another time."

"Is that an order?"

"You've been doing a hell of a job for us, Jan. Let's not ruin it now."

Jan straightened out on her seat so that she faced front. "What are you doing in there?"

"Protecting Ginger. I told you this was serious, Jan, and when Henry radioed in how she was behaving, we moved fast. We're in the vacant apartment next to hers."

"And how did you arrange that on such short notice?"

"Patriotism, the building manager's."

"So you're up there waiting?" Jan said, looking back at him.

"Said the spider to the fly," Windish gravely answered. "Now if you don't mind my asking, what brings you down here in the middle of the night, Jan?"

"Richie Denmark."

Windish absorbed that for a full minute before saying, "Who's that?"

"It's someone Frank White says you know."

"Frank said that?" Total innocence.

"But he says you don't know him any longer. Can't. He's dead. His girlfriend too, along with one of your men."

The agent behind the steering wheel shifted uneasily on his seat, but Windish ignored him, concentrating on Jan as if he really wanted to help her sort through all this. "When did all this supposedly happen?"

"White was thinking of a case the two of your were working on around Christmas."

"Yes," Windish allowed, remembering, "that much is right, but the rest of it . . . I don't know who he's mixed up with me, but . . ." He made a helpless shrug.

Headlights played across the rear window as a car pulled up to the mailbox behind them. Shielding her eyes, Jan stared into the back-seat.

"What *did* you and White work on?" she asked.

And he told her, with admirable detail and sterling conviction. For several minutes he erupted with the facts of their joint investigation, but never once did he mention a Richie Denmark or a girlfriend or one of his men dying. In his story, they ran an investigation into the death of a mule for one of the cartels. Case unsolved. He and Detective White had worked well together and shared a few beers, and, personally, he was at a loss to explain what case the detective was referring to, although in White's defense the agent did point out that the caseload for anyone in law enforcement was monstrous.

"White doesn't drink beer," Jan said, doubting that it was true but refusing to let all this pass uncontested.

"He quit, huh?" Windish said it without missing a beat.

"Are you about done?"

He wasn't. For another few minutes he went on about how he appreciated her concern for Ginger, but that there really was nothing to stay up all night over. They had the A team on duty.

"Was this Hammer involved with Richie Denmark?" Jan asked when Windish wound down.

Windish got busy denying that until Henry interrupted to say, "There's someone going in front."

All heads swiveled toward the building where a Jeep Wrangler with a lit advertisement panel on top that said MIDNIGHT PIZZA had pulled curbside. A stocky man in a leather jacket and billed cap bounded toward the main entrance balancing a warming box like a tray on his palm. They watched him open the entryway door and step directly up to the lobby's security door.

"He's not buzzing an apartment on the intercom system," Jan said.

"He knows the code," Windish added.

"He's inside," Henry said, grabbing up his pistol.

Windish, meanwhile, was fumbling with a portable two-way stuck in his trenchcoat's pocket. Once he finally ripped it free, he said into the radio, "Uncle Festus, company's coming."

"Copy," came back across the radio. Uncle Festus sounded suspiciously like Henry's uptight partner, Tommy.

Jan didn't hear any more because she was out her door and charging after Henry, who ran in a crouch, both hands holding his gun. He'd reached the front door before Jan was halfway across the street. Through the lobby windows she saw the delivery man take the stairway instead of the elevators. Windish, who had by then struggled out of the rear seat, shouted this out from behind Jan. By the time she'd reached the building's entryway, the first flaw in the agents' defense had been exposed: Henry didn't know the building's security code. He was pointing his automatic at the numeric pad controlling the door lock when Jan joined him.

"Shoot," she said.

"What if it freezes the lock?"

They were still staring helplessly at the keypad when Windish arrived, panting so hard that he had to brace a hand against a wall and gulp air a moment before he had the breath to tap in the security code. His first attempt failing, he wiped his eyes and bore down on himself. The second time he entered the code, the door lock clicked and they were inside the lobby, by then empty.

"The stairs," Windish gasped, shoving Henry in that direction.

Windish himself plunged toward the elevator with Jan close behind. When she later recalled all that happened in the space of the next few minutes, she was amazed that she couldn't recall any terror. Somehow all her body's systems but her eyes had shut down, and even those were operating on a kind of tunnel vision that took in only what was directly in front of her.

"Stay here," Windish told her, but he didn't try to push her back when she stepped on the elevator with him. On the way up all he said was, "Stay low." She, for some reason, couldn't take her eyes off his wide, green tie, not even when he drew out his gun, a snub-nosed thing that she thought looked like a toy, not a reassuring thought, nor was the way Windish held it, with his pinkie extended, a confidence builder.

On the way up she listened for gunshots but heard none. On eleven, they were alone. Moving sideways, Windish jiggled far enough down the hall to see that Ginger's door remained shut. About-facing, he hurried to the stairway at the front of the building. Ten feet shy of the stairway door, he hit the deck with a thud and a grunt. Both hands were wrapped around his pistol as if it was slippery. Jan took up a position slightly to his left, lying flat enough to smell carpet shampoo.

For once neither spoke.

A minute passed before the radio in Windish's pocket crackled and Henry's faraway voice triumphantly announced, "Got him, Casper."

While continuing to aim at the stairway with his right hand, Windish used his left to tug out his radio.

"Copy," Windish said. "Where?"

"On four."

"Steady," Windish advised over the radio. "We want him operational."

Sucking down air, he pushed himself up to his hands and knees, peeked sideways at Jan, and when he found her looking back, said, "Good work." The slow rise to his feet was reminiscent of a deep-sea diver afraid of the bends. Once upright, he started to holster his gun but thought better of it, holding it at his side instead. For a moment, he checked up and down the hall, as if making doubly sure nothing was out of the ordinary, but also catching his breath. On the way to the elevator, he confided to Jan, "I never thought it would be this easy." Perspiration shined on his upper lip.

On four they found the delivery boy spread-eagle in the hallway in front of apartment 420. His stubby fingers were digging into the red carpet and his head was twisted sideways. His billed hat had been knocked off, revealing stringy, platinum blond hair; his pizza-warming box had landed near his unlaced tennis shoes. A blubbering sniffle echoed around inside his throat and escaped out his pierced nose. He looked all of eighteen going on seventeen; his huskiness was all baby fat. Henry stood over the desperado in a two-handed target stance, his pistol pointed at the base of the kid's skull.

"Claims he's really a delivery boy," Henry said.

"Jesus Christ, man," pleaded the delivery boy, "just call my boss."

Windish ordered the boy to shut up, put his hands behind his head, and face straight ahead. The kid straightened out as if shot. Windish then planted a foot squarely on the boy's back and motioned for Jan to lift out his wallet, a canvas and Velcro job. Inside it she found twenty-one dollars—a five and sixteen ones—a wad of portrait photos of the type submitted to high school yearbooks, and a single rubber, whose worn wrapper declared the contents to be lubricated and ribbed. She also found a driver's license whose picture matched the kid on the floor.

"Thomas VanDyke," she read. "Lives at four-three-two-nine Thirty-third Avenue South. That's here in the city."

She held the license out to Windish, who couldn't be tricked that easily and waved it off. The sheen of perspiration had spread to his cheeks and forehead.

"What are you doing here, son?" asked Windish.

"Trying to deliver three goddamn veggie supremes."

"The profanity won't get us anywhere," Windish said, putting more weight on the boy's back.

"Hey man," the kid cried, exhaling forcefully.

"I'm going to ask some questions," Windish said, keeping the pressure on the boy's back, "and I don't want you to think about your answers. Just say them. Agreed?"

"Umpfft," was all the kid could manage.

"Good," Windish said, lifting away enough of the weight for the kid to suck down a breath. "How did you know the security code downstairs?"

"The cops who called in the order gave it."

"Come on, sonny. You'll have to do better than that."

"Hey, man, the guy who called said they were cops on a stakeout. That's why he couldn't come down to the lobby and why he wanted me to slip in and take the stairs. They couldn't let anyone know they were here, man."

"And that's all the he said?"

"Said they were starving," the kid answered.

Jan glanced at Henry who looked dumbly at Windish who fixed Jan with a murderous glare, as if to say she was to blame for diverting their attention. She could see the coloring of his neck streak through several shades of crimson. Grabbing for his radio, he blustered into it, "All clear, Uncle Festus. Over."

No answer from Uncle Festus.

Windish repeated the message twice more as he broke for the elevator. During that time no one opened an apartment door any-where on the fourth floor, even though by then Windish was shouting into his radio, and his run could best be described as a stampede of punch presses. Jan actually had trouble keeping up. The last she saw of the delivery boy, Henry still had him covered from point-blank range.

# TWENTY-THREE

THE FIRST TIME THE HAMMER HAD killed someone for hire it'd taken three days for the local paper to cover the murder, and then the rag had assigned it a single, small paragraph, buried on page twenty-two. It'd been a storybook hit too, fast, efficient, symmetrical—right between the eyes—and certainly deserving of more than one lousy two-inch column placed on the same page as an advertisement for men's cotton briefs. Worse, the crime boss who had footed the bill had wanted to make an example of the dead man, and as he put it, "Page twenty-two isn't so much an example."

On the same day the local paper had awarded front-page coverage to a high school honors student who had beaned his father with a computer monitor after a disagreement over a graphics package. The blow had killed the old man right on the spot, which happened to be the shag carpet in the family living room. As far as the Hammer could see, the homicide had been nothing more than a lucky accident, but that fact hadn't mattered to the myopic managing editor, who no doubt imagined himself a spiritual descendent of Hearst.

From that date on, the Hammer chose a different weapon for every contract, his choices ranging from the bizarre to the inspired.

Having been shown the value of showmanship, he'd gone on to say good-bye to victims with a ball-peen hammer—hence his moniker—a potato peeler, an antique buffalo rifle, a Volkswagen Bug, a slingshot, and a javelin, among other things. He was pleased to say that the change in tactics had earned him more than his fair share of ink, which was why at midnight, after relieving a hospital security guard of his ID and keys, he wandered into a kinky sex shop in the city's all-night district and purchased a red wedding veil they happened to have in their boutique section. Actually, the veil was part of a belly dancer's costume, but he preferred to think of it as part of a bride's ensemble. He had a gut feeling that this woman security guard would face her end as bravely as he would face his own when the time came, and he wanted to do something special for her.

A taxi ride past Ginger's place revealed that the DEA knew his fastidious habits well enough to remain on duty. The man behind the wheel of the surveillance car was speaking into a radio transmitter as they drove by, a fact that failed to worry the Hammer. The more the merrier. It was easier to confuse a group than a single man. A mile farther down Hargrove he had the cabbie drop him off near an all-night pizzeria, where he pulled a nylon over his face and hijacked a 4Runner from one of the delivery boys. Five blocks later he screeched onto a side street, discarded the lit advertisement panel that said MIDNIGHT PIZZA, and doubled back to the municipal parking ramp situated alongside the DEA's surveillance car.

On the way the Hammer discovered three things about his stolen vehicle: the rearview mirror had a baby spoon on a gold chain dangling from it; there were two barely concealed handguns within easy reach of the driver's seat; the vehicle was outfitted with a cellular phone, which the owner shortly used to tell the Hammer about a shit storm full of razor blades that was headed his way. The Hammer informed him that he could pick up his 4Runner in front of the Fifth Precinct station, which he'd just passed, in the morning. The threatened shit storm quickly died away, and the Hammer soon found a spot on the parking ramp's third level that faced Ginger's building.

At that height he looked out slightly above the tops of the spruce lining the street. Although tree boughs blocked out the surveillance car, through the treetops he did have an unobstructed view of the entrance to Ginger's high-rise. There he sat, checking his watch, locking his gloved hands together to do isometric exercises, and, having neglected to pack a toothbrush, picking at his teeth with a pizza coupon he'd found stashed above the sun visor.

The only time he got out to stretch, he jogged to the northmost end of the ramp from where he had a side view of Ginger's building, which stretched a half block back to a service alley. He spent fifteen timed minutes doing calisthenics while studying the high-rise from that angle. The lowest balcony stood fifteen feet above the rear service alley, and since he couldn't jump, or even pole vault, that high, he returned to the 4Runner to rummage through its back in hope of finding something useful. In the wheel well reserved for the spare tire he didn't locate any rope but did come face-to-face with a metal carrying case that had a combination lock. Liking the way the delivery boy had threatened him over the phone, he didn't bother trying to open the case.

Returning to the driver's seat, he settled in to outwait his adversaries, which he knew wouldn't prove difficult, not given the stunted attention span of government employees. Hunting was the only remaining profession that prized patience, which gave him a sizeable advantage over almost anyone, and particularly over civil servants, who as a rule were driven by a type of mass fear common to lemmings en route to the sea. His hunting style, a mishmash of Native American hocus-pocus and high-tech accuracy, made him a giant compared to such competition. On top of which, he had added incentives. If the government employees lost and he coffined Carmen, they went home to their subdivisions by the sea to read about pension plans. If he missed and got caught, he got a government entitlement too, the last thing he wanted.

Several years ago a fellow executioner had been fingered by a girlfriend and now sat waiting for the lawyers to quit charging fees and for the State of Florida to seat-belt him in for one last ride. Aside from making the Hammer a fanatic about protecting his identity, the story made him determined never to be taken alive. As might be expected, he had the usual criminal's fantasies about going out with his six-guns barking.

While sitting there he saw two county ambulances flash by; the closing of restaurants and bars; the passing of pizza delivery vehicles, all of which appeared to be four-wheel drives manufactured by foreign companies that believed in team management. He concluded that all of the drivers were probably delivering more than sausage and pepperoni. He also wondered when they found an opportunity to use their four-wheel drives.

Twice he saw a dazed Ginger wander down to the building's lobby as if expecting someone. For a moment he had the absurd notion that she wanted him to know she was home. Something about the way she wantonly leaned against the lobby's picture window while searching up and down the street made him think it. She looked pale and her footsteps were unsteady. Both times on the way back to the elevator she tripped over the edge of a rug.

Not long after Ginger's second visit to the lobby two more government agents arrived, one in need of a corset, the other a handful of Quaaludes. They conferred with the man in the surveillance car before crossing to Ginger's building where they used the intercom system to summon a man in a swanky smoker's jacket to the lobby. Only a building manager would wear an outfit like that. The Hammer hadn't seen a lounge coat that shiny since his father's. By holding up identification to the glass door, the agents talked their way inside.

It was when the security door opened that the Hammer flashed on a possible plan of attack. As the agents leaned on the manager in the lobby, the Hammer grabbed his cellular phone, obtained Ginger's number from information, and called her. He counted ten rings before she haltingly answered. Given the tiny size of her apartment, it was impossible to imagine how she could have needed more than two rings to reach the phone. The delay pleased him.

"H—Hello."

"I'm in the lobby," he said softly, watching the round agent make grand gestures as the building manager escorted them to the elevator.

Ten seconds slipped by without an answer.

"I'll be right up," he half whispered.

And then she did the unexpected.

"I'll be waiting," she said, and hung up.

He couldn't help but laugh out loud. The hitman he'd replaced had told him the same thing, and as he now hung up, he had to admire the woman's balls. For an instant he felt a twinge below his left eye, followed by an honest-to-goodness shiver of regret over what he had to do. Discipline got him past the stirring of what he supposed must be his conscience. Over in Ginger's building, the lights went on in the efficiency next to hers. The agents appeared to be making themselves at home, but Ginger never fled in terror as he'd hoped. If she'd shown up down on the street and he had moved with his usual swiftness, he would have only had to handle the chump in the surveillance car.

The second opening came shortly after 3:00 that morning. By then the only vehicles on the street belonged to pizza fly boys and groggy cabdrivers. The sky remained overcast, as it had for most of this tour, but the cloud cover had thinned enough for a ghostly half moon to burn through just above Ginger's building. From her balcony it wouldn't have been visible, not that the woman was spending any time out-of-doors since his call, but it added a nice, haunting touch to the scene.

Then he saw the other woman security guard, the one he'd hit on unsuccessfully in the hospital elevator—J. Gallagher, he remembered. She was walking past the entrance to Ginger's, moving tentatively until even with the surveillance car where she momentarily stopped before making up her mind and jaywalking across the street. A pizza delivery jeep had to switch lanes to avoid creaming her. She stayed on course without seeming to notice. Before she reached the opposite side, the spruce trees obscured her, so he rolled down his window and heard voices that were too far away to make sense of. Minutes later, when the DEA agent wide as two came bursting out of Ginger's building, the Hammer heard opportunity knocking.

First he ordered up three pizzas, making up his story as he flew. It didn't even occur to him that misrepresenting himself as a cop might be funny or ironic or a slap in anyone's face. At the moment it was what worked.

By the time the pizzas arrived he'd taken the stairs to the street level and crept as close to the surveillance car as possible. When the delivery boy skipped inside Ginger's building as instructed, the crowd from the surveillance car gave chase as if the Hammer was choreographing their footsteps. The instant the trio was inside, he charged across the street, let himself in with Ginger's security code, and raced to the building's back stairwell, which he took two at a time all the way to eleven. He didn't sprint but took the steps in a measured way that barely winded him.

On eleven he peeked out the stairway door in time to catch the wide agent and woman guard boarding an elevator heading down. In no time at all he stood in front of Ginger's apartment with her spare key in hand. Higher mathematics said there was one agent still a door away. Knowing he had to hustle, he grabbed the door handle but never had to apply the key. No need. The door was unlocked. Ginger really was waiting.

He nudged the door in far enough to spy the neck of an empty airline vodka bottle littering the miniscule entryway. The apartment beyond was dark, which meant he would be silhouetted against the hall light as he entered. Thinking of the handguns in Ginger's closet, he threw himself into the room as low to the floor as he could manage without scraping off his nose.

The first shot whistled overhead. After the firing of the gun died away, the room sounded twice as silent. There was no second shot, at least not right away, so he rolled on his back to aim his own gun, a sturdy little Colt autoloader, which until recently had been safeguarding the delivery of pizza and sundry items, toward the hallway from where a DEA agent should soon come rushing. Ginger, he figured, must be huddled somewhere beyond the bed, praying. Hearing her thumb back her revolver's hammer ruined the beauty of that theory. He called out the first thing that came to mind, "Got any Chinese?"

A pause that sounded like a freight train passing. A door opened nearby.

"Enough for two," Ginger answered.

Her slurred voice drew his attention just as an agent slammed in from the hall. Before he could flip about to greet the cavalry, Ginger did so twice. Her first shot stood the agent up, the second pitched him back into the hall.

For distraction, the Hammer shattered one of the tiny liquor bottles against a wall and drew shot number four. The muzzle flash gave away her location in the corner behind the bed. Even though he held a gun in hand, he found himself rushing her in a crouch. One punch to the jaw crumpled her, but not before she managed a fifth round that shaved close enough to his flank to burn the folds of his jacket.

From his coat pocket he unfurled his wedding veil, which he twisted into a tight cord and had all the way to her lovely neck, actually feeling the press of her throat against his knuckles, before he lost control of his hands. Gears locked up in his wrists. How long he looked down at his fingers in wonder he couldn't say. Probably only seconds.

For the first time in his career, he'd lost his nerve, although that thought didn't hit him until later. At the time all he knew was that his body wasn't responding. He lifted one arm and shook it, watching his hand flop. He didn't even have to look in the victim's eyes. She was out cold. Maybe that was part of the problem; she would never know she was leaving. One thing was certain though: whatever the hang-up was, he didn't have time to analyze it. Unable to move his hands, he tried bending his back, which created enough momentum to free up his hands and fold her over his shoulder. He didn't remember her being so light.

The run to the rear stairway was uninterrupted. He displayed perfect balance all the way down to the second floor, where he flopped her down in the stairway landing, only then noticing she was still armed. Her grip was so tight on her Smith & Wesson that he had to pry her fingers loose one at a time, which started to bring her around. He slugged her again before leaving her in the stairwell as he kicked in the door to the first apartment on the left, number 248, which turned out to be a storage room holding mop buckets, stand-up vacuum cleaners, and cleaning supplies. With the hallway clear, he toted Ginger inside and laid her down as gently as possible, which left him in a vulnerable position directly above her as she came around again. This time she moved more quickly and had enough sense to try kicking his crotch, as any smart woman would. She missed, stamping her heel against his thigh. With the contact, he felt a sudden rage and strangled her without a thought. Once she was lifeless, he tied the veil in a bow, lifted an NFL sticker from his pocket, wet it on her extended tongue, and pressed it against her cheek.

By then the wail of sirens was building outside. He let himself out on the apartment's second-floor balcony, dropped to the alley, and made his way back to his hotel unseen. On the way he dialed 911 from a pay phone and informed them they better send the meat wagon to 1281 Hargrove, apartment 248. That was strange too. Normally he preferred to let his work ripen without interference, but this time it bothered him to think of her lying there without being able to breathe. There was something else too, something he couldn't quite put a finger on but which left him anxious to the point of nausea. To get his mind off that, he found himself calling his parents, which he hadn't done for over a dozen years. When his father answered, the Hammer blurted, "You killed him," then hung up before his old man could answer. For some reason he was breathing heavily.

# TWENTY-FOUR

JAN SLEPT LIKE A ROCK DROPPED in a bottomless lake. She slumbered through the day after Ginger's body was found and through a good chunk of the evening too. At about 9:00 that night she shuffled out to the kitchen without saying a word to those daughters assembled in front of the TV with their homework. Her mother was sitting at the kitchen table stuffing inserts into envelopes for her latest community awareness project. Jan didn't say a word to her either. What was there to say? The way they all avoided looking at her, they had to have known what had happened, no doubt thanks to TV.

She put some water on the stove, emptied a packet of hot chocolate that already contained tiny marshmallows into a mug, and filled the cup with water that hadn't had a chance to boil. She'd forgotten to turn on the burner. It didn't matter. She never tasted it anyway. The cup sat on the counter in front of her as she stared out the kitchen windows at the driveway where her youngest had abandoned her bicycle outside the garage. She never said a word about that either. Five minutes later she shuffled back to bed.

About 4:00 the next morning she found herself all slept out and lay immobile in her bed, staring up at the ceiling, which her mother had insisted on painting but a few months before owing to nights exactly like this. Two hours later when her mother stirred, as usual, before the alarm rang, Jan had yet to move. Claire leaned over her face as if checking whether she was alive.

"I see you in there."

Jan made no answer.

"This won't bring her back," her mother said.

Jan thought of several crisp answers but couldn't lift her tongue.

"I'll get you some breakfast," her mother said with a sigh.

Jan was aware of Claire turning off the alarm, tugging on her robe, stepping into slippers. Before Claire left the room, she announced, "You'll have to come to the kitchen to get it."

In her mind, Jan waved her mother away, but her hands lay flat at her sides. She had to strain to picture Ginger's face, and then suddenly she couldn't remember it at all. Instead, she found herself looking at Detective Frank White's large nose. She also saw his bedroom and the two people in it the night before. Something wet grew in the corner of her eyes, but she couldn't do anything about it. Her hands still wouldn't move. Leaving the detective's earlier wouldn't have made any difference. She was waiting for someone to tell her that.

The phone rang. The extension by her bed sounded as though part of her inner ear. Still, she couldn't reach it. Three rings erupted before Claire answered from the kitchen.

"It's the hospital," Claire called down the hallway.

Jan managed to close her eyes. Her mother called out twice more before giving up.

Soon Jan heard groans from her daughters' bedrooms, followed by the daily race to the bathroom. Whoever lost peeked in the bedroom but didn't wander close enough to be identified. That probably meant it was Amy, who kept her distance because she didn't currently approve of her mother's job.

Water ran in the bathroom. Jan tried to will it off. Couldn't. A sign of things to come? Yes. She couldn't stop the day from progressing either. Gray light invaded the bedroom windows. The cooking timer used to control bathroom privileges went off. Ten minutes to a customer. The telephone rang, this time only once. Her daughters were now on the scene, screening calls.

"The hospital," Leah shouted from the kitchen.

An argument over a sweater. Another daughter peeked in on her. A posse was rounded up to find a schoolbook, which was tracked down behind the TV. The front door began opening and slamming shut. Tess, the youngest, stuck her head in the bedroom doorway.

"Need a sick note, Mom?"

Katie went by and tugged on the ribbon in Tess's hair, sparing Jan from having to answer.

Then nothing. School buses had carried them all way. Then the phone.

"It's that detective," Claire said, standing in the bedroom door again. When Jan didn't respond, her mother picked up the bedroom extension and said, "She's playing dead at the moment. I'll tell her you called."

Wasn't that just like her mother? To be so insensitive as to say Jan was playing dead after what had happened. And it didn't end there. Claire trooped right into the bedroom and started getting dressed as if nothing out of the ordinary had happened. She was putting on her checkered, square-dancing outfit, which meant it was Thursday morning and she was heading to the community center for seniors' do-si-dos. Fine. Let Claire go dancing. Was she putting on her gold earrings? God, she was. And rubbing perfume behind her ears and on her forearms and a dab on her gums. She added some color to her cheeks too, enough for an autumnal sunset. All done right at her vanity, which until a month ago she'd kept covered with a black shawl. Jan managed to roll on her side to avoid watching.

"I'm leaving," Claire said. "If you want to feel sorry for yourself, you'll have to do it alone."

With pleasure.

Except that right now Jan couldn't quit seeing Ginger's face, even with her eyes open. She lay there for what seemed like a short time, although the phone rang on three separate occasions. Finally she had to get up. It was that or wet the bed.

She sat in the bathroom until hearing the phone again. Standing, she opened the medicine cabinet so that she wouldn't have to look at herself in the cabinet's mirror. The phone again. She stared into the cabinet until the ringing stopped. Closing the cabinet door, she saw herself in the mirror anyway, very much alive. She knew there was nothing she could do about that, or about Ginger, but at the same time a part of herself was hoping she was wrong. What she could do she didn't know. But there must be something. That little lie got her moving, got her ready for work.

Not until she got behind the wheel of her car, turned the ignition, put the car in reverse, and looked in the rearview mirror did she slap the steering wheel and openly cry.

Even if her car could back up, she couldn't. There wasn't any going back now.

# TWENTY-FIVE

THE HAMMER SLEPT LIKE A FLAT stone skipping across a deep lake. Each time he dozed off, a sense of being airborne jerked him back to wakefulness. He tried several tricks—meditating, hot chocolate, counting past jobs—but nothing worked. He brushed his teeth a half-dozen times without results. Staring at the ceiling was out because it reminded him of the last night he'd spent in the woman security guard's apartment. He couldn't turn on the TV because the voices bothered him. He couldn't hit the TV's mute button because then he wouldn't know what they were talking about, which was worse. Whenever he jerked awake, he had an unexplainable urge to wash his hands.

Several times when he nodded off it felt as though he was about to catch a glimpse of his future. Ridiculous as it sounded, the precognitions unnerved him. He'd now missed Carmen twice and was beginning to wonder if a hand that was much, much larger than his own might be involved. A clammy sweat settled on the low of his back, and he spent a half hour immobilized on his bed, trying to calculate whether he felt any remorse for all that he'd done in his life. The sum of his calculations was zero, which wasn't reassuring.

Finally he decided that the only way to get any rest at all was to tire himself out by continuing on with his duties.

Getting dressed, he went down to the hotel's breakfast shop where the conventioneering shrinks were loading up on coffee, swapping stories about psychosis, and pretending they'd quit smoking. The Hammer took a seat at the counter, surprised to feel somewhat comforted by the living, breathing bodies around him. With all the people cluttering up the world, it was hard to imagine his subtractions from the populace as anything other than a tonic for society in general. He ate toast to settle his stomach.

After a cup of tea, he retired to a pay phone at the back of the restaurant to put in a call to his answering service, whose switchboard was behind the bar of a honky-tonk in Roadkill, Oklahoma. Jesse, the owner of the Two Dot Bar and Dance Hall, had vacationed with the Hammer in Central America some years before where the then-young Hammer's cold-blooded enthusiasms had made an impression. The older mercenary had taken him under his camouflaged wing and helped the Hammer through some atrocities, as they liked to joke. The Hammer had stuck at the freedom-fighting business for a couple of years until tired of tropical mountains, generals with press secretaries, and Panama City binges. Through some contacts he'd made during that time he eventually fell into his current line of work. The only soldier of fortune he kept in contact with was Jesse, who was as close to a friend as the Hammer had in this world. Or the next. They hadn't seen each other in person for years, but still the Hammer trusted him, which explained why he didn't bother to come up with a new answering service even though Carmen Romero-Muehlen had twice tried reaching him at the Two Dot. The fact that the DEA would inevitably come sniffing around Jesse's didn't matter. The heat wouldn't faze Jesse, and who else could the Hammer trust?

"Two Dot," answered Jesse.

"How's the weather over Panama?"

"Clear."

It was an almost daily ritual that never varied unless someone had tried to reach him. Messages usually amounted to a first name and telephone number.

His second call went out to his current employer, who was developing an attitude.

"We paid for quick and dirty."

"When it goes down," the Hammer said, "that's how it'll be."

"It's way past quick."

"I'll double up on the dirty."

"I'm hearing you missed again."

"All part of the plan," the Hammer assured him. "How about the name of a croaker?"

"Go to a Dr. L.L. Adams. In the yellow pages, I'm told. Tell him Rex referred you." His voice deepened dramatically, which was par for the course. "I'm expecting a happy ending out of all this."

"You'll be in stitches," the Hammer promised.

Call number three went to Randi in Atlantic City. When she answered, violin music was still playing in the background.

"Yes?"

"It's the Hammer."

The music cut off, her voice lost its dewy husk. "It's been a while."

"Haven't been your way. Did you free up Friday and Saturday?"

"From late Friday on can be arranged. But I'm not wearing all that crazy football gear again."

"That was a one-time gig, believe me. This is something much simpler. You won't even have to take your skirt off."

"Don't think I haven't heard that line before."

"No," the Hammer said. "I mean it. All you have to do is fly out here, pick up a plant, deliver it to a very sick man, and fly home."

"Nothing kinky with the dying man?"

"Word of honor."

"What's he got?" she asked, choosing not to comment on his word of honor.

"I'm the patient, if that will relax you any. And it looks like I'm going to have a drug overdose."

"And you're paying me to come visit you?"

"That's about it."

She exhaled. He could imagine her blowing cigarette smoke up at the ceiling while searching for an advantage.

"You know how I hate to fly," she said at last.

"I think I've got just the medicine for that."

And he did. Five thousand dollars worth of elixir, plus traveling expenses, which was of course a great deal of money, but he was paying for more than her time. He was buying a still tongue if anything went haywire. The price tag on that kind of muscle control was always steep. Once the price was fixed, they took of care of most of the details within minutes. Randi was expecting a matron from Rhode Island.

After phoning an airport hotel to arrange a double for himself and Randi, he called the hooker back to give her the reservation info. Her answering machine was again on duty but he hung up and redialed until she answered. The fifth time did the trick, as Randi interrupted her recorded message and he was able to give her the name of the hotel.

He got Dr. L.L. Adams's number from information and set up an appointment for late in the afternoon. He tried offering a bribe, which the phone receptionist said she'd be delighted to accept, but that it wouldn't move up when he could see the doctor, who was involved in an important convention until tomorrow. When he tried to get the appointment switched to an earlier slot tomorrow, she informed him he was lucky to get in at all. She'd certainly never heard of anyone named Rex, so as a referral it didn't cut any of her ice.

"The reason for your visit?" the receptionist asked.

"Genetic counseling."

"Dr. Adams is a psychiatrist."

"Exactly," the Hammer said and hung up.

* * *

Leaving the hotel, he asked the doorman for directions to a florist, where he selected an enormous arrangement of potted mums, one large enough to cheer a dead man. He spent more time choosing the pot than the plant, and when he at last found a large molded plastic pot with a recessed bottom that suited his needs, he instructed the florist to transplant the mums while he stepped across the street to a drugstore. At Eagle Drug he purchased packaging tape, a cardboard shipping box, and a toothbrush that caught his eye.

Back in his hotel room, he pulled his portable armory out from beneath the bed and removed a seven-shot automatic, a stiletto, a set of identification cards that included a Blue Cross of Greater New York ID, and his medic's kit from which he lifted a syringe, spoon, lighter, and some street H. Calling room service, he ordered up a bottle of Jack Daniel's. Spreading his junkie's paraphernalia out on the dresser top, he brewed up a concoction guaranteed to freeze a heart.

Unwrapping the green foil from around the base of his mums, he taped his loaded hypo, the keys stolen from the hospital guard, and the small-caliber automatic to the indented bottom of the pot. Thinking about the size of Manos's chest, he rearranged everything until able to fit in a second clip for the automatic. Setting the flowers on top of his cardboard shipping box, he outlined the base of the pot with a complimentary pen from the hotel and sawed the circle out with his stiletto, then crammed the cutout into the recessed bottom and secured it with tape. After wrapping the mums back up, he had no trouble sleeping for sixteen hours straight.

# TWENTY-SIX

JAN ARRIVED AT HER DESK ELEVENISH and found two pink office messages waiting for her. Both had *urgent* circled, both were from Detective Frank White, both said *call me*. The top slip had been written up the first thing that morning, the bottom one, late the previous afternoon. The backward-slanted handwriting with the loopy serifs belonged to Miss Pepperidge, but one look across the aisle warned Jan not to bother asking if the detective had mentioned anything else. The secretary peered back as if a barnyard rock had just been lifted, leaving little doubt who she thought responsible for Ginger's death. It wouldn't have been an opinion the secretary had formed all on her own, but one she would have caught, probably when the Little Admiral sneezed. At the county, blame was infectious. Jan found herself wishing she was back in bed, the blankets pulled over her eyes. She felt a draft. Someone from Social Services passed by without saying hello.

Pulling herself back to her desk, she tapped out Frank White's number, to hear a friendly voice as much as anything. It turned out to be a mistake. Right away he went overboard with sensitivity and concern.

"I heard about last night, Jan. How are you holding together?"

"It looks like everything's attached."

"I know how you must be feeling, Jan. We lost a man last year and . . ."

"I don't want to talk about it," she said, apparently a little too loud. All papery noise and keystrokes in the vicinity of her cubicle ceased. Forcing herself to tone down, she conceded to the detective, "Not yet, anyway."

"You're vulnerable right now, Jan, whether you realize it or not."

"I'm going to hang up now, Frank."

"There's something else you better know about," he hurriedly said.

"Only if it's important."

"It might be," he said, all apologetic. "We've got a case I thought you should hear about. Does the name John Frazer mean anything to you?"

"No. Should it?"

"I doubt it. He was a driver for Premier cabs. We found him in his trunk yesterday, dead for several days."

"There's a reason I should know this?" she asked, shielding her eyes with a hand as if the office light had become too bright.

"He choked to death."

"That doesn't sound like a reason. It doesn't even sound like a homicide."

"It does to your new friend Windish." He was trying to make a joke but the laugh died feebly in his throat.

"Windish?" she said. "Why get him involved, Frank?"

"The cabbie normally worked the stand by your hospital, for one thing. That and the fact that in all the cases we've opened a file on, we've never seen a murder weapon like this one. When Windish hit town, he requested notification on any oddballs."

A long pause. Not a creak from Miss Pepperidge, who normally conducted a symphony of rattling forms, scratching pens, and dropped paper clips.

"Are you going to tell me about the weapon?" Jan said, cupping a hand over her phone receiver to muffle her voice.

"A chunk of chicken breast," he said, resigned to how ridiculous it sounded. He cynically added, "We're working on who cooked it."

"Why are you so sure it's murder? Why not his supper?"

"In his car trunk? Besides, he was wearing pajamas, and the cab was abandoned in the parking lot of a police station."

"And it took how many days to find him?"

"Three, best guess of the ME. It probably would have taken longer if someone hadn't tried to burgle the trunk and left it open when they saw the contents."

Pressing her eyes shut to concentrate, she asked, "Was there a football sticker anywhere at the scene?"

"That's what Windish asked," he said slowly.

"So you've had time to think about the answer."

"Too much time," he said, clearing his throat. "There was an NFL sticker on the chicken, yes. I don't suppose you'd be willing to tell me what that's about?"

"What aren't you telling me about Windish, Frank?" She had a sudden intuition that he was loosening his tie and looking guilty.

"Listen Jan, this guy they call the Hammer, his head must rattle like a gourd. I think you've got to be damn careful, considering everything." He added lamely, "I'm thinking that for selfish reasons."

She didn't know what to say to that, but figured she had to come up with something if she ever hoped to end the conversation, and suddenly she hoped to. Agent Windish was knocking at the entrance to her cubicle, red-faced and out of breath.

"I'm running late," she said into the phone.

"I miss you," Frank White answered, his voice low, probably to prevent anyone on his end from overhearing.

"Can't talk now," she said. "Bye."

Windish brushed an unwashed bang of hair off his broad forehead and tried to say in a routine way, "She wants to see you." His hurried movements threw the planned carelessness of his effort off.

"Who?"

"Our patient," he said, impatiently waving for her to join him. His pink shirt had underarm rings, his sparse beard was showing up like a connect-the-dots picture, and he had the smell of something that had been hiding in a laundry hamper for several hot days. He'd switched to a dark blue tie that was even wider than his horrid green one. "The ipso facto for why we're all enjoying each other's company. Carmen Romero-Muehlen, her highness."

"You're not going to say anything about Ginger, are you?" Jan said, refusing to budge from her chair.

"I'm trying not to," Windish agreed.

"The woman's dead."

"We *were* trying to guard her."

Jan stood, and although she was a head shorter and well over a hundred pounds lighter, it was the agent who rocked back on his heels. Shoving past him, Jan led him away from her cubicle before Miss Pepperidge overheard anything worse.

"So what does your patient want?" she asked when away from Security's ears.

"To talk to a woman. She says."

"What's wrong with her nurses?"

"She's convinced you can amuse her."

"Tell her I don't know any card tricks," Jan said, pushing open the doors leading out of the administrative wing.

"She'll pay you," Windish said, right behind her.

"Why would she want to do that?"

"Perhaps she's used to buying things?" he suggested.

Jan waved off that idea and led the way to the elevators where they waited for a car side by side.

"What's she offering?" Jan asked, more intrigued than she cared to admit.

"Hundred an hour."

The elevator arrived and Jan stepped on first, next to someone from Medical Records who stood behind a shopping cart piled high with patient charts. Windish crowded in next to her.

"What's she want to talk about?" Jan asked as the elevator doors closed.

"That's my question," Windish said, sounding cranky enough for her to believe that for once he actually was as much in the dark as she was. His pupils may even have been dilated.

At the patient's insistence, Windish shagged the two nurses out of the isolation room and followed them out himself, leaving Jan alone with the patient, the bodyguard, and the muted images of a game show on the TV. Windish and nurses lined up outside the room's glass windows, bickering about who had the authority to order what, or at least Jan assumed that was why they were all talking at once and pointing fingers at themselves. She couldn't make out their words, not with the door slid shut.

All she could hear was the private bodyguard humming a Spanish lullaby under his surgical mask. Jan had had to tie a mask on too, along with a hospital gown over her uniform, and she had to snap on a pair of tight plastic gloves that made her palms sweat. She did her best to ignore the bodyguard, especially when the patient ordered him to pay the lady for her time. Pulling a silver lamé billfold out of the back pocket of the scrubs he wore, his gloved hand separated a hundred-dollar bill from its family, extending it toward Jan, who continued to look away from him. He floated the bill on to the bed in front of Jan and withdrew to the door where the top of his head nearly reached the bottom of the TV. Jan let the bill lay.

"I better warn you up front," she told the patient, "I'm not so good at girl talk."

"Then we have something in common."

Halfway through her sentence the patient stiffened in pain. She lay on the bed as if pinned under a great deal of water. Her limp hair fanned out on the doubled-up pillow; her arms had greenish-blue bruises in several places from IV sticks. Someone had pinned her dark hair away from her puffy face with two red butterfly clips, a garishly feminine touch, considering the sterile surroundings. Her skin had a faint yellowish red cast, as if swabbed with Betadine, a disinfectant; the whites of her eyes carried the same jaundiced hue. The only part of her that seemed truly alive, instead of preserved, was the swirl at the center of her brown eyes. Once the pain abated, her body slackened and she took several shallow breaths before saying, "Have you wondered why someone would go through all this?"

"You don't want to die," Jan said, glancing away, suddenly embarrassed.

"True. But why? Have you thought about that?"

"Some," Jan said, curious enough to turn back. "Maybe you're afraid."

"Oh, I am. But not for myself." Carmen Romero-Muehlen rocked her head slightly to emphasize this. Her voice became protective. "I have a little girl. She's five, right now. About to start school. Does that help you understand?"

"Maybe."

"Someone's got to be there for my little one."

"No father?" Jan asked, feeling more sympathy than she'd expected.

"He's standing by the door over there," Carmen Romero-Muehlen said without flickering her eyes toward the bodyguard. "A moment of weakness." Her mouth rounded for a sharp, painful breath and her eyelids lowered halfway. When her discomfort passed, she said, "I think we all want most what we can't have. Don't you?"

"I haven't figured that out yet."

"Ah. Well, I know I have. I wanted respectability, but . . . what I got is standing by the door over there. You begin to see how it is?"

"No problem seeing that," Jan said, refraining from glancing toward the guard.

"True," the patient said with a sad chuckle that she quickly cut off with a grimace. After catching her breath, she formally asked, "Have they told you who I am?"

"Mostly."

"That's not so important except it means I have money. Enough to give you some."

"You've already tried," Jan said, nodding toward the hundred-dollar bill.

"More than that. Much more. Would you like that?"

The woman had a talent, one she'd groomed. Her voice carried a charming insinuation, as if they were already in league together, and she was only sharing what she had because of that closeness. Jan's vision drifted away from the patient and out of the room; she said nothing, simply waited to hear what would come next. Beyond the room's glass wall one of the nurses was repeatedly checking her wristwatch while the other spoke heatedly into a phone. Both glanced anxiously into the unit at frequent intervals. Agent Windish did everything but press his oversized nose against the glass as he peered at Jan, trying to read her reaction.

"Scruples?" Carmen Romero-Muehlen wheezed when Jan didn't immediately respond. "I respect that."

"To hell with scruples," Jan said, faking some toughness. It was dawning on her that she might be about to find a way to atone for Ginger. "I've daughters too."

"I respect that more. I'm talking about a good deal of money, my dear. Say fifty thousand."

"What would I have to do?"

"Deliver something for me. A payment."

"How dangerous?" Jan said.

"There's some, but minimal, I think. For a smart woman. What I'm interested in is that you can be trusted."

"And what makes you think that?"

"I've seen you arguing with my overstuffed benefactor," she said, rolling her eyes toward Agent Windish at the window.

"Who would I be delivering this payment to?" Jan asked, without commenting on Windish's finer qualities.

"An old friend of mine."

"He can't come to you?"

"He's tried, twice. We used to call him Eveready, like the batteries, but around here I believe you know him as the Hammer."

"I see," Jan said, glad to have her expression hidden by a surgical mask she wore.

"Haven't you wondered," Carmen Romero-Muehlen speculated, "what good a new liver will do me with someone like the Hammer out there?"

"Now that you mention it."

"That is why I need your help. I want you to contact the man, and make him a handsome offer on my behalf. Tell him I want to live and that I'll pay him for the privilege. If he accepts, I want you to act as a go-between. I think he might trust someone who's not with the DEA."

"Trust me to be dumb," Jan said. "Why wait until now to ask him?"

"What makes you think I have?"

"All right, so what makes now different?"

"He's tried for me twice and failed. Maybe he'd like a way out."

"He doesn't strike me as a quitter," Jan said.

"Me either," Carmen Romero-Muehlen answered with a mirthless laugh. "But what other choice do I have?"

Jan watched her a moment before saying, "I do all that alone?"

"It would have to be that way, yes. You'll never get close enough to him any other way."

"What's to stop him from killing me?"

"Nobody's paying him to, my dear, but if it worries you, pick a public place. He's the best at what he does, but he's no magician."

"Say it works," Jan said after a moment of consideration, "what's to stop them from sending someone else after you?"

"My man over there can handle anyone else my cousins might send."

"For fifty thousand?" Jan said, not wanting to sound too eager, which wasn't difficult.

"From where I am, it sounds like a bargain."

"How much does the Hammer get?"

"Two million. That's a bargain too."

"When?" Jan asked.

To which Carmen Romero-Muehlen let her eyes close in relief as she said, "Bless you."

Afterwards, when Windish rushed up to her, Jan brushed by him, saying, "Girl talk." A response that caught him flat-footed. Jan continued on her way, saying with some satisfaction over her shoulder, "I'll be in my office if you need me."

But she didn't have to rearrange paper clips in her desk drawer for long to see that only a fool wouldn't involve Agent Windish. Anything else would be making the same underestimations as Ginger. More infuriating, when she paged the agent to arrange a meeting, he didn't sound at all surprised. They soon met in a vending machine area, and he listened patiently to what she had to share, then put both his hands on her shoulders and gazed into her eyes.

"Will you do it, Jan?"

His lack of surprise made her shake off his hands and say, "You knew what she wanted from the start, didn't you?"

"No," he said. "But I knew about it almost as soon as you did. We have her room bugged. Will you do it?"

She paced away from him, muttering, then returned to jab a finger at his blue tie. "Only if we can make it reasonably safe."

"If we can't," he said, "I'll call it off."

"You're damn right we will. Why will you do any better job protecting me than Ginger?"

"For one thing, we won't have you to distract us."

Unable to tell whether he was serious or making a poor joke, she dropped the matter, asking instead what came next.

It took the agents less than an hour to set up shop for a phone call to the number Carmen had provided Jan. They commandeered a nurse's office between the third and fourth MICUs and carted in their equipment. Aside from a bookcase crammed full of computer printouts, the room had one window whose blinds were closed, three chairs, a phone set up with a headset in addition to the normal receiver, and Agent Sonny looking incorrigible as he probably had when he'd received his first plastic cop badge as a kid.

"Does she even have the money?" Jan asked as she took everything in.

"She had a million for your hospital," Windish said. "So why not? And if this goes right, you can keep your bonus from her, minus the IRS, of course."

"Ha," said Jan. "How are we going to play it?"

"Once you get him on the phone, explain who you are and why you're doing it. All straightforward."

"Why am I doing it?" she asked, not so sure herself.

"Money," the agent answered, thinking she wanted to know what to tell the Hammer. "It's the only reason he'll believe."

"Then what?"

"Propose a meeting."

"In a public place," Jan inserted.

"Good," Windish said, rubbing his hands together. "We can cover you there."

That wasn't as reassuring as the agent imagined, but Jan went ahead, saying, "What if he won't meet somewhere public?"

"Then it's off," Windish said with a firm nod. "That point's not negotiable."

"Why are you being so nice to me?" she asked, intending brave humor. He took her question seriously though.

"Because I think you've got potential, Jan."

She cocked her head sideways and squinted at him but couldn't see why he was flattering her when she'd already agreed to do it.

A male voice answered the long-distance number that Carmen's instruction sheet provided.

"Two Dot."

"I want to leave a number for the Hammer."

"Who?"

"My cousin, the Hammer."

All this was scripted out on the sheet of paper handed her by Carmen Romero-Muehlen's bodyguard.

"Shoot."

She gave him the phone number.

"He'll get it."

That simple. The rest of the afternoon was spent trying to think of something else while waiting. That wasn't so simple. Within an hour Windish had twice explained all the ways she'd be protected. A half hour after that everyone had grown tired of looking away from one another whenever their eyes met. Eventually they all tried reading the literature on hand, unfathomable tracts on critical-care nursing—respiratory assessment, cardiac catheterization, and the ever-popular placement of gastrointestinal tubes—plus thick notebooks crammed with interdepartmental notes dating back over a decade. Soon they were back at dodging each other's eyes.

At 6:00 that afternoon Windish said, "We call it a day. It's no good to let him think you're too anxious. Report back here at eight tomorrow."

At first the dismissal felt like a reprieve, but the giddiness had dissipated before she was out of the parking ramp. Lately, every time she left the ramp she found herself thinking of an ambulance that recently departed forever by the same exit. Tomorrow began to feel like a piece of tape she couldn't shake loose.

On the drive home she thought that she might well be doing the most foolish thing in her life, outstripping even her marriages. The idea was oddly comforting, as if it proved she was still alive, although it may have been comforting for a much simpler reason: It saved her from feeling guilty about Ginger.

What she didn't understand was where she got such instincts from. An answer for that was waiting at home. She'd no more than pulled into the driveway than her middle daughter Katie was madly waving to her from the kitchen doorway.

"Grandma wants to talk to you," Katie called out. When Jan didn't move fast enough, she added, "It's long distance."

That increased her foot speed.

Picking up the kitchen phone, she said, "Mother, where are you?"

"Las Vegas," Claire matter-of-factly replied.

"What in the world . . ."

"Everything's fine, dear. I'll be home next Tuesday. Leah should be able to handle anything that comes up until then. She is almost eighteen."

"So you keep telling me."

"I wanted to do something for myself," Claire suddenly said. "Something unpredictable. And fun. That's all."

Claire hung up, which left Jan with no alternative but to do the same. When she looked around the kitchen, she found all four of her daughters looking at her as if they wanted some answers. She suggested they take a number.

# TWENTY-SEVEN

THE OUTER OFFICE OF DR. L.L. ADAMS belonged around a kidney-shaped swimming pool, not on the third floor of a suburban professional building. The low, pink chairs were inflatable poolside ones that could float, the plants inflatable palms, and the receptionist, a young blond with a fifties bouffant and heavy black-frame eyeglasses, had a mole on the side of her neck that at first glance resembled a valve stem. There was a bicycle pump in a corner, the wall clock was numbered backwards, and the room's pictures were all of icebergs in milky-green seas. The Hammer had the last appointment of the day, and as he stood waiting, not about to be caught in one of the chairs, the receptionist locked up the office, pulled on a fake leopard-skin coat, and told him as she let herself out, "L.L. will be with you shortly."

Five minutes later he was about to let himself into the inner office when that door opened and the doctor emerged with his patient, an anemic-looking adolescent dressed in what appeared to be a prep school blazer. The fact that Adams apparently was a child psychiatrist at least helped explain the toyland decor. Doling out words of encouragement that verged on fatherly, the doctor nudged the boy out of the office before turning a critical eye on the Hammer.

"You're the one Rex sent?"

The doctor's question didn't sound like a compliment. In contrast to his flaky office, he was conservatively dressed in a dark suit and tie. With his dark good looks, the guy probably could have made a handsome living modeling tweed jackets and Ivy League sweaters. He had the kind of superior attitude that usually tempted the Hammer to smash mouths.

"I'm your five-thirty appointment," the Hammer answered.

"I thought I told Rex I was all through with this monkey business."

"Maybe tomorrow you're all through," the Hammer corrected. "Today you're still peeling bananas."

The Hammer slowly reached out to brush off the doctor's shoulder with his fingers, as if sweeping dandruff aside. The doctor glanced from his shoulder to the Hammer without speaking, his expression one of contempt.

"Now why don't we get on with this," the Hammer said. "I'll be sure and tell Rex what you said."

Taking the doctor by the elbow, the Hammer led him into the inner office with enough menace to shut him up completely. Dr. Adams stared straight ahead, apparently experienced enough with Rex's associates to know better than to resist. The inner office was completely traditional, with leather couches, diplomas, and one-pound books.

"What exactly is it that I can do for you?" the doctor said, easing himself out of the Hammer's grasp and sliding behind his desk. Unlocking a drawer, he pulled out a prescription pad and tossed it on the desktop without any eye contact.

"I'm thinking of checking into a hospital," the Hammer said, standing close enough to view exactly what the doctor reached for in his drawer.

"What would be ailing you, Mr. ah . . ."

"Nothing at the moment," the Hammer said without supplying a name. "That's where you come in. I'm planning on being admitted to a hospital."

For the first time the doctor looked up, sharply. "What kind of business is this?"

"Nothing out of the ordinary, doc. All I want from you is a script and some advice."

"Leave it to Rex," he muttered. "Is there any specific reason you want to be admitted?"

"I need a nice comfortable bed in an ICU."

"What type of ICU would we be speaking of?" the doctor asked, insinuating that such distinctions were probably beyond his new client. "Surgical, medical, or maybe a nice neurological?"

"One that caters to overdoses."

"Medical then. Am I to assume you foresee an overdose in your future?"

"Doc, you must have been first in your class," the Hammer said in a folksy way, wagging his head in admiration. The shrink was smart enough to redden and clam up. "Now," the Hammer went on, "the kind of overdose I'm shopping around for is something that will keep me up there a day, two at the most, then leave me able to walk out on my own."

"This sounds like a dangerous business."

"That's why I love it," the Hammer said without intending any humor.

"Medicine isn't an exact science," the doctor said, hedging. "There's no predicting how the human body might react to a given substance."

"Why do you think I'm here, doc? I figure pharmaceuticals are the safest way to go."

"You want me," the doctor said, pointing a slender finger at himself, "to help you almost kill yourself?"

"That's what I'd be paying you for," the Hammer said, nodding agreeably.

"What if they trace it back to me?" the doctor said, stalling. "My license number will be connected to any prescription I order."

"Doc, I'll be using different names for picking up the script and admitting myself into the hospital. Think of it this way—I'm a professional too."

"I'm warning you up front," the doctor said, still not buying it, "this is substantially less than a brilliant idea."

"How much would it take to make it brilliant?"

The doctor made a sucking sound between his teeth before shaking his head in submission and saying, "The idea is preposterous."

"Let's not pretend that I have to wear you down, doc. How much?"

"A thousand," he said, hoping to overprice himself.

"You'll do it for five hundred," the Hammer said, counting out the cash. "And Rex is hearing about it."

"What's your pleasure," Dr. L.L. Adams asked with resignation as he watched the green bills accumulate on his desk. "Oral, intravenous, or suppository?"

"Gotta look like street business."

"In the arm then, I suppose. Unless you're talking about a gay street." Glancing up at the Hammer, he shook his head *no* at that idea. "I'd say we're talking morphine." The doctor's voice grew stern. "You make the injection subcutaneously or you may not last until the hospital. Do you understand?"

"No veins," the Hammer said easily.

"That is essential. Now, as to amount, we must be extremely cautious. You weigh how much?"

"Two-oh-three."

"Your age?"

"Thirty-eight."

"You're in good health?"

"Tip-top."

"Have you taken narcotics before?"

"Only for shrapnel."

Consulting a thick book he pulled down from a shelf behind his desk, the doctor eventually scribbled out a prescription, saying as he wrote, "Push no more than five milligrams. Do you understand?"

"Five, max," the Hammer said, turning his head sideways to read the prescription.

"And who's my patient?"

The Hammer showed him a special air force ID he'd brought along for the purpose.

Copying the name on the form, the doctor said, "And you'll leave my name out of it, right?"

"I'd be ashamed to mention you."

"You must be in an emergency room no more than a half-hour after you inject," the doctor said, ignoring the Hammer's answer. "Fifteen minutes would be optimal. Tell them you think you got a bad batch. Tell them exactly how much you have taken and of what. No fooling around. Do you have clean syringes?"

"Covered," the Hammer confidently answered.

The doctor repeated his instructions with an air of indifference, directed him to a pharmacy where the service was commendably discreet and showed him the door without a good-bye. The last the Hammer saw of him, Dr. L.L. Adams was gazing thoughtfully at the five C-notes piled on his desk, looking like someone caught squarely between the Hippocratic oath and the deep blue sea.

# TWENTY-EIGHT

EARLY FRIDAY MORNING JAN FOUND HERSELF in heavy negotiation with her daughters, who had mobilized themselves around a kitchen table cluttered with cereal boxes, open schoolbooks, and cosmetics that were passed around until reaching her youngest, Tess, at which point Jan retired them from circulation over everyone's protests. The topic of the day was tickets to a rock concert, and the girls were holding out for all they could get. The conviction of their expressions told Jan that much.

For the last week, her daughters hadn't seen much of their mother, so discipline was fraying. Plus, now that Claire had abandoned them for the wilds of Las Vegas, there was a touch of rebellion in the air. Claire's absence also created two pressing problems: Friday and Saturday nights. Galling as it might be, Jan had to pin down a baby-sitter before returning to work. A world that included hitmen made it impossible to imagine leaving her youngest daughters unchaperoned for two nights, and the world did include hitmen as well as enough other possibilities to prematurely gray a teenage mother.

"Here's the deal," Jan announced. "Leah, I'll spring for your concert this weekend."

"All right!"

"Mom!" the three youngest cried at once.

Jan held up her hands for quiet.

"Hear me out," she told them. "In return, Leah, you'll have to help baby-sit your sisters while your grandmother's making her fortune and I'm at work."

Groans all around. A half-sister to the youngest, Leah usually felt outnumbered and flaunted her seniority accordingly.

Her daughters were all swooning over a heavy metal concert scheduled for Saturday night, Whipped Cream being the demonic artists in question, emphasis on the *whipped*. Actually, it was Leah who had started the chant for tickets, at roughly twenty a pop, plus tax. The unrest had spread from there. Tess, age eight, didn't totally understand who the group was, but she wanted inclusion, a term picked up from her grandmother, who'd become a fiend for activism since discovering the senior citizens' community center.

Most of the time, Leah, age seventeen and on the pill—secretly, she thought—didn't bother with asking permission for anything, and at her advanced age she hated taking any steps backward. This time around, however, she had purse problems, as in the empty variety. She'd recently been discharged, as she put it, from her cashier position at the local video store. Reason? Lack of enthusiasm, as she put it. Whatever the rub—and Jan didn't currently have time to check her story out—it left Leah without financial backing for the creamiest concert of the year.

Did their mother have a heart, or what?

When they tried pinching Jan's wrist to detect a pulse, she withdrew her arm and told them they wouldn't find one. There had been pouting all around until she announced her alternate proposal. Then came the gnashing of teeth.

"There will be ground rules," Jan warned. "No stereo after ten. Meals eaten at the table, just as if we're civilized. And . . ." here she checked the stunned faces of her youngest three, ". . . no ganging up. Understood?"

Sour nods.

"Leah," Jan said, catching her eldest making a triumphant face across the table, "if it doesn't work out tonight, no concert tickets tomorrow."

"I'll be at their mercy," Leah protested.

"Not exactly," Jan said, raising her voice above the celebrating mob. To the youngest three, she said, "You know how you're always asking your father to take you out on the town? Well, the night of the concert, I'll arrange for him to do it, unless of course Leah tells me of some reason I shouldn't."

Stunned silence. The younger girls clearly found it difficult to imagine their estranged mother and father agreeing on something that big.

"Mom," Amy, age fourteen, reminded her, "this isn't Dad's weekend to take us."

Their father had custody one Saturday and Sunday a month, when he didn't cancel out.

"But if I can arrange it?" Jan went on, undeterred. "Do we have a deal?"

Guarded agreement, which left her with four long faces to think about while speeding to work that morning.

Before joining Agent Windish, she stopped at a lobby phone and punched up her second ex's number, which she regretfully knew by heart. She hadn't called from home because of the girls. Reasoning with Karl usually got ugly. Owing to her ex's rotating policeman's schedule, it was impossible to know when it was best to call him, but she preferred early mornings. There were petty reasons she liked calling early—she might interrupt his breakfast with some woman or his sleep if he'd just gotten off a graveyard shift—but most of all she called then to avoid having the prospect of talking to him hanging over her all day.

"It's me," she said.

"Which me," he groused and then laughed in a way that reminded her on a cellular level of his hangovers.

"Favor to ask," she said, knowing better than to get sucked into one of his games. "Can you take the girls out Saturday night? It would mean a great deal to them."

"And to you?" His laugh turned meaner.

"I'll spring for it," she said, refusing to pass anything personal on to him.

"No can do, kiddo. I've got plans."

She saw the whole conversation unfolding before her. The thing about Karl that drove her up and down the walls was his refusal to alter his schedule. When it came to keeping appointments, he was hell on wheels—unless the appointment was with her. Since their divorce there had been never-ending friction over timetables.

"You owe them for being such a shit last month."

"I'll make it up to them next month."

"Why not this Saturday?"

"Always trying to jerk me around, aren't you, Jan?" No laughter this time.

*Have it your way,* Jan thought. Out loud she said, "I hear you're dating."

"That's right. A real woman."

"Glad to hear it," Jan said. "How'd you like it if I had a chat with her, unreal woman to real?"

"Say," he said, always slow on the uptake, "how'd you like me to have a beer with a certain loser over in homicide. I hear you've been seen hanging all over him."

"Go right ahead," she said, sounding tougher than she felt. "Maybe you can get him to quit bothering me."

The bluff, if that's what it was, saddened her, for she sensed there was some truth to what she'd said. Flattering as Detective Frank White's attentions were, the spark between them kept going cold. Apparently the same could not yet be said for Karl's latest squeeze, for after some less-than-tender words, they reached agreement. Karl would pick the girls up at 5:00 on Saturday evening and return them Sunday morning. In return, Jan would refrain from sounding the asshole alarm to his new girlfriend.

It was a quarter past 8:00 before she managed to join Windish and

Sonny, who were by then pacing the hall. Fortunately, the phone hooked up to the recorder had yet to ring, which saved her from charges of irresponsibility. Even so, her tardiness drew a reproachful look from Windish and an envious one from Sonny. Within minutes they'd each settled into their separate nonchalant poses.

When the call came through at slightly past 10:00 that morning, Jan banged her knee against the desk, Agent Windish sat up with such a start that he grunted, and Sonny poked himself in the eye while putting on the extra headset. Jan let it ring four times before reaching for the receiver. By then Windish was convinced she had stage fright and was fiercely pantomiming to pick up the phone and speak. When she did put her hand on the receiver, a chill crept all the way up her arm to her elbow. Only the sight of Windish's bulging eyes goaded her onward.

"Who is this?" she asked without saying hello.

There was a long pause before the man on the other end said, "I didn't know I had a cousin at this number."

He sounded near as the next room, which set her heart pounding even faster.

"Distant cousin," she said, scowling at Windish, who was now encouraging her to talk by opening and closing his fingers as if working a hand puppet. Jan went on, "I'm calling to give you a message."

"From Carmen?"

"How did you know that?" she said, barely averting a stutter.

"You sound like that woman security guard hanging around her."

The cockiness with which he identified her tied up Jan's tongue.

"I've been expecting to hear from her again," he said when Jan didn't respond. "What's her offer?"

"H—how do you know I'm calling to make one?"

"What else is she going to do, lady?"

He made it sound like plain old business as usual, which strangely enough calmed her. When Windish tried coaching her by opening and closing his hands again, she turned her back on him.

"Two million to let her live," Jan said, woodenly reading off the note Carmen's bodyguard had provided. "Half of it up front. One hundred thousand for every six months she's alive after the operation."

"Generous," he said, impressed. "What kind of reason did she give you to help her?"

"Reason?" Jan said, having trouble with any words she couldn't read off the paper before her.

"It's Carmen's special way of motivating people," the Hammer explained. "She always comes up with some extra reason to help her, something beyond greed and power. Let me guess. She used her daughter on you, right?" When Jan didn't respond, he said with a chuckle, "Don't feel bad. She really does have a daughter. Probably loves her too."

"She's paying me," Jan stiffly answered. "That's how she got me to help her. So are you going to get bought off too? Or what?"

"What do you advise, J. Gallagher?" he asked, his voice going creepy.

Hearing her name sent the coldness in her phone arm past her elbow.

"Do you think," the Hammer continued, "that I should take some time off and try to improve my backhand?"

"Be nice if you did," she said, her voice remote. The only backhand she could imagine him using was against someone's cheek.

"Let's say I'm interested," he said. "How are you going to get me that first million?"

"I hand deliver it."

"And the rest?"

"She'll transfer it into a blank account for you, wherever you want it."

"Word of honor?"

"She's not foolish enough to think you couldn't find her if she cheated," Jan said. At the bottom of the instruction sheet from Carmen it said in bold letters **Appeal to his vanity.**

"She's foolish enough to offer me money," he said with satisfaction. "Where would you deliver the first payment?"

"Someplace public."

"But open," he added.

"Safe for us both."

"Such as?"

"There's a bus stop on the backside of the hospital at Charles and Twenty-first," Jan said, unconsciously crossing her fingers without knowing whether she wanted him to say yes or no. "At rush hour it's crowded enough with people to protect both of us."

"The DEA in on this?"

"Call them and ask," she said.

"Any sign of them and you'll be penalized."

"How many yards?"

"A major penalty." But he spoke more decisively now, as though he'd made up his mind. "This is how I see it. You be on that corner this afternoon at five sharp with the cash. Wear a red headband so I don't have any trouble spotting you."

"That's way too soon," she protested.

"No second offers," he said, hanging up.

With a dead phone still in hand, Jan pointed the receiver at Windish and said, "He knows my name."

For once that gave her the last word. For once she could have done without it.

Up until lunch, she was kept busy meeting with Carmen, who took hope from the Hammer's attitude, and with accompanying the bodyguard to a local bank to collect the payoff million. Except for when he stepped into the safety-deposit room and told Jan to wait in the bank's lobby, she and the bodyguard didn't say a word to each other during their field trip. Throughout all this, Jan kept up the charade of handling everything alone, without the DEA's interference. Back in the patient's room, she lifted the locked briefcase containing the money and commented it felt heavy as a dead cat. Nobody laughed. The bodyguard quietly relieved her of the briefcase while Carmen assured her that an additional fifty thousand was being transferred into a local account and would be available for her withdrawal by tomorrow. As a matter of principle, Jan refused what felt like an offer of blood money until Carmen pointed out that she had her girls to think of.

After lunch, Jan informed Windish she wasn't going anywhere without a gun. Encouraged by her zeal, he promptly provided her with a .32 caliber small enough to fit in her windbreaker's pocket. It'd been years since she'd received firearms instruction from her ex, but she refused to ask for a refresher course. Later, she took a few minutes in a locked bathroom to reacquaint herself with the little beast. She'd banned them from her house, along with her ex, and now she found herself doing business with both of them.

Then came several interminable hours during which Windish ran, and reran, the plans for taking the Hammer alive when he tried to pick up the cash. They viewed him as a witness with tremendous potential, a man whose knowledge of drug kingpins possibly rivaled that of Carmen's. They postulated that he might arrive by bus, taxi, through a manhole cover, on a parachute, and too many other ways and guises for Jan to remember. Some of the suggestions were so wild that she began to wonder who was using drugs. Mostly, she felt light-headed and couldn't avoid replaying over and over the way the Hammer had known her name.

As they fit a bulletproof vest on her, she watched the six hand-picked agents who'd volunteered to help protect her. They all looked happy as your usual army volunteer. As for Windish, he wore a billed cap that said DEA on the front. He paced a good deal. Everyone else was dressed in street clothes and trapped on folding chairs crammed into the office where Jan had talked to the Hammer. At least it kept her out of MICU Four, where she'd last seen Ginger alive.

At 4:30, she returned to Carmen's bedside to claim the briefcase and receive any last-minute instructions. There were none. Leaving the unit, she felt as though she was jumping out the cargo bay of a plane. Her jeans and windbreaker failed to relieve a curious sense of nakedness. The red headband lining her forehead felt prickly. There was a pistol in her pocket, and she wasn't particularly glad about it.

Outside, the clouds had again cleared away and a bright blue sky made her squint. All the glass at the corner of Twenty-first and Charles added to the glare. Everywhere she turned were windows. To her back slouched the seven stories of General Jack's oldest building, not exactly a high-security facility, particularly since hospital security had been kept in the dark about today's activities. Kitty-corner, the twelve unfinished floors of a medical office-building offered plenty of open viewing. Across Charles Street was the south end of the four-story warehouse the Hammer had already made use of once. Across Twenty-first Street was St. Stanislaus, with its dark, stained-glass windows of death, angels, and resurrection. Adjacent the church was the juvenile detention center, which had the honor of being the oldest county building in consecutive use. It looked as though it had once housed Romans. Apparently, they had windows back then too.

Somewhere out there, behind one of those windows, the Hammer had to have a spyglass on her. She itched in various private places and had to repeatedly remind herself not to scratch.

On the street level the rush-hour traffic multiplied and divided and spread like a cancer. From one hundred to two hundred people lined up on the sidewalk, waiting for transportation home. Whenever there was a lull in the traffic, county employees could be heard bitching to one another about being county employees; office workers gossiped about asbestos in their building and who was pregnant; discharged patients, bandaged in great profusion and propped up by crutches, swore to God they'd never set foot in another hospital.

The Hammer could have been one of the business suits whose faces were hidden behind any of a half-dozen *Wall Street Journals* within striking distance. Or he could have been driving one of the motorized wheelchairs weaving through the crowd to the special handicapped bus stop. That would have been classic misdirection. And as if all those possibilities weren't sufficient, a nearby bicycle lockup area attracted men whose features were concealed by crash helmets.

After five minutes Jan had whiplash from turning in so many directions. The plainclothes agents protecting her felt as useful to her as a fig leaf. Standing nearest her was Agent Henry, acting as though she wasn't within hailing distance. Not even a flicker of reassuring eye contact from the tough guy. To the other side of her stood the redheaded agent with the Texan accent. He was made up like a bus driver, a seat cushion under one arm and a ten-year service pin on his hat. She didn't bother searching out the other agents. It was better not to know. They were somewhere nearby, close enough to swarm all over the Hammer when he tried to make the pickup. At least that was the idea. As plans went, Windish's was simple-minded, which was the one sure thing going for it. In Jan's experience, anything requiring teamwork was iffy.

An unannounced addition to the circus was Carmen Romero-Muehlen's bodyguard, who tried to blend into the background by standing behind a light pole to Jan's rear. He'd made a pitiful effort at disguising himself by sticking a baseball cap on backwards, wrapping on a pair of gangster sunglasses, and draping a gigantic poplin trench coat over himself. A short length of nylon clothesline stretched between his hands, which seemed big as oven mitts, and he entertained himself by popping the rope taunt. Crowded as the bus stop was, a small clearing spread around him. When it came down to it, the bodyguard gave her more confidence than all the DEA guards combined.

So there they all stood, cozy as flies in amber.

By five after 5:00, Jan had removed her red headband, which had made her forehead feel too much like a target. She'd identified that fear when ducking in reaction to pigeons flying off St. Stanislaus's dome. She kept her right hand buried in her jacket pocket, gripping her pistol. Her left hand felt numb from the dead weight of the briefcase.

At 5:06 she told herself he wasn't coming. At 5:08 she promised herself ten more minutes and then she quit. At 5:09 she wondered if it was really 5:09. She had been estimating the time in her head and it seemed as though two or three generations had passed since she'd taken up her position. Having forgotten to wear a watch, she'd been sneaking peeks at a secretary's wristwatch until the woman had boarded a 52E bus. Now all that she had to help gauge the passage of seconds was a time-temperature clock above a bank four blocks farther down Charles Street. That digital sign had been stuck on the same reading since mid-winter when a cold snap froze its mechanism and the feds froze its assets. According to that clock, it was 9:33 and the temperature was at minus seven.

She was telling herself it had to be at least 5:13 when it happened.

A scream.

Jan jerked to the right in time to see Carmen's bodyguard crumpling as if his legs had turned to ash. A crescent the size of a thumbnail blossomed in the middle of his brown forehead. The cry had been wrung out of the throat of a thin man who was backpedaling in terror away from the falling bodyguard.

"Down!"

Agent Henry shouted that from nearby, but she was too busy dropping the briefcase, drawing her gun, and crouching to answer. Someone tackled her from the side. She rolled with the body clipping her and told her hand to shoot. Her hand needed to have its hearing tested. An instant later she realized it was the agent dressed as a bus driver whose weight was crushing her to the sidewalk. Instead of a sense of relief, she was angry at herself for hesitating. What if it hadn't been the agent?

Meanwhile, agents converged from everywhere. One may have dropped out of the sky.

There was no sighting of where the first shot had come from. The agents couldn't reach a consensus on the direction; they couldn't even determine which way Carmen's bodyguard had been facing when he'd caught it square between the eyes. At least no one else had been dropped.

That was the good news, what there was of it. At Jan's feet the dropped briefcase had cracked open, releasing cut newspaper. That was the start of the bad news, or perhaps it would be more accurate to say that that was the start of *more* bad news.

# TWENTY-NINE

THE POWER IN HIS TRIGGER FAILED before he could pull off his second shot, and then the blur of someone protectively lunging at J. Gallagher made a follow-up shot meaningless. It didn't matter, he told himself, knowing it was a lie but not knowing what other options he had but lying about it. At least he'd nailed the more important target, the one that simplified his current job by half. J. Gallagher was mop-up. Why he'd let slip that he knew her, he couldn't exactly say; it was disturbing, as a matter of fact, but hardly worth bothering about, not considering the rest of what was on his mind. Besides, the chances of her reconstructing where their paths had crossed were slim at best.

His real regret was having to resort to something as ordinary as a 30-06 for a fellow professional. He had been thinking that chopsticks would be a lovely way to bid Manos adieu, a classy pair of ivory sticks, say from a historic dynasty, but he just couldn't fit it in and would have to save the artistic touches for the grand finale with Carmen.

Speaking of whom . . . he ought to send Carmen a thank-you note for setting this much up for him. She must have been delusional to imagine he wouldn't see through her offer, and if she was that far gone, she might soon be completely gone if a donor didn't appear. Death by natural causes was the last thing he wanted for her, and while he'd waited inside the church for 5:00 to arrive, he'd offered up a modest prayer that the wonders of modern medicine could keep Carmen fresh at least long enough for him to finish her off. It might be hairsplitting, but it wasn't enough that she be sent on her way to the next world. He had to be the one who gave her the push. Otherwise he wouldn't be satisfied.

He'd once bagged a man who turned out to be an organ donor and whose heart had ended up beating in someone else's chest. Knowing that the heart was still out there pulsing was such an unsettling feeling that the Hammer had gone back and finished off the heart's new home free of charge.

After squeezing the trigger, he knocked out the stick propping open a small ventilation window he hid behind. Swinging around the corner to the empty church balcony, he pried out a piece of wainscotting that he'd earlier loosened, unfastened the rifle's stock, and placed the entire assemblage in the hollow space between the wall studs.

"Sweet dreams, baby," he said, patting the rifle scope where he'd affixed an NFL sticker.

Tapping the wood panel in place, he picked up an open gallon of eggshell-white paint and hurriedly, but without spilling, retreated back around the corner. With even strides he passed the ventilation window without looking out, descended the stairs past the circular, stained-glass scene of Christ ascending to heaven, and reached the church's vestibule, looking totally union in paint-speckled white bibs and cap. Stepping on top of a drop cloth, he resumed painting over a Pepto-Bismol pink wall near the main entrance.

Two minutes passed.

Only one parishioner entered, a shriveled old lady in a paisley shawl; her eyes were milky and her English was Polish. It took him a minute to realize that she must have said something equivalent to *Bless me father* while passing by him.

No DEA agents burst in with splatter guns drawn and Miranda cheat sheets tucked in their breast pockets. That meant a more methodical search would soon be underway. With the wall in front of him half painted, he replaced the cover on his paint can, neatly folded up his drop cloth, and put his brush in a plastic baggie that he made airtight with a twist tie. He left the miracle of the half-painted wall for the church elders to scratch their beards over.

Outside, traffic continued to rush in every direction. Across the way at the hospital bus stop a knot of timid spectators hung back from the fallen Manos. A nearby huddle of DEA beef received rapid-fire instructions from a human windmill whose stout arms gestured everywhere. Descending the church steps undisturbed, the Hammer turned into the narrow alley separating St. Stanislaus and the juvenile detention center without attracting attention. A fly streaked down the alley in the direction of Manos. Otherwise, no excitement. At the back of the church, in one of the slots reserved for priests, he loaded his paraphernalia into the back of a van he'd rented under the name of a former football placekicker and made what was known in some trades—his included—as a clean getaway.

# PART THREE

# THIRTY

As far as Jan was concerned, surgery waiting room number one was the only place inside General Jack deserving an air-pollution rating. Too much anxiety and grief and anger were routinely pent up within the confines of that space for even the country rulemakers to ban tobacco, as they had everywhere else within the hospital. She wouldn't have minded lighting one up herself, even though she'd quit in what felt like another lifetime. Floor lamps hazily lit four separate groupings of furniture that were durable far beyond human flesh. It was a place to wait, a limbo that smelled stale as poker night with the boys. The windows had a nicotine skin and the armrests had burns. Tidy stacks of Christian pamphlets stood on two end tables. A card table in one corner had a partially finished jigsaw puzzle of Bambi in the midst of woodland greenery and friendly creatures. Jan stared at the puzzle for several seconds before recognizing the scene.

Early Friday evening, barely two hours after the bodyguard's death, found Agent George Windish smoking just inside the waiting room's door. He didn't need a cigarette or match to do it either. With so many contingencies and countermeasures and forebodings whirling and dinging around inside his dedicated head, spontaneous combustion was inevitable. Every agent who could be spared from his post had gathered in the surgery waiting room. Sonny and Bug slouched, professionally strung out as ever; in his civvies, the red-headed agent with the soft Texan accent and newly bandaged ribs—from tackling Jan—stood with his hands tucked behind his brass belt buckle, a posture he somehow made appear natural; Agent Henry stood beside a lamp fingering one of the religious pamphlets; three other guys in assorted suits and ties milled about like floorwalkers waiting for the doors to open on the biggest fire sale of the century.

Representatives from hospital security had assembled too, including Eldon Hodges, who gripped the arms of his chair as if strapped in and waiting for the juice. Jerry Cody sat next to the Little Admiral, constantly tugging at his collar and generally acting like an organ grinder's monkey. Among the security guards present, Action Jackson had retired in boredom to a corner, arms crossed, thoughts at least a continent away. Stanley Charais rocked back and forth on a loose-jointed chair next to Jackson's; Leo Kennedy *helloed* anyone who strayed in front of him. Lastly came Jan, who'd staked off a small square of turf for herself and acted stoical as possible. With no one paying the slightest attention to her, her efforts went unnoticed.

Other families were as big and happy. The Corleone clan came to mind.

Finally, two last DEA agents with blank expressions straggled in. Windish closed the door and quit puffing out his cheeks.

"Two things," Windish announced without preamble. "Now that we're having *full* cooperation with hospital security, it's come to my attention that our man is in possession of a hospital employee ID and a full set of security keys, meaning he has access to almost any lock on the grounds."

"Who should we thank?" the redheaded agent asked.

Windish made an open-handed gesture toward the Little Admiral, as if to say he was on, but Eldon Hodges responded with stone talk, a nice gabby granite. After a half minute of dead air, Windish picked up the slack.

"Our man subdued Security Officer Cody," Windish said, nodding toward Jerry Cody, who currently concentrated on his shoe tips, maybe wiggling his toes or wishing himself invisible.

"Tied him up," Windish said, "stole the officer's ID and keys. We can only assume that he intends to make use of them to get closer to our charge. Other questions?"

Everyone looked at someone else.

"You're paid for your minds too," Windish reminded them.

"How do we know we're dealing with the Hammer?" Sonny asked.

"Educated guess. A hospital employee was mugged. Aside from keys, the only thing taken in the attack was an employee ID, not exactly a hot street item, unless you're our man."

"But he left him alive?"

"It appears that way," Windish said, drawing a snicker from the back of the room. Cody's head bobbed up.

"Isn't that unusual?" Jan asked, speaking up because she disliked the way everyone was acting as though they would have defended themselves more ably than Cody had. "Leaving him alive, I mean."

"Apparently he wanted to make sure we got a message," Windish said. "Would you mind sharing the message, Officer Cody?"

Jerry Cody mumbled, "He wanted Ginger to know that Duke sent his love."

A sudden stillness grabbed the room.

"And would you please tell everyone where it happened?" Windish said.

"In the private parking lot off Twentieth. I was escorting two nurses to their cars."

"And when?"

"Tuesday, late, ten after eleven."

"And we're just finding out about it now?" Jan said when no one else raised the point.

"Communication outage," Windish answered with a meaningful look at the Little Admiral. "We've straightened that out, I think. But the lag means he's had three days with the ID and keys. Speculations?"

Everyone sank into their chairs and looked sideways and kept their mouths shut.

"Come on, people," Windish groused. "Burn some gray cells. Maybe he's going to pose as an employee. Or maybe he wants us to think that he's going to pose as an employee. Or maybe he wants us to think that he wants us to think that he's coming as an employee. That way we'll focus our energies elsewhere and not pay enough attention to employees. Either way we'll be ready. For now we concentrate on all employees with access to the patient and double our coverage everywhere."

There was a lot of foot shuffling. Windish held up a hand for quiet.

"This brings us to my second point. A possible donor has been found for our witness."

Everyone stiffened.

By the time they were adjourned, Agent Windish had lit a sizeable bonfire under everyone but the Little Admiral, whose dampening powers approached those of an inland sea. Everyone else moved quicker though, acted more keyed up, suspected that for once Windish might be on target: If the Hammer was going to strike, it would have to be soon or Carmen would be gone. There hadn't been one word mentioned about the bodyguard's death, and the fifty thousand Jan was supposed to have earned for derring-do appeared to be printed on the same newsprint as the Hammer's million.

# THIRTY-ONE

EARLY FRIDAY EVENING, AFTER TWICE WIPING every surface in his hotel room, the Hammer packed and checked out. Armed with a false set of IDs, he rented a car, an eminently nondescript compact, and drove to the airport motel where he'd reserved a room for himself and Randi, who wasn't arriving until later. He left her the mums and a note summarizing her itinerary, along with the name he would using, Vince Lombardi, one of football's coaching immortals. He asked her to bring a get-well card too, something sentimental, he thought, since she was supposed to be Mrs. Lombardi. Once she'd delivered the mums on Saturday morning, she was to head directly back to the airport, changing cabs at least twice on the way. He'd already wired her payment, but with his note enclosed an extra five hundred for pin money.

Having set that in motion, he drove back to the center of the city, on the way stopping at the bus depot to ship his portable armory cross-country again. He then visited a discount store to hunt up a change of clothes more appropriate for his upcoming hospitalization. He emerged with chinos, T-shirt, and sneakers—all black—as well as a shaving kit and some accessories that he imagined were suitable for a junky. Complementing his black ensemble was a Princess Daisy wristwatch, silver-tinted sunglasses, and finger jewelry right off the hand of a fortuneteller. He may have worked for a drug cartel, but all that he knew about street addicts came from the movies.

Returning the rental car, he walked to a new hotel, one with some cockroaches, since he was now a druggie, and checked in under an assumed name, this time an ex-football halfback who spent more time in drug rehabilitation than on the field. An hour later he'd shaved his head and chest bare. During the next twenty-four hours there would be a number of strangers getting a close look at him, and he wanted them to remember the veins on his head, not the shape of his nose.

At a quarter past 10:00 that evening, he rolled up his sleeve, filled his syringe from Dr. L. L. Adams's prescription vial, checked his Princess Daisy, which had already lost five minutes, took a deep, calming breath, and parked the needle in his arm. There wasn't much sting at all. Floating out of the hotel's seedy lobby, he flagged down a cab, waited for the driver to open the door, and said, "Jackson General. Jackson General. Jackson General."

The middle-aged nurse at the emergency room's front desk greeted him as if men with shaved heads and hoarfrost eyes was business as usual.

"And how can I help you?"

"I got into some bad shit," he answered.

"And what kind of bad shit would that be, sir?" she asked, her voice cheery as an enema.

A security guard standing behind the nurse gave the Hammer a once-over with the dead eyes that all cop-types learn from some-where. To the nurse's right, partially concealed by a partition, an-other nurse was wrapping gauze around the bloody wrists of a young woman whose eyes were even deader than the guard's.

Wide halls cut away from both sides of the front desk at ninety degree angles. To the right stretched a line of high-backed, wooden wheelchairs filled with patients tenderly holding various parts of themselves while watching closely to see if the Hammer managed to cut in line ahead of them. Down the hallway to the left lay a pair of closed doors marked with a red NO ADMISSION sign. The doors had narrow window slots that revealed a bright and crowded emergency room where hospital staff shuffled beds, conferred in groups, and explained the fine points of the health care system to patients strapped down at the ankles and wrists. Two brown-uniformed paramedics pulled a decaying old man in the entrance doors the Hammer had just drifted through. Although the patient was still gasping for breath, it smelled as though his bowels had gone ahead to the hereafter without him.

"Can you tell me your name?" the nurse was asking, ready to write his answer on a form.

"Rob . . ." and there the Hammer stopped, almost having said his God-given name, which he hadn't uttered for years. The slip made him realize how difficult this was going to be. Without his full faculties, he was far more vulnerable than he'd ever been before. Summoning all his powers of concentration, he said, "Vince Lombardi."

"OK, Rob Vince Lombardi, you going to tell me what kind of bad shit you got into?"

"I think heroin," he said, trying to remember Dr. L.L. Adams's instructions.

"You're not sure?"

"It doesn't feel like H."

"You got a habit?"

"I've got lots of habits."

The funny stuff bounced right off the nurse. "How much did you take?"

Why was her voice so loud? Even the scratching of her pen was magnified.

"A needleful."

"When did you take it?" She was reaching for his arm to check for tracks.

Why did she sound so distant? And how could she be loud and distant at the same time?

"Maybe I should come back later," the Hammer said, glancing down at his arm to check his Princess Daisy wristwatch as if he had a pressing street-corner appointment. But the watch was gone. He didn't have any idea what had happened to it either, at least not until he checked his other wrist and saw it strapped on there.

"Don," the nurse said, raising her voice to summon the guard.

"Which cube?" the guard asked, snapping on a pair of disposable gloves.

"Sixteen's open. Stash him there."

"Just relax," the guard said, pressing him down in a wheelchair.

"Your hands are cold," the Hammer told the guard.

But when the guard belted him into the chair all of a sudden it was his own hands that were freezing. And the lights were damn near blinding. And Jesus!—why was this half-dead guard pushing the wheelchair a hundred and twenty miles an hour? He considered bailing out, but couldn't rouse a single muscle.

An orderly assisted the guard in transferring him to a gurney that lay five feet from the old-timer just hustled past the front desk; the old boy was curled in a fetal position and sucking greedily on a corner of his bedsheet. For some reason the Hammer couldn't take his eyes off him.

"He an OD too?" asked the Hammer.

"Just relax," the orderly said, pulling a curtain that shut him off in a world of white. Something was being attached to his upper arm, then came a tightening. He tried rolling away but didn't have the control.

"Relax," the orderly repeated. "All I'm after is your blood pressure."

He could hear voices beyond the curtain. They didn't seem to be talking about him. In fact, nobody seemed to give a damn whether he lived or died.

"Now your temperature. You're going to feel something in your ear."

What kind of bullshit was that? Worse, this orderly, who looked as though he spent all his free time getting sand kicked in his face, caught the Hammer's wrist and forced his arm down to the bed. Could he believe that?

"Relax, mister. It's a new kind of thermometer. That's all." The orderly held up a plastic device the size and shape of the instrument docs used to peek in ears.

Relax? He felt so fucking relaxed that he could have been a living puddle. By the way, where were all his bones? What was wrong with his thermostat? And why did time have a wavy distortion to it, as though moving forward, backward, and hanging up at all once? He gulped a breath and pressed shut his eyes.

"I'm Dr. Hunnicut," a male voice said.

*Reruns,* he thought.

"Can you tell me what you've taken?"

Something sharp speared the center of his chest. Popping his eyes open, he saw a gloved knuckle digging into his breastbone. He batted it off.

"Four-point him," the doctor said.

Two security guards stepped forward out of a black void in the time-space continuum. Wait, they were only wearing black uniforms and holding leather restraints more alive than either of them. His flight instinct kicked in, attempting to save his ass as it had so often in the past when black or blue or gray uniforms were about to ply their trade.

A chunk of time broke lose; he grabbed hold of it. Sitting up, he chopped the Adam's apple of a guard leaning over him. He felt heat from the contact and turned the heat into motion. Kicking out at the other guard's crotch, his leg struck the bed's side rails. The collision tore something out of his mouth, maybe his tongue, maybe just a scream. With the one guard down, clutching at his throat, the other guard, a fat son of a bitch, tried using his gut to pin down the Hammer's legs. Then, without warning, the orderly blindsided him, ambushing his arms, but the Hammer ripped them free and tried springing to his feet. He didn't quite make it.

How could he? Every corpuscle in his body was shackled to a cold, heavy weight. Time reeled backwards, fast, dragging him away from the emergency room without anyone knowing it. For a flash he vaguely sensed them up top swearing at him. Then they were gone and it was dark and cold as the bottom of a well on a winter's night.

He awoke to find himself confined in a white padded room. Something was wrong with his arms. They wouldn't move. He tried his eyes and could see a camera mounted in one corner of the ceiling. Leather straps lashed his wrists and ankles to a hospital bed. Some time later a bolt clicked on a door with a small, screened window. A nurse, two new security guards, and a doctor filed in.

"How you feeling, friend?" the doctor asked, applying that chummy voice the medical profession resorted to whenever it wanted him to turn informer on himself.

"On my way to recovery," the Hammer said.

"Sure you are, buddy," the doctor said, patting him on the shoulder. In his professional tone, he said to the nurse, "Start him out with two milligrams of Norcan. Repeat it at three-minute intervals and let's reevaluate when you hit ten millies." Back to palsy-walsy for the Hammer. "We're going to take good care of you, buddy. Just hang in there." To the nurse in a secretive voice, "Let's hustle this one up to an ICU."

"Yes doctor."

"Make him a seventy-two hour hold."

"Yes doctor."

"And get him out of here before we've got a statistic we don't want."

"Yes doctor."

"You doing anything after work tonight?"

"Yes doctor."

He came to in a hospital elevator. Somewhere above him a man was speaking, a woman answering.

"We taking this guy up to the floor where Madonna is?"

"What are you talking about?"

"Up on four, they got some kind of high-security deal going down. I heard it was either a movie star or the president's daughter."

"Just keep an eye on the patient, would you?"

"Why? He's doing all right. Look, he's grinning at something."

He found himself in an ICU being transferred from one bed to another. Two nurses were talking.

"You think he'll make it?"

"If he's still with us tomorrow, probably."

"You voting to strike?"

"You're goddamn right I am."

"Is Nola still fucking that government spook from down the hall?"

"Geez, your mind doesn't quit, does it?"

With the coming of Saturday's dawn, he slowly regained warmth in his extremities. By midmorning he managed to reestablish contact with linear time. Nurses lifted his wrist to check his pulse, nurses adjusted his IV drip, nurses fluffed his pillows. Occasionally a doctor stood bedside and touched his chart. Before noon Randi brought his flowerpot and coolly kissed his forehead. Gradually it came back to him why he was there.

# THIRTY-TWO

FROM FRIDAY EVENING ONWARD JAN GALLAGHER spent the duration of Carmen Romero-Muehlen's operation on duty. For some bothersome reason, Agent Windish refused to believe they could come close to managing without her. In fact, he insisted on it. Perhaps it was his childish way of acknowledging the fact that she could have been potted along with the bodyguard.

"Too many potential disasters," he told her after dismissing the rest of the troops from the mass security meeting. "I need your insights."

She mentioned that she'd been running since before 7:00 that morning and was too worn down for any insights. Having been on duty since 6:00, he wasn't impressed.

"He may pose as an employee," he told her.

She pointed out that Jackson General employed over three thousand people of whom she knew but a fraction. He wasn't convinced.

"We're at our most vulnerable while she's in that operating room," he told her. When she asked why, he veered off on a lengthy tangent involving the science of probabilities.

She brought up her daughters, who sounded ready to torch the place the two times she'd managed to call home.

"I need you tonight," he told her, overruling all ifs, ands, or daughters. "Not tomorrow. Not the next day. If you're not here tonight, I'm not sure that we can pull this off."

Almost. She almost said that she didn't care, that she was having nightmares about untangling his messes, but . . . There was Ginger, or rather the lack of Ginger, which Jan was thoroughly tired of trying not to think about. Continuing onward still seemed the only way to lay all that guilt to rest.

Once she agreed to stay on, she became Windish's closest confidant. That was another of the agent's acts she was ready to stone.

The fun started in earnest shortly after 10:00 Friday evening as she raced from one DEA agent to another with the usual news from Windish that the sky was falling. A stairway door opened a crack as she passed and someone hissed, "Psst!"

She kept her distance, saying, "Who is it?"

"Hodges," came a hushed reply.

He had to open the door wider before she would believe it was the Little Admiral.

"What do you want?"

"Your cooperation."

"You're setting your sights too high," Jan said.

Lesser bureaucrats would have reddened around the jowls, but Hodges only had to take in an extra breath. "Help me with this, Gallagher, and life will be easier for you."

"Can I get any details on that?"

They stared hard over each other's shoulders until Hodges coaxed forth a threadbare smile.

"I take it that you need some time to think it over?"

"Don't hold your breath," Jan advised, letting herself out of the stairwell.

Within five minutes she was second-guessing herself, but even as she thought about it she knew there was no backing out now. The Little Admiral had a memory that would outlast his mind, whatever that meant.

* * *

The fun got a booster shot around midnight when Windish dispatched her up to the rooftop of the Old General, where he'd stationed an agent with night binocs. The guy had a radio and was to report anything out of the ordinary, but until something out of the ordinary occurred he was to maintain a blackout in case the Hammer was monitoring the airwaves. Another example of the feverish rationale that possessed Windish. Jan was to check on the lookout periodically to make sure he was still able to pee in his plastic jug and didn't have an NFL sticker attached to his forehead.

She was about to cross Wabash Street to reach the Old General when a parked Mustang honked at her and pulled forward on her side of the street. A startle reflex nearly put her in flight until she recognized Detective Frank White behind the wheel. She dialed up *annoyed* and waited to greet him.

"We need to talk," he said through his open window, making it sound as though this was for her own good.

"What are you doing down here?" she asked, remaining on the curb.

"I could ask you the same thing," White said, killing his motor. "Didn't I warn you about this Windish?"

"How did you find out where I was?"

"Your eldest daughter squealed."

"So how long have you been parked out here?"

"Goddamn it, Jan," the detective complained, "I've been worried sick about what I might have gotten you into here."

"Consider me warned."

"Look at what happened to that dizzy blond you work with." Instead of looking at her he toyed with the keys in the ignition.

"You drawing comparisons between me and a dizzy blond?"

"She got her head blown off."

"Her dizzy head, and she was strangled."

"What about the cabbie we found in the trunk?" Now he looked up at her.

Jan shook her head at him and said, "Tell me what you want, White. Would you do that?"

"I want you to leave this to the professionals."

"I suppose that's you?"

"That's beside the point."

"Are you still holding something back about Windish?"

"Goddamn it, Jan."

"I asked Windish about Richie Denmark. He denied all of it."

"Goddamn it, Jan."

"You aren't fooling anyone, so out with it."

"Goddamn it . . ."

"Do the decent thing, Frank," she said, softening. "Tell me."

"Goddamn it," he said, this time weakly addressing his steering wheel.

"What other choice do you have?" she asked.

"God . . ." His mouth worked a moment, but his heart wasn't in protesting anymore and sounds quit coming out. Eventually he said, "I didn't actually give him your name."

"Huh?" she said, not understanding.

He repeated himself.

"So how in the world did he get it?" Jan asked, lowering herself to her haunches to look directly at the detective.

"He already knew it."

"Then why come to you?"

"Some way or another," White said with a woeful shake of his large head, "he heard that you and I knew each other. He wanted somebody to vouch for him."

"You?"

"He couldn't find anyone else," the detective said, chagrined. "And he claimed it was essential to get your trust."

"Why my trust?"

"I don't know," the detective admitted, miserable about it.

"But you went ahead anyway."

"I did."

"Because you thought it might bring us together, or something?"

"That's part of it."

"What's the rest of it?"

The detective looked away before turning back and confessing in a small voice, "He promised to give me the name of a witness in the Richie Denmark investigation."

"And you waited until *now* to tell me?"

"I didn't want you thinking whatever it is you're thinking," he said, searching her face for some clue. "I was hoping I wouldn't have to mention it."

"So much for that."

"Things are getting out of control, Jan."

She raised a hand at him but could think of nothing worth saying, so lowered it. The detective dipped his chin as if he had something more to divulge. If there hadn't been a gap in the traffic on Wabash, she wouldn't have heard what came next.

"He said something about needing a small woman with black hair."

"Black?" Jan said, absently touching her head. "Why?"

"Don't know."

She couldn't think of a sensible answer herself. After a moment of watching the passing traffic, she suddenly asked, "Do you want to know why I broke up with my second ex?"

He averted his eyes and his voice dropped so low she couldn't hear his response.

"What?"

"I already know," he said, louder.

"You already . . . how?"

"I talked to him."

She took a step away, her hands grasping for something to tear in half, but then she spun around. "What gave you the right?"

"He came to me."

"Oh, well," Jan said, making an expansive gesture. "That makes all the difference in the world. I suppose he bragged about his other women?"

"It doesn't matter."

"He bragged," Jan predicted. "I know that one. But here's what the real problem was, Detective Frank White. The real problem was that he was always trying to tell me what to do. Does that sound familiar?"

"Goddamn it," White complained, "maybe somebody has to."

Jan straightened, saying, "I think you better leave."

He started to open his car door but she leaned over, bracing her hands against it.

"I mean it," she said.

"If you think this gives you an excuse to end it between us. . . ."

"What would you think?"

When he couldn't come back on that, she left him with his mouth twitching. As she stormed around the front of his Mustang, he found his voice, but whatever he said registered as an angry buzz in her ears until she was across the street and he shouted, "I'm sorry!" Seconds later he squealed away.

Caught unprepared for an apology, she pulled up to watch his taillights while trying to remember if she'd ever heard a man tell her that before. She must have but for the life of her she couldn't pinpoint when. So what? Was she supposed to be grateful? Her mind pulled up lame with that thought. Knowing what stunts she was capable of when indignant, she searched out a drinking fountain inside Old General and ran some tepid water over her wrists. How much that helped was debatable, but she wasn't in any mood for arguing with herself. Lately, she never knew who would win.

The remainder of the night needed new shock absorbers. Stanley Charais squared off with a DEA agent who remarked that he didn't look old enough for his job. Jan had to mediate. Action Jackson caught an orderly, who had taped a picture of the real Madonna on his employee ID, trying to help a nurse deliver an overdose admit to one of the fourth-floor ICUs. Jackson wouldn't let them off the elevator without Jan's OK, and Jan refused to sign off until the ER charge nurse left her hectic duties to come up to four and vouch for the orderly.

A few minutes after that, Bug showed up missing at Carmen's currently-empty ICU where he was supposed to be ensuring that there were no unscheduled deliveries. He stayed missing only as long as it took the German shepherd left on duty to start growling when Jan approached the linen-cart barricades. Within seconds the agent appeared from inside the unit, his fly unzipped. Jan didn't make further inquiries.

Interspersed with those highlights was a steady stream of nonsense from Windish to his satellites, all of which she was chosen to transmit; two more sightings of the Little Admiral in unlikely places; and a call from her eldest daughter reminding her that she had a Saturday night concert and that Claire remained in Vegas. For all of those reasons Jan didn't troop right up to Windish and demand to know why it was essential she have black hair. She wanted her wits about her for that scene.

# THIRTY-THREE

Two days before and several hundred miles to the southeast, the vice squad of a large city staged an early-morning frontal assault on a crack house. Three seminude chemists shot their way out the back to a Ford Bronco with which they smashed through a wooden privacy fence and made the street. Vice gave hot pursuit.

Five blocks away a thirty-five-year-old single parent named Lollie Jefferson was struggling to get her three-year-old daughter Lakesha buckled into the backseat of her Geo. She was running late for a job she couldn't afford to lose. As she backed out of her drive a jumbo jet lifted off from the city's nearby international airport. At the same time her daughter launched a tantrum. If not for those distractions Lollie might have heard the sirens and avoided pulling into the middle of a high-speed chase. When she looked up and saw the flashing patrol car bearing down on her, she punched the accelerator in an attempt to save her daughter. In that much she succeeded.

As for Lollie, she was rushed to a level-one trauma center where a CAT scan indicated a massive epidural hematoma between her skull and brain. A neurosurgeon attempted to ease the pressure on her brain without encouraging results. Her pupils failed to respond to light, she required a respirator for breathing, and her EEG read-out had lines flat as a ruler. She was brain-dead, which in that state, as in most states, was the legal definition of death.

Lollie's driving license stated she was an organ donor, and her closest living relatives, her parents, agreed that something good should come of their tragedy. They applied their heavy hands to the release forms that would allow her organs to be recycled. The hospital's transplant coordinator took it from there. Since that medical center performed only heart transplants, she arranged destinations for Lollie's kidneys and liver, as well as her cornea and other body parts, including bone, tendon, ligaments, and connective tissue. The human body was worth considerably more than it once was.

Ideally, Lollie's donations would have gone to the most needy recipients within range, the ones who had the best blood and tissue matches. The United Network for Organ Sharing, a nationwide agency, supposedly oversaw this dispersal of life-giving organs to the fourteen thousand plus terminal patients in its database. But since when did a bureaucracy function smoothly? No, there were surgeons' egos to consider, and rivalries between transplant centers which had patients desperate for an operation, and finally there were the news media that could short-circuit the entire, fragile distribution network by playing up the need of a particularly helpless recipient.

None of which even touched upon the question of whether major organ transplants, with their huge expenses and unpredictable, sometimes modest, extension of life spans, were the best way to improve the health of the country as a whole. There was the issue of who donated the organs. The poor? Minorities? People most likely to be killed in a crossfire right outside their doors? And who received the organs? Not likely that it was the poor. But all those grisly questions went out the window as soon as one patient like Carmen Romero-Muehlen showed up with end-stage chronic hepatitis. Surgeons cut, surgeons healed. Prestige was at stake, money wasn't far behind. Those hospitals that performed transplants managed to convince the general public of their skill, thus attracting other patients, thus increasing the weight of their coffers, thus making the board of trustees appear farsighted, thus allowing the purchase of new equipment and the initiation of new programs, thus attracting the best physicians. . . . and so on.

In other words, the number of hospitals performing transplants was spreading fast. Meanwhile, there remained a critical shortage of available organs for transplantation. Lifting the fifty-five mile-an-hour speed limit was a boon to transplant units, true, as was the proliferation of handguns, but there remained many more patients waiting for new hearts, kidneys, livers, or whatever, than there were parts to go around. This meant that as the number of hospitals performing transplants multiplied, competition for resources—namely dead bodies—increased. In the end what the placement of Lollie's liver came down to was this: the head of transplant surgery at Lollie's hospital owed the head of transplant surgery at General Jack a favor for a heart received a month before. And that's how Carmen Romero-Muehlen received her liver.

So Lollie Jefferson's liver ended up in the exceedingly well-trained hands of Dr. Mark Purcell of the Jackson County Medical Center. He and his surgical team had flown in a private jet, one donated by a local corporation for the tax write-off, to the site of the harvesting, and after an hour of intense labor were able to lift Lollie's oyster-gray liver out of her abdomen and gently lay it in a stainless-steel bowl. Quickly flushed and washed to remove Lollie's blood, the organ was packed in a cooler chilled to zero. From there it was rushed hundreds of miles to the waiting patient. The surgical team had roughly six hours to get the liver reconnected to a human body.

The precious cargo that the transplant team carried back could certainly be thought of as the miracle of miracles. Weighing in at roughly three pounds, the liver can hold up to a quarter of the body's blood supply. It performs hundreds of necessary metabolic functions, including the making of at least a thousand enzymes. It retires worn-out red blood cells, turning them into bile. It helps with the absorption of fat, turning it into carbohydrates. It creates blood proteins

233

and coagulants, and it detoxifies numerous poisons. To duplicate its efforts would require an international effort, and even that wouldn't be enough. Some of its processes can't yet be re-created by science. Without the liver, the body's chemistries go out of whack within minutes.

Before the private jet was halfway back to General Jack, Carmen Romero-Muehlen was waiting beneath the operating room's bright lights, holding on to the hand of a nurse and praying as she stared upward, wondering if there were angels just out of sight or if something else was up there. As soon as the liver arrived, she was anesthetized and removal of her own liver commenced. Now it was a race against the clock to reattach the donor's liver to Carmen's major blood vessels before tissue began to die. Of the six hours on the clock, they had used over two of them in transit.

With everyone present focusing on a single task, the concentration above the operation table was palpable. This wasn't the cutting out of an appendix or the removal of your garden-variety gallstone. There was no time for banter or horseplay or comments about the size of the patient's vulva. Removing and replacing a liver was one of the most complicated operations known to modern medicine, surpassing even a heart transplant. Depending on complications, the operation could stretch on for upwards of twenty hours; there were that many blood vessels to be reconnected. The undertaking was one of the true wonders of human achievement, but in this case it turned out that it wasn't wonder enough.

From the beginning Carmen Romero-Muehlen began to hemorrhage. So severe was her loss of blood that even a rapid infusion machine couldn't replace it fast enough. For twenty minutes, the activity above the operating table was frenetic. Arms crisscrossed over the patient at hummingbird speeds, but in the end Dr. Purcell dropped his hands to his side and made a simple declaration.

"We've lost her."

Carmen Romero-Muehlen's hopes, dreams, and family moved beyond the reach of her physical remains. Even her surgeon was no longer at her side. He had moved on to opening up another patient who might survive thanks to Lollie's gift. Back in Carmen Romero-Muehlen's surgery suite everything was still. The only movement was a straight line on an EKG monitor that hadn't been turned off.

In the halls of General Jack no bells tolled, no lights flashed. There was no wailing of mourners. News of the expiration stayed strictly within the operating room, where everyone was too intent with the business of saving the next patient to pause over the loss of the last. Throughout the night and on into the next day General Jack did what it could for the living and left the dead to fend for themselves.

In Labor and Delivery a twenty-eight-week-old preemie was delivered, as were four healthy infants and one stillborn. On Urology a kidney-stone patient bellowed for Demerol. Ortho had a ninety-seven-year-old woman who managed to fall out of her bed and fracture her other hip. In the locked psych unit an attempted suicide laughed until dawn. Oncology quietly lost a lung CA. Coronary Care gained four myocardial infarctions and it wasn't even snow-shoveling season. A nurse on a medical floor accidentally stuck herself on a needle carelessly left in the room of an AIDS patient. In the Emergency Department the medical staff was inundated by a wave of humanity that leaked, creaked, spit, and moaned. Honors for the story of the night went to a heroin OD who walked in off the street, announced that his name was Vince Lombardi, that he'd won two Super Bowls, and who went berserk when a security guard tried to restrain him for his own protection.

During the sixteen hours it eventually took to transplant Lollie Jefferson's liver in the patient flying standby, Agent George Windish remained in the far end of surgery waiting room number one, unaware that he'd lost his witness. He stayed away from the windows, which allowed him to avoid his reflection and the inevitable thought that he needed to lose weight. His own physician had warned him that he was a bypass operation waiting for one last muffin smothered in butter. From bypass surgery to transplant surgery was a short jump, in the agent's mind at least, but over the years, thanks to his training and tenacity, he'd learned to deflect his thoughts away from his own excesses by focusing on someone else's. That's what he did for the sixteen hours during which the medical staff was too involved in their second operation to think of letting him know of Carmen Romero-Muehlen's fate.

Cooperation between the agent and the liver-transplant team was limited at best, a cold war confrontation with each side making demands of the other that couldn't realistically be expected to be fulfilled. Only after tying off the last stitch did Dr. Purcell bother to search out Agent Windish and inform him of the outcome. It was then shortly after noon on Saturday.

"Your witness didn't make it."

By that time Windish had been purifying his mind and wringing his hands and avoiding his reflection for nearly thirty nonstop hours. Coffee made his gestures look as though hurrying to catch up with his thoughts. His eyes appeared to have sunken into his face.

During that same thirty hours Dr. Purcell had also been awake. And cutting. Adrenaline and good pharmaceuticals kept his eyes from crossing. He'd had his hands inside the abdomen of a patient he'd lost; he managed to salvage the day by saving another's life. Afterwards all that appeared left of him was his hyperactive fingers that flitted about as though still cutting blood vessels and tying knots. The rest of his lanky form was an exhausted tangle of prematurely gray hair, eyeglasses, and jogging shoes covered by the sterile tissue liners of the operating room. Too weary for lengthy explanations, he said, "Sorry, she was a bleeder," and started toward the door.

"I think you're wrong about that, Doctor," Windish said, somehow making the ridiculous sound respectful.

"Trust me," the doctor answered, stopping short. "She's dead."

"Sometimes," Windish said, speculating, "a dead person can do us more good than when they're alive. I'm surprised someone in your line of work wouldn't have noticed that."

"If that's supposed to be a joke . . ." the physician said, half turning.

"They're more cooperative."

"Fine," Purcell said, taking a step toward the door. "She's down in the morgue, take it up with her."

"What if we have a plan, Doctor?"

Purcell lingered.

"Some good can still come of all this," Windish promised. "If we hurry. If you help us."

The doctor massaged the back of his neck and silently cursed.

"There's still the matter of Carmen's financial donation to your transplant unit," Windish reminded him. "The money may not be clean, you know."

"I was wondering when we'd get around to that."

"All I'm asking is this," Windish hurriedly said. "Let's keep a lid on Carmen's status for awhile."

"And what else?" the doctor asked, slumping into a nearby chair.

"Let us put someone in her place."

"What can that possibly gain?" the surgeon asked, but then abruptly stood before Windish could respond. "You're still after this hired gun, aren't you?"

"It's a golden opportunity."

"Out of the question. I won't endanger the lives of my people for your games."

"What if we replace your staff with our own people? Look, all I'm asking is this: Your people keep Carmen's condition under wraps. Let the rest of the hospital, and the world, think she's alive."

"What's it gain you?"

"Time. Answer me this, Doctor, if Carmen had made it this far, what would you be doing for her right now?"

"Watching her," Purcell guardedly said. "Watching for rejection, for side effects of the immunosuppressants, for chemical imbalances, for infection."

"And how long would that go on?"

"As long as the patient's alive."

"How long would it go on here at the hospital?" Windish doggedly asked. "Typically, that is."

"There is no typical."

"Well, I'm not asking for much time. Let's say a week. That should do it. If nothing's happened by then, we'll clear out and forget where the money Carmen put in trust for you folks came from. How's that?"

Shaking his head in sad bemusement, Purcell complained, "You can't keep something like this a secret that long. Not in a hospital. Maybe someplace else, but not here. Somebody will talk, an orderly, a nurse, a morgue attendant. See? And even if they slipped up and didn't, the lab would notice that the blood chemistries are out of whack. Or maybe the medical examiner won't like it, or . . . who knows?"

"Details," Windish said with relish. "I didn't say it would be easy. But if we've got a woman in the patient's bed, who's going to argue with that?"

"Administration, for one."

Picking up a nearby courtesy phone, Windish thumbed through a pocket-sized notebook, got the number he wanted, and dialed. Getting Executive Averilli on the line, he apologized for bothering him at home on a weekend and then briefly outlined his proposal, including a heavy-handed reference to Carmen's money along the way. After a couple of *yeses* and *noes,* he formally extended the receiver to Purcell, who identified himself, listened, and turned away for some confidential words that Windish, full of confidence, didn't bother to eavesdrop on.

Hanging up, the doctor said, "A week's too long for this nonsense to hold together. Say I route the bloods to my experimental lab and pay a courtesy call to the ME . . ."

"That's the spirit."

". . . there's still going to be a leak."

"So we speed things up."

"This is about as fast as I care to go."

"What happens if you release the news that you've performed a successful transplant?" Windish asked, framing an imaginary headline with his hands. "That ought to quicken our man's pace, make him wonder how much longer he's got before Carmen's moved out of here to someplace he might not get at."

"The woman's dead," Purcell said, "and I'm not saying anything to the contrary. Not in public, not in private. Not at all. There are certain ethical standards. . . ."

"I understand completely," Windish assured him. "But you must have performed a successful transplant recently, haven't you? I mean, someone got a liver who's still alive, right? So your press release keeps the name of the patient confidential to protect their privacy. Just a standard news release. Or better yet, say I convince a local station to do some in-depth reportage on your program in exchange for some hot tips on the status of the local war on drugs. How would that make you feel?"

"Like a bastard."

"That sounds encouraging," Windish said, putting his hand out to seal the bargain.

The doctor wasn't pressing any flesh though. Turning on his heel, he said, "Have your guinea pig down in the operating room within the hour."

# THIRTY-FOUR

By Saturday morning Jan tingled as though her fingers had been stuck in a hundred-and-ten volt socket from dusk to dawn. At 6:00 a.m. Windish had solicitously asked if she wouldn't like to sneak some shut-eye. There wasn't enough time for her to go home, he had said, not with the operation still in progress, but one of the cots they'd set up in the ICU would be empty. She'd been worn too smooth to talk back. By then, as far as any of them knew, Carmen had been under the knife for ten hours. Thanks to Windish's less than brilliant, and much less than successful, attempt to have the surgical team strip-searched before the cutting began, not a peep had come out of the operating room. When Jan's head hit the pillow, she cursed George Windish, blinked twice, murmured good night to her daughters, and set sail for Nod.

She dreamed. She was damned tired of that too.

Behind Jan's closed eyes, Agent Windish licked a hand and wet down his unruly hair before proposing to her. She accepted, except that in the dream she was Ginger. They arrived at the church, half of which remained empty except for Jan's mother, who had a slot machine in front of her. The priest was Detective Frank White, who was packing a shoulder holster and got stuck on *Speak now or forever hold your peace.* No one piped up. Agent Windish said *I do.* Quivering, Jan parted her lips to repeat the same. Before she could utter a syllable, the roof blew off the cathedral and she woke to the creepy sensation of being watched from above.

Rubbing her eyes and lifting her head, she found Agent George Windish studying her from three feet away. He was seated on a folding chair he'd turned backwards and was rolling the tip of his blue tie around one of his fingers. His worried expression shifted into a smile.

"I need a word, Jan."

"So do I," she promptly answered, raising her head off the pillow.

"There's been a little mishap down in the operating room," Windish quickly said, before Jan could unload anything.

Jan stared at him a moment before saying, "How little?"

"They lost our witness."

The agent made it sound as though something had been misplaced, a forceps or scalpel or pint of blood.

"Oops."

"What we've got to work on now," Windish determinedly said, "is salvage."

He got up to pace, and Jan pushed herself up on her elbows to watch. He tightened his belt, loosened his tie. Stopping, he grew all visionary.

"I like to believe we can all, in our own way, do some good in this world, Jan. Leave things better than when we found them."

"How lucky for you."

"We've got a man out there somewhere," Windish said, making a grand, sweeping gesture to the lands beyond the hospital, "who imagines he's a master subtracter. It's my sworn duty to bring an end to his kind of arithmetic, and if we can convince him that Carmen's still hospitalized, then he'll come for her. The operation won't be an entire loss. Does that make sense?"

"I hope not," she said, dropping her head back to the pillow.

"What I'm trying to get at is this: If you would take Carmen's place for a little while, I think we can hold this thing together. You look enough like her to make it work."

For a moment, Jan saw double. Two of Agent Windish blocked her view of two of everything else. At last she said rather dreamily, "Trust me."

"I don't . . ."

"You forgot to say *trust me,*" Jan interrupted.

"You'll have the best protection that modern technology can provide," he said, stopping in front of her and putting a hand out as if to help her up. "I absolutely guarantee it."

Jan closed her eyes but it didn't help any. In fact, it made matters worse. With her eyes closed she couldn't avoid seeing Ginger's angry face. Maybe there were times in her life when Jan said no to crazy ideas. Surely there must have been. But at the moment she was at a loss to summon a one of them, and meanwhile that contrary streak came welling up inside her, the way it had when she'd agreed to marry a second time, the way it had when she'd made up her mind to sue the county for discrimination, the way it did whenever someone told her not to do something, which was exactly what the little voice in her head, the one that always sounded like her mother, was telling her now. *Better not, honey.* Opening her eyes, she slowly turned her head toward Windish and said without any doubts, "You were banking on this from the start, weren't you?"

They pointed Jan at a dressing room and told her to slip into a gown, one of those unisex, backless things that made her feel as though men were leaning out of doorways behind her. Next they had her stretch out on a gurney in patient recovery, adjacent to the operating suites. The bed was hard and cold. Bright and smelling of floor wax, the room was minimally staffed and drafty, although when she complained about the breezes everyone acted as if she was making it up. Only one other patient was waiting to regain control of his central nervous system after the anesthesiologist was through with it. The covered belly-hump of that older male patient reminded her of a pregnant woman, maybe because the last time she'd lain in a hospital recovery like this had been after the cesarean birth of her last daughter. A nurse appeared at her side and stuck an IV in her arm.

"Nothing but saline," the nurse muttered and was gone.

"Show time," said Windish.

Jan snapped the surgical mask in place, and they whisked her out of patient recovery, the agents forming an armed phalanx around her. Every time they reached a corner or doorway, it seemed as though another agent joined the wedge. Radio chatter met them as they rolled through each checkpoint. At times they moved so fast the gurney's wheels wobbled, and the agents had to jog to keep pace. Windish puffed away up front, the point blob, making sure nothing obstructed their path.

Her convoy traveled in fits and starts, holding up every time they reached a new set of closed fire doors. Raising her head slightly, she could spy past the sheet covering her feet to the next section of corridor where disgruntled medical staff were being evacuated to make way for her. The employees were all straining backwards for a glimpse at what was passing through, and seeing their reactions forced Jan to realize that the plan was working. Normally these stretches were full of doctors careening from door to door, patients bellyaching about the color of their Jell-O, and portable IV pumps trailing sinisterly behind anything that moved and owed money to the General. Not today. Everyone was mistaking her for someone else today, someone returning from the operating room, someone in need of bodyguards and cleared hallways and a full range of security measures. And if they were all tricked, why wouldn't the Hammer be taken in too? She heard something chattering and locked her jaw to stop it.

For the remainder of Saturday afternoon Windish had a ragged but invisible drum and fife corps marching behind him as he deployed and redeployed his men. He assigned twelve-hour watch tours, ordered all his supporting cast in to the hospital, quartering two or three of them in the communications hub at all times.

That left Sonny at the linen carts; Henry at the rear service elevator and stairs; hospital security covered the public elevators; Bug and one of the Texans drew street duty down on Wabash, across from the taxi stand. And don't forget the dogs, who were constantly on hand except for duty tours outside. In fact, the dogs were the only ones whose eyes didn't appear turned inside out from lack of sleep, whose steps weren't crooked, and who didn't talk in concentrated bursts, as if short-circuiting. The only problem with the dogs was that nobody knew how to handle them properly. If the Labrador wasn't making friends with strangers, the shepherd was barking at dust motes.

The final joke in her protection was the pistol she insisted on having underneath her bed covers. As tense as her arm felt, she wasn't sure if she could lift it.

# THIRTY-FIVE

THE HAMMER DREAMT THAT MANOS WAS about to kiss him full on the mouth, about to lay on a nasty, wet, French job, about to poke a formaldehyde-preserved tongue past his lips to lick his gums. That's what happened when he didn't brush his teeth before bed and dreamland. It never failed. Somebody, some ungrateful newly-dead wretch, always tried to get amorous whenever he forgot to brush. It was the bacteria multiplying in his mouth that attracted them.

Waking saved him from the dead man's embrace, but what roused him remained a mystery. He sat bolt upright, fists bunching up starchy bed covers. The head of every nurse, doctor, and visitor in the intensive care unit around him was cranked his way with varying degrees of alarm. Maybe he'd shouted something obscene, although at present he couldn't hear anything but the wheezer on his left and the moaner on his right, neighbors whose bedsides smelled liked embalming rooms.

"What happened?" he asked his nurse, who stood nearby, looking startled and about to drop a tray of medications. She was a young, platinum blond whose perky pageboy and sunny ways struck him as a cover-up for inexperience. That much seemed promising.

"There's nothing to worry about, Mr. Lombardi."

"Did I say something?"

"You sort of screamed," she said, sounding as though it was sort of cute.

"Screamed?"

"You were waking up, that's all." She cast an apologetic glance at another nurse, who rolled her eyes sympathetically, as if to say they'd all had screamers.

"What exactly did I scream?"

"Well, mostly you screamed *no.*"

"Mostly?"

"You said something else, Mr. Lombardi, but I really wasn't close enough to make it out."

"Call me Vince," the Hammer said, relieved that he hadn't given anything away. Wanting everything to return to normal, he said in as friendly a voice as he could manage, "What should I call you?"

"Lisa," she said, hesitating enough to reveal that he frightened her.

"Got a boyfriend, Lisa?" he asked, trotting out some lounge-lizard charm.

"You're supposed to be concentrating on getting better, Mr. Lombardi."

"You know what I think?" he teased.

She checked the chart at the foot of his bed without answering.

"I think you've got potential," he said.

Blushing furiously, she pretended to have urgent business in the unit's supply closet. Counting paper towels, or something. Closing his eyes to rest, the Hammer guessed she'd do fine. The question was, would he? To avoid worrying about the job ahead, he had to expend a great deal of energy. Then, when he closed his eyes, he recalled what he'd shouted after screaming *no.* He'd shouted *I can't.* Just before his dream had exploded, Manos had changed into Carmen. It was the touch of her lips that woke him up screaming.

\* \* \*

Pretending she was a deathly ill patient recovering from a nearly fatal operation drenched Jan's back in sweat. They had her hooked up to so many monitors and intravenous lines that she felt like Gulliver held down by AT&T.

A nearly constant stream of hospital employees descended upon her, and since Windish was worried that one of these people might be the Hammer's inside source, he waved them all ahead in their duties after subjecting each of them to dog noses and highly personal questions. Phlebotomists arrived almost hourly to draw blood. From housekeeping came a Southeast Asian woman whose English amounted to *yes-ee*. A chaplain marched in like a Christian soldier and wouldn't retreat until having said several prayers for Jan's recovery. The head of the transplant team stopped by to say the ruse was hopeless. Soon thereafter, a respiratory therapist—who it turned out had the wrong patient orders—pushed in her cart. The mix-up wasn't discovered until after Jan had received a full treatment of inhalations. The nursing supervisor, who came by to find out if the nurses on duty needed any support, didn't act convinced that Windish was a private nurse brought in at the DEA's request; she didn't seem to believe that he knew which end of a bedpan to hold up. Finally, a dietician dropped off a menu that listed three clear liquids from which to choose.

The only break in the procession came when she convinced Windish that if he didn't let her call home, she was getting up and walking out of there. That bought her a phone. She was glaring at Windish, who at the moment was masquerading as a nurse in scrubs, when her youngest daughter answered the phone in tears.

"What's wrong, Tessy?" Jan asked, forgetting Agent Windish and the way a flack jacket made his scrubs tight across his chest. His mouth and nose were concealed by a surgical mask, and his head covered by a surgical cap. As if to top off the irony of his appearance, he had been encouraging Jan non-stop to *look natural*.

"Dad isn't coming," Tess blubbered, "and Leah left us all alone for her concert."

The sentence ended in a wail as shouting filled the background.

Since Murphy's Law had nothing on Gallagher's, Jan didn't delve into what had happened to the girl's father. It wouldn't be anything original.

"What's going on now?"

"Kate and Amy are hitting each other."

"Get them on the line."

Some frantic screaming accomplished that much. Amy laid claim to the kitchen line; Kate had to scramble all the way back to the bedroom extension. Both yammered their defenses until Jan ordered, "Quiet!" Teenager silence followed, the most vengeful kind. Before sending everyone to separate corners of the house, Jan vowed that a baby-sitter with full life-and-death powers would be there shortly. That set off a new round of grapeshot that completely ventilated her heart. She vacated the line before making promises she couldn't keep about coming home. When Windish approached her bedside, she told him, "I *am* looking natural."

The Hammer's covers felt leaden when he flung them off. Swinging his bare legs out of bed, his feet almost overshot the cold floor and landed him on his knees. He managed to stand with all the grace of a buoy in heavy chop. His nurse caught him just as he reached his pot of mums.

"You *must* be feeling better," she said, guiding him back to bed by the elbow. "I'd say it won't be long and you'll be on your way out of here."

"You wouldn't be trying to get rid of me, would you, Lisa?"

"Not at all, Mr. Lombardi," she said, embarrassed by his familiarity. "I only meant that you're doing so well, and all, that I wouldn't be surprised if tomorrow morning they transferred you to a floor bed and had a serious talk with you about what's happened here."

"Here?" he said, pulling to a stop three feet shy of his bed.

"All I meant," she said, flustered, "was why you ended up visiting us. We certainly wouldn't want it to happen again, would we? Not with all you've got to live for, I mean. A beautiful wife who's smart too."

"My . . ."

The approach of a hospital security guard, who moved as if wearing Mr. Universe bikini briefs, saved him from asking what wife. Taking up a pose at the foot of the Hammer's bed, the guard gave nurse Lisa a come-hither look. She warned him off by shifting her eyes toward the head nurse's desk and back. Just moments before the charge nurse had sent an under-medicating doctor packing, and at the moment she was homing in on the security guard's triangular back. Undeterred, the guard hoisted a hairy forearm to show his silver-banded wristwatch. Lisa flashed five fingers at him before returning her complete attention to her patient, touching his elbow to urge him on.

"Why the guard?" he asked once the hunk had gone.

"He's helping protect a patient down the hall," the nurse answered in a whisper.

"From in here?" he asked, irked by the reference to Carmen.

"No-o," she said, as if he was teasing her again. "He's guarding the elevator out in the hall. How's your appetite, Mr. Lombardi? Can I get you something to eat?"

"Pass," he said. "But I could use a toothbrush."

"Coming right up," she said, relieved to have something else to talk about. "Regular or gel toothpaste?"

Within the next hour Jan had pounded out the phone numbers of friends she resorted to in emergencies, and friends she hadn't talked to for months, and friends who were really no longer friends. It being late Saturday afternoon, all the calls did was elevate her blood pressure. After several moments of intense debate with herself, she obtained Frank White's number from information and tapped it out without taking her eyes off Windish, whose surgical mask currently made him look like a member of some ridiculous harem.

The detective answered precisely on the third ring, creating the impression he'd been counting.

"White," she said, "I've got a favor to ask you, and since you helped get me into this mess, I figure you owe me one. Big. And don't think this means anything. We're not exactly a match made in heaven."

"At least we're talking," he said, daring to sound hopeful.

"Don't press your luck."

He didn't, and when she explained what she needed, he agreed. That was how she landed her baby-sitter.

With that crisis out of the way, she found herself wondering how she would defend herself if despite all Agent Windish's assurances, the Hammer succeeded in reaching her. The prospects weren't encouraging. There was the pistol of course, but considering the jangly state of her nerves, she didn't have much confidence in her markswomanship. What's more, if the killer succeeded in getting this far, she didn't imagine that Agent Windish and crew would be in any condition to help her. Once beyond the shock of that thought, she started searching for any advantages the isolation room might provide. Other than beneath her bed, there wasn't anywhere to hide, not even a private toilet, so she ruled out a disappearing act. It would be better to play possum than cower under the bed. She spent a good deal of time evaluating the lethality of every gadget in sight and reached the IV cart to her left before finding anything that could conceivably prove lethal. On top of the cart lay a remote control for the TV. Reaching for it, she asked Windish, "This thing working?"

"You're too sick to need it. Remember?"

Ignoring him, she familiarized herself with the control buttons, cranked up the volume to maximum, and armed with a gun in one hand and a TV clicker in the other, turned off the tube and settled in to wait. The wall clock had tortoise legs. Their conversation was all used up. For an hour nobody but DEA agents dressed as medical staff came and went from the unit.

It happened during supper. A distant crack carried in from the hallway. The report sounded like two freight cars coupling several blocks away.

"Gunshot," Sonny called out from the hallway.

Every agent jerked his clefted chin toward the doorway, whipped out his pistol with varying degrees of practice, and pretended he wasn't wetting his pants. A dog yelped as if Sonny had stepped on its tail. Windish waved two agents out into the hallway before crouching beside Jan's bed and bracing his shooting arm on the bottom rail at the foot of the bed.

Jan was moving too, although not far. She squeezed the remote control with her left hand, grasped the pistol with her right. The rest of her was paralyzed. If her heart wasn't in her throat, something that size with a pulse was.

The head nurse had no more than left for supper when the security guard came sniffing around the Hammer's nurse. While Romeo and Juliet did their balcony scene in front of an infectious-waste bin that was partially concealed by a curtain, the Hammer slipped out of bed, feeling fairly steady, if chilled. He pulled on and belted his robe, then made it to the arrangement of mums without being noticed. A get-well card leaned against the flowerpot, but he'd regained sense enough to skip reading it. Unwrapping the green tinfoil protecting the plastic pot, he pried off the cardboard base and removed the small automatic, spare clip, hospital keys, and hypodermic stashed there. The extra clip, capped needle, and keys he dropped in his robe's left pocket, the automatic he jammed in the right. To the gun, he whispered, "I'm glad you're here."

What he did next came automatically, without any hesitation. He was thankful for that much.

Approaching his nurse and her boyfriend, he lifted his gun, leveled his arm, and pumped two shots into the guard's chest before the man's look of astonishment could turn to terror. As the guard crumpled backward, the Hammer felt a power surge. The nurse's bewilderment filled him with a sense of accomplishment. Before she could react, he corkscrewed one of her thin arms behind her and jammed his automatic into the small of her back. Her spine bowed and she took mincing steps as he steered her. As they left the unit, she sobbed, "Please," which made her just about a perfect little hostage, all dressed in white and looking every bit as helpless as she actually was. For the first time in days everything was going right.

Before they'd covered twenty feet, three agents in scrubs burst around the corner at the far end of the hall, maybe fifty yards away. They had to be agents. He didn't imagine for an instant that the medical staff had started arming itself. To protect himself, the Hammer hunched as much of himself as possible behind his shield. That was like trying to stuff three dimensions behind two, but it did the trick. When the agents pulled up twenty feet shy of the nurse, one crank on her wrist disarmed them. Herding them back the way they'd come, hands on their heads, was no problem at all.

He definitely couldn't complain about progress. Other than a wobble in his knees, he felt fine and even managed to scoop up one of the agent's discarded pistols for insurance. When they paraded past a closed-circuit camera set up in the hall, he couldn't resist a wink for posterity. Around the corner were two dogs, but they turned tail when he pointed the gun at him. Everything was under control as they entered the unit where Carmen lay.

"Out where I can see you," he ordered. Turning cordial, he added, "I think it's time we introduced ourselves."

In addition to the three agents he'd already caught, another three filed into the center of the room, arms raised, two shuffled from his right, one from the left.

"Stay together," he said. "Don't get all spread out."

A fat one who'd come from Carmen's bedside to his left told them to do as told.

"That's close enough for a first date," the Hammer announced, bringing everyone to a halt. The three men he'd ushered in from the hallway stopped halfway between the agents converging from the two sides. The six of them stood in a single line in front of him, the three in the middle with their backs to him.

"Do you want me to point out the obvious?" the fat one on the far left asked. His voice was raised much louder than necessary, as if a raging flood lay between them.

"Maybe another time," the Hammer suggested, mimicking the loudness. "Who the hell are you?"

"Special Agent George Windish. And being in charge here, I feel obliged to warn you that you'll never get away with this."

"Well, since you're in charge," the Hammer obligingly said, "maybe you'd like to tell everyone to lay their hardware down and step away from it, carefully, as if this nurse's life depends on it." He applied some torque to the nurse's arm to get his point across.

"Everyone do it," the fat man named Windish grimly said.

"One at a time," the Hammer added.

"One at a time," Windish repeated.

Singly, the three agents caught in the unit stepped forward to lift their automatics out with thumbs and index fingers. Their constricted expressions caused the Hammer to chuckle and suggest they relax, but the one named Windish was the only one goofy enough to comply. As he stooped to lay his snub-nose revolver beside the other guns, he said conversationally, "Do you mind if I ask you a question?"

"Only one?"

"Why the NFL stickers?"

"Ratings," the Hammer said. "These days you got to have a gimmick." With a toss of his shaved head, he motioned for Windish to back away from the weapons. "Now where could Carmen be?"

"Right this way," Windish said, gesturing toward the isolation room with the proprietary air of a maître d'.

"Minus you," the Hammer told him. "I want everyone kneeling out here where I can keep an eye on you." Raising his voice, he commanded, "On your knees."

When they didn't start genuflecting, he yanked the nurse's arm, squeezing out a whimper that got results.

At a distance of twenty feet with a glass isolation wall in between, Jan couldn't be sure of a hit, so she kept the pistol under the bed covers and tried not to shiver.

"Foreheads to the floor," she heard the man with the shaved head bark at the agents, the order straining his neck cords. She knew he must be the Hammer, but she tried not to think it.

Once satisfied that everyone was prostrate, the Hammer began sidestepping toward the isolation room, keeping his petrified hostage between himself and the agents at all times. The pair of them almost seemed to be floating, if a chunk of stone like that nurse could defy gravity. At the moment, anything seemed possible, even inevitable. Agent eyes helplessly watched the levitation as best they could from either side of noses pressed to the floor.

Positioning his hostage squarely in the center of the isolation doorway, as if setting up a window display, the Hammer whispered what almost seemed like an endearment in the nurse's ear, causing her to vigorously nod *yes* and continue nodding as he left her. As he neared the foot of her bed, Jan had the unwanted feeling that she could see his skull. The way he was grinning at her put a terrible tension on his jaw and temples. He studied her a long moment, staring at her midsection as if afraid to look her in the face. He acted worried about something, but gradually, his confidence seemed to grow and he lifted a hypo from his robe's pocket. Sounding slightly surprised, he said, "This shouldn't be a problem at all."

She couldn't budge her right arm, but did find enough strength to press the *on* button of the remote control. Behind the Hammer, the TV came to life, "Entertainment Tonight" blaring across the room.

Spinning with what would have been called *lightning reflexes* in the Wild West, the Hammer shot out the tube, causing the hostage to shriek before remembering to run. At the same time, Jan managed to raise her right hand far enough to blow a .32 caliber hole in her bed sheet and spin her target to her right. When the Hammer fired wildly back, blowing out an innocent EKG monitor, Jan squeezed off another round, missing everything, as far as she could tell. The roar in her ears sounded like an approaching 747, and she didn't manage another shot because she was too busy jerking out lines as she rolled off the bed for cover.

Out in the unit agents were grabbing up pants legs, clutching armpits, and digging at the small of their backs—for hideaway guns, Jan hoped.

The Hammer pinned everyone down with three shots as he

lunged toward the hall as if someone had a hold of his ankle, maybe Agent Windish's invisible fife player. From the back stairway, the agent named Henry arrived in time to have half a "Halt!" die in his throat along with the rest of him. The Hammer shot him point-blank without a pause. After that, it looked as though the Hammer was talking to his gun.

In the center of the unit, the remaining agents had latched onto their derringers and were plunking away. They upset the Hammer's balance twice without bringing him down. Then they were all aiming at an empty doorway.

# THIRTY-SIX

A GUNSHOT FROM THE HALLWAY PUT the brakes on any hot pursuit. Sonny dashed to the door first, pulled Agent Henry into the unit by his feet, and pressed two fingers against his throat to check for a pulse. Second to the door was the redheaded Texan, who dropped to his stomach and peeked three times into the hallway before waving on the next man, who shoved a portable IV cart in front of himself for cover.

Jan watched Windish swallow twice before working up enough spit to broadcast an all-points bulletin. The foot chase that news flash triggered would have winded the Keystone Cops. In addition to the DEA's cavalcade, hospital security guards suddenly appeared from the direction of the other MICUs and were sucked along. Even the Little Admiral added his waddle, miraculously appearing from a nearby nowhere. There weren't any railroad tracks for a cow-catcher scene, but the DEA's two skittery dogs soon took up the slack, tangling everyone's legs with their leashes. Dressed in nothing more than a hospital gown and holding a gun with four rounds left, Jan hotfooted it after everyone else for no better reason than she wasn't about to be left alone with Agent Henry's remains. When the head of the column reached a corner, she froze with everyone else. Her arm smarted where she'd jerked out the IV needle, she felt a draft on her back, her bare feet were ice cold.

Fresh droplets of blood splattered the tiled floor every two or three yards and led the posse to within twenty feet of the rear service elevator, where they found the black Labrador licking up the trail. Jan rounded the rear corner in time to witness Sonny aim a kick at the Lab, but the dog dodged his foot easily, causing a hard pratfall. Nobody laughed, not even the German shepherd who was parked before the elevator as if he'd treed something dangerous. The light panel showed the elevator car to be headed down to one.

Everyone hit the stairs running—that included the dogs, pressed into service as trackers. As soon as the stairway door opened, the canines did the sensible thing and cross-cut everyone, bolting for higher ground. The resulting pileup of arms, legs, and oaths took some slapstick to sort out, but once there was order, everyone thundered down the stairs as if being chased by a billowing cloud of black smoke.

"We need him alive," Windish shrilly shouted.

Jan brought up the rear, tailgating the last agent in line, who was caught in the back draft of the guy in front of him, and so on down the line to the front where Sonny spurred on the two dogs who hadn't chosen this direction to begin with.

After sending the service elevator to the first floor, the Hammer fired one panicky shot at the empty hallway behind him, just to provide food for thought, and limped through the stairwell door. He went down three steps before halting, gripped by an instinct that told him to reverse directions and head for higher ground. Without questioning why, he labored up a full flight, losing his footing but once.

Opening the last door with his master key, he stepped onto the flat roof and made his way toward the service elevator's tower some thirty feet away. A little rest and he'd be ready for new tests. Falling hard, he had to crawl the last five feet. Coming to, he found his nose pressed against the tar roof. Something was leaking deep inside him, soaking his gown and robe. He'd fix that once he'd opened the door to the tower. The keys weren't in his hand. Who'd taken them? He strained to lift himself, couldn't. In a moment of clarity, he saw that even if he got the keys back, opened the tower door, and managed to hide inside, all he would succeed in doing was bleed to death.

He heard someone whimper. It sounded like a child. Looking around, he saw no one near him.

Resting for three bubbly breaths, he managed to roll over on his back. After several more breaths he pushed himself into a sitting position against the elevator tower.

For a moment he sat admiring the small automatic in his hand, and then, with much effort, he raised it to his head. Poking it in his ear didn't feel right. Pressing it against his eye felt even worse. Jamming it tightly against the bottom of his chin gave him no satisfaction at all; he tried his nose. The smell of the recently fired gun failed to make his mouth water, but that was when he understood what he was supposed to do. Lowering the barrel, he attempted to slide it into his mouth.

No go.

He couldn't open his mouth. The barrel clicked against his teeth and he could taste the meal waiting for him, but no matter how hard he jammed the barrel, another part of himself cried *WAIT*.

He found himself dreamily staring at the sky as if expecting some kind of sign. After several moments without sighting a shooting star, he had a nonsensical thought: He was afraid to die. It didn't make sense, but in his weakened condition it explained why he'd three times failed to get close enough to take care of Carmen. A wave of shame swept over him, followed by denial, followed by something wet sliding down his cheek. When he rolled his eyes heavenward, he saw a perfectly-clear night sky and passed out wondering how it could be raining.

Halfway to the third floor, Jan dropped out of the footrace in frustration. She was too far back of the head of the pack to help anyway. Sitting down, she stared at her handgun, which she'd deposited one step below her. She'd done what she could, she'd done more than anyone could reasonably expect of her, and she told herself to be satisfied with that much. She told herself that two or three times. Then she told herself it was too late to take Ginger's place anyway, an impulse she supposed lay at the absolute bottom of her recklessness.

A collision of bodies, followed by curses, drew her immediate attention to the lower floors. Peering over the stairway's metal railing, she caught flashes of movement below—a man's shoulder, a dog's tail, a hand gripping a pistol. Before all the scrambling ended, the black Labrador came loping up the stairs, startling her into scooping up her gun and almost firing. She laughed in relief and nabbed the dog's leash as it trailed by, causing the Labrador to whine and strain against its lead as if on the trail of something wounded.

"What am I trying to prove here?" Jan asked the dog. That was a question she'd heard before, and one that a dog was as likely to answer as anyone. In her experience, answers always came long after the time when they might do any good, so when the dog strained to yank her onward, she went along.

The Labrador pulled her past the fourth floor and higher. On the half-flight landing between four and five Jan spotted a droplet of blood. After that sighting, the red splats increased in frequency, soon one to a step, then two and three to a step, as if a spigot had been slowly loosened. The last half-dozen steps to the top were a blur as Jan became an increasing drag on the leash. Every third or fourth step the dog tired of tugging Jan onward and paused to glance imploring back at her.

The fifth level was a locked psych ward, but the dog ignored that unit's rear door and pulled Jan down a short hallway to three steps that led to the roof. The floor was splattered with crimson spots the size of nickels, dimes, and quarters, some of which were smeared by dragging feet. Jan pressed against the wall to avoid wetting her own bare toes. In one place he'd slipped and left a handprint, but what summed up his weakened condition best was the pool of blood on the step below the roof door, that and the fact that he'd left a set of master keys in the lock.

"Unless he's got a helicopter in his pocket," Jan said, holding the dog back, "we got him." As she reached toward the doorknob, another thought occurred to her and she added, "Or he's got us."

Rather than consider that possibility, she went into a crouch and touched the knob as if testing for heat. Turning the master key, she pushed, just intending a peek. The dog bolted through the opening though, forcing Jan into a quick choice. Pride won out. As she dove out on the flat roof, rolling to the left, nothing hit her forehead but a cool breeze.

At first she was unable to see anything but the glow of floodlights from over the edge of the building. The darkness was interrupted by the black geometric shapes of vents and the elevator tower, plus one break in all the shades of night. In front of the largest black square slouched an oblong, white spot as fluttery in the evening breeze as a ghost. The Labrador was wagging its tail in front of the figure, which wasn't pointing anything at Jan, although it took her several seconds to reach that conclusion. The robed man wasn't pointing anything at Jan because he was too busy leveling a gun at his own head.

"Lord."

She braced herself for gore, but upon approaching him couldn't spot any extra openings in the killer's head. Propped against the door of the elevator tower, he'd dragged himself that far but no farther. Lowering herself to one knee, she had to touch his neck twice before detecting a pulse.

"Alive," she said, tugging the gun from his mouth and out of his hand.

The Hammer's eyes fluttered at the sound of her voice, his lips did a trial run without producing any sound, then two pitiful words escaped before he passed out.

"Save me," he said.

From above, the night sky seemed to be trying to pull her prisoner away, and she kept a light hand on his chest to make sure that didn't happen. She hadn't looked—really looked—at the Milky Way for what seemed like ages, and now, kneeling beneath the enormous sky, she gazed upward. The spread of stars reminded her of a picture from a childhood book, a story about men coming down from a mountaintop with the gift of wisdom. She wondered if a woman might come down from a rooftop with the same. She said good-bye to Ginger.

# THIRTY-SEVEN

THEY CUT THREE SLUGS OUT OF the Hammer; the lowest had burrowed into his right buttock, the highest his shoulder. In between was a divot from his gut that would have put lesser constitutions to rest. For a messenger of death he had a remarkable will to live.

During the next thirty-six hours Agent George Windish hovered like the angel of Moroni just beyond the Hammer's IV drips and monitor readouts. His wing tips got in the staff's way though, and he was soon banished from the unit's airspace, forced into a holding pattern in the hall. When the patient climbed back to consciousness, Windish swooped to his side with offers of immunity, plastic surgery, plastic cards, and a leak-proof identity. In between the aspiration of mucus from his throat, the Hammer agreed to deliver the goods.

Within forty-eight hours Windish had arranged the patient's transfer to the very unit where Carmen had been billeted, and Windish, with a skeleton crew, stayed on, guarding the man they had been previously guarding against. Thanks to Jan's track record, she drew the high honor of helping to coordinate the Hammer's safety. The joke in the halls ran this way: Business as usual. The Hammer even requested that the canaries be moved back in from the communications hub. If he was going to be a songbird, he wanted company. He tried to make a joke of it, but the effort came out jittery and weak.

That Monday Jan and her daughters received a postcard from Las Vegas. The front of the card had a nighttime photograph of a small stucco building shaped like a Spanish mission and lit up by a bluish neon light that said *Little Chapel of Silver Bells*. There were two bells outlined beneath the name. The back of the card had a handwritten note.

*Ned and I have decided to stay on another week in Las Vegas, as husband and wife. Don't forget to feed Milhous. Love Claire.*

Milhous was her parakeet.

The girls, in particular Amy, claimed to be thrilled by their grand-mother's elopement, and the whole tribe greeted the newlyweds at the airport with flowers and rice, but once back home, the girls went through the same denial and period of mourning as when their father had moved out. Nobody had much to say to Jan, and what came out had an edge of accusation. Leah claimed to be glad Claire was gone. Amy played the invalid and holed up in her room. Katie asked if Granny didn't like them anymore, and Tess wanted to know if it really was Jan's fault that Claire had gone away.

Once over the shock, Jan had to admit it felt liberating to once again have a bedroom to herself. Her newfound freedom also may have had something to do with why she eventually gave in and agreed to sup with Detective Frank White. Soon enough she found herself on the couch next to the antique radio where the after-shave rolled off the man of the house in waves. The crystal wineglasses rested on coasters, and a puppy dog was trapped behind the detective's eyes. When he leaned toward her, she held him off.

"I don't want us kidding ourselves that this is love," she said.

"So what are we doing here?"

"Pretending," Jan said, pulling him closer.

\* \* \*

After ten days without incident the Hammer was discharged from the General and warehoused in an undisclosed location. The last Jan saw of Special Agent George Windish, he was rallying his troops to cross the next Delaware. That left MICU number four empty, except for canaries, which she inherited and took home as a gift for her daughters. The peace offering was accepted.